The
BROKEN
HEARTS
Bakery

Books by Carla Laureano

MacDonald Family Trilogy
Five Days in Skye
London Tides
Under Scottish Stars

Supper Club Series
The Saturday Night Supper Club
Brunch at Bittersweet Cafe
The Solid Grounds Coffee Company

Discovered by Love Series
Jilted (novella)
Starstruck (novella)
Snowbound (novella)
Sunswept (novella)

Haven Ridge Series
The Brick House Cafe (novella)
The Broken Hearts Bakery

The Song of Seare Trilogy
Oath of the Brotherhood
Beneath the Forsaken City
The Sword and the Song

Provenance

The

BROKEN
HEARTS
Bakery

CARLA LAUREANO

LAUREANO
CREATIVE MEDIA

ACKNOWLEDGMENTS

You'd think after having written fifteen books, the process would get easier, but the truth is, every book is a new and exciting (terrifying?) adventure. I'm eternally grateful to be surrounded by an amazing group of people who make this job so much easier and more fulfilling.

A huge round of thank yous go to: my amazing and intelligent Haven Ridge Beta Squad (Meaghan Ahlbrand, Jessica Baker, Elisabeth Callahan, Kim Campbell, Leslie Florea, Denise Hershberger, Mindy Houng, Amy Parrish, Brenda Smith, and Susan Snodgrass)—your contributions to this story were unmistakable; my editor, Jocelyn Bailey, who helped make this book the best it could possibly be; my copyeditor, Denise Harmer, whose attention to detail puts me to shame (and I'm pretty darn detail-oriented!); cover designer extraordinaire, Hillary Lodge—this cover is a whole thing of its own and I love it so much; my writer friends Amber Lynn Perry, Jen Turano, Lori Twichell, and Courtney Walsh, who keep me going when all I want to do is sit on the sofa and eat chocolate—love you guys!

And last, to my fabulous readers. This book wouldn't exist without you, and I'm so grateful for your support, which allows me to do the thing I love most in the world. Thank you!

CHAPTER ONE

IF GEMMA VAN BUREN HAD LEARNED ANYTHING in her thirty years on this planet, it was that heartbreak demanded chocolate.

Or, as she preferred, chocolate wrapped in flaky butter pastry and baked to a perfect golden brown. Which was why when she walked into the lobby of the Family Law Offices of Merivale and Mercer on Monday morning, she shoved a pink pastry box across the countertop to the young receptionist.

Alicia looked up in surprise, the rim of red around her eyes giving away her mood despite her flawlessly-applied makeup. "You didn't."

Gemma leaned onto the counter with a sympathetic smile. Everyone in her office knew what a pink box meant: consolation treats. It didn't matter whether the heartbreak was personal or professional; it would be accompanied by baked goods. At first, some of the pricklier attorneys had given her a hard time about letting on that she had a softer side, but that had gone away the minute they saw her in negotiations. Forget the velvet glove—Gemma's iron fist was sheathed in puff pastry.

Alicia flipped the lid open and sighed in pleasure at the smell of sugar and butter. "Bless you. How did you know chocolate croissants were my favorite?"

"I didn't. But it's every woman's favorite when she's kicked a no-good boyfriend to the curb."

"Oh, but I didn't—"

Gemma held up a hand and gave her a significant look. "You traded up in life. Right?"

Alicia gave her a little sideways smile, the first such expression Gemma had seen since Alicia's boyfriend of five years gave her the *it's not you, it's me* speech..

"The best part is, we've decided that consolation pastries have no calories."

"In that case. . ." Alicia picked a croissant from the box and took a bite, rolling her eyes in pleasure. Gemma hid her smile and moved past the desk amid the click of her high-heeled pumps before Alicia called out, "Oh, I almost forgot. . . Mr. Mercer was looking for you a few minutes ago."

Gemma froze in mid-step. "Right now? I've got a deposition at eight."

"He didn't say specifically, but. . ."

She groaned. "Great. Thanks for the heads up." Gemma continued walking the hall toward her office as if it were a minefield, ready to explode with the first unwary step. It wasn't good if one of the partners was looking for her this early, particularly since he should already know her schedule—each associate's digital calendar was available for viewing by everyone in the office. If she could just slip into the conference room a little early—

"Gemma! Have a minute?"

Too late. She put on a noncommittal smile and turned to face her boss. "Actually, John, I've got a deposition in the Clearwater case—"

"This won't take long." John smiled what she thought of as his courtroom smile—his likable smile—and gestured with his head toward his glassed-in corner office.

Gemma gathered herself. "Of course. I can take a few minutes. Let me drop off my briefcase first."

She made a quick trip to her own office before she returned to his, then lingered just inside his door, hoping he wouldn't insist on her sitting. No such luck. He gestured to the chair in front of his mahogany desk and then settled behind it, unbuttoning the coat of his well-made, very expensive three-piece suit. She seated herself casually, crossed her legs, and folded her hands in her lap while she waited.

He waited, too. It was a common enough negotiation strategy: stretch the silence out until someone cracked. But she was good at Chicken, and frankly, if he was going to waste her time with a meeting that probably could have been an email, she had no problem wasting his.

"So, I understand you met with Cameron Lowe yesterday."

Inwardly, Gemma did a fist pump at winning the staring contest, and her own amusement at the childish game put more of a smile on her face than she intended. "I did."

"And you told him you couldn't help him."

"I did."

"Gemma, he's a return client of the firm."

"Yes, I realize that."

"Then why did you tell him you didn't represent adulterers?"

It was actually better than the words she'd been thinking at the time—she'd doubted her first impulse would be appropriate even given the reason he was a "return client," and it was never acceptable to use questionable language in her law firm. "John, I was very clear on the kinds of cases I'd take and clients I'd represent—"

"As an associate of this firm—"

"Which you well remember, because it was you who pursued me. After . . ." She pretended to think. "It was the Rollins case, wasn't it? If I recall, you were opposing counsel." She smiled calmly at him, her courtroom face. She actually got to use this face more often than her colleagues, because unlike them, she would take a case all the way to court if she felt the other side was being unreasonable. And more often than not, the judge sided with her clients because she didn't represent creeps, cheaters, or abusers.

A smile crept onto John's lips. "Yes, I remember." He should. He'd been so impressed by her performance in the courtroom that he'd handed her his card in the hallway and asked her to call him for an interview the next day.

Gemma rose. "Good talk, John. I have a deposition."

His smile faded. "Gemma, sit down."

She froze, her heart stopping for a moment before it resumed double time. Normally John would just roll his eyes and wave her off, the subject tabled until next year when he found the need to remind her of his nominal authority over her. But this? This was new. She sat.

"Eli and I have been talking."

And now she understood. John Mercer might be the partner who oversaw the everyday workings of the firm, but Eli Merivale was a forty-year career attorney with the fees to match. He took the highest-profile cases, such as celebrity divorces and custody disputes, and he overruled John only when something particularly egregious pinged his radar.

Somehow, Gemma had gotten on his radar.

"I can't imagine that Eli is upset with my performance. I have the highest satisfaction rating of any attorney in this firm, and I out-billed the nearest associate by at least thirty percent last quarter."

"It's not your performance, Gemma. We all agree that you're a very competent attorney—"

"Competent? I'm more than competent—"

"But the number of clients you turn down doesn't sit well with Eli. It reflects badly on the firm if prospects can't engage the attorney that brought them here in the first place."

"You mean, if I turn them down, they go somewhere else. It sounds like you should be having a talk with the other associates, not me."

"Gemma, someone in your position can't be so choosy."

She frowned. "What does that mean, 'in my position?'"

John took a deep breath and let it out slowly, a placating expression on his face. "Eli thinks you're a little high-minded for an associate. He's been willing to overlook it until now because your work is outstanding and you have the highest referral rate in the firm. But when you alienate long-time clients like Cameron Lowe, who has a great deal of influence in this town . . . he's starting to believe you could be a liability."

"That's ridiculous. I pick cases I believe in, people who need help. Just because I refuse to represent clients who would leave their spouses in the lurch after thirty years of marriage doesn't make me a liability. Besides, I don't have room in my caseload to take every client who comes my way, so the point is moot."

"You spend twenty percent of your time on pro bono work."

Gemma stopped, stunned, understanding the unspo-ken message in that statement. "He wouldn't."

"He would. He's serious, Gemma."

"So unless I take on clients whose cases I don't believe in, I can't take the cases that I do?"

"We can't tell you what cases to take on your own time. But you won't be able to handle them here, under the firm's umbrella."

Gemma closed her eyes, pressing her fingertips to her temples. This was what she had been afraid of. This was why she had made a very specific agreement as to her autonomy when she was hired. This job was just about money to Eli and his ilk—it truly didn't matter to them who got the house in Vail, or the original Matisse, or the use of the condo in Hawaii over the Christmas holidays. And if she was truthful, that didn't matter much to her either.

But those clients let her take on the other cases for free, the ones that did matter. Those clients didn't argue about material possessions. They just wanted their nightmare to end, for their children to be safe from their spouse's rages, to not have to start all over from scratch when they were betrayed by the people for whom they'd sacrificed their own dreams. They were the ones who needed a do-over. They were the ones against whom the system was stacked when it favored power and money and education over the truth.

They were the ones who would suffer if she didn't do what Eli wanted.

And yet that would make her exactly the person she'd promised herself she wouldn't become when she chose this course for her life.

John's expression had turned sympathetic now, as if he sensed her internal turmoil. "Take some time to think about it. You don't have to make a decision right now."

"What is there to think about? I was very clear about my criteria when I came to the firm. You assured me . . . you promised me . . . that I would be allowed to choose my cases and I didn't have to compromise that for you or anyone else."

"Gemma—"

"We both know that an oral contract is legally binding in California. If I wanted to, I could fight this. I could bring a wrongful dismissal suit."

John looked pained. "You could. But I wish you wouldn't. Family law is a small world, Gemma, even in Los Angeles. Win or lose, in the long run, you would only be hurting yourself."

She didn't let it show on her face, but he was right. Even if she were able to convincingly argue wrongful dismissal in court, she would first have to force Eli to fire her before she even had a case. For good or ill, Gemma never walked into court without knowing her chances of winning, and right now, she didn't like her odds.

He must have sensed her wavering, because he folded his hands on the desk, his expression softening. "You have some vacation time. Why don't you take next week off and think about it? I'd hate to lose you, but I'm afraid there's no room for negotiation in this."

And there was no room in his expression for argument. She knew John too well to think she was going to talk her way out of this one. Either she came back to work, ready to take on whatever clients he deemed fit, regardless of how it might violate her personal ethics, or she didn't come back at all.

"Okay. I'll clear my schedule. It's fairly light anyway." She stood and began to smooth her skirt in a nervous habit she thought she'd broken, then clenched her hands by her side. She wanted to give a parting shot, but there was nothing left to say. Not right now.

She gathered herself and headed back down the hallway, feeling like the proverbial ground had just shifted beneath her feet. In five minutes, her world had changed, and she had no idea what she was going to do about it.

Looked like Alicia wasn't the only one who would be needing the consolation pastries today.

CHAPTER TWO

GEMMA SLEEPWALKED through the rest of her day, moving with robotic efficiency from deposition to new client consultation—another one she passed off—to lunch with a colleague, all the while her mind spinning through the ultimatum she had been given. The only advantage of her whirling thoughts was that her evening drive through horrific cross-town traffic seemed like a blink; she only knew it had been bad because it was past seven o'clock when she pulled into the driveway of her Santa Monica home. Unfortunately, she was no closer to knowing what she wanted to do.

She scooped her shoes out of the passenger seat without putting them on and walked up the rough concrete and brick driveway in her bare feet to her front door. It was a tiny house, barely thirteen hundred square feet, bought when she'd taken the job at Merivale and Mercer for an exorbitant price that now felt like a steal considering the current real estate market. Built in the 1950s with all of the function and none of the style of the mid-mods down the street, it was nevertheless fully remodeled in soothing shades of white, gray, and cream.

Gemma dropped her purse and keys on the entryway table and paused to preheat the oven before she proceeded to her bedroom to change. Off came the business suit and silk blouse, on went the sweatpants with a paint smudge on the thigh, her well-worn USC Gould Law School T-shirt, and a thick pair of Scandinavian knit socks that were much too warm for the climate. She padded back into the kitchen and was halfway through measuring ingredients for cream puffs before it hit her, the abstract becoming concrete.

It wasn't just her job she was risking if she stood up for her principles. It was her entire life. She could give up her car without a second thought—the sporty sedan was a splurge she could do without. But her little haven here from the bustle of the city? She wouldn't be able to afford this lovely little house with its huge kitchen and marble countertops in a quiet neighborhood, her respite from apartment living. Given the fact she'd been putting all her extra money toward paying off her student loans, her savings were far more meager than her lifestyle would suggest. She'd underestimated how expensive it was to live in LA, even with a more-than-decent income.

And yet, even though that idea hit her with a wave of sadness, it wasn't the money that concerned her most. It was the loss of purpose, routine, the rhythm of a life she loved. Being a lawyer was the only thing she'd wanted since she was sixteen years old. One didn't just walk away from the top family law firm in the city and expect that future employers wouldn't ask questions. If she stood up for her principles and lost her job, there was no guarantee that she would find another one. What good would her principles do her then?

Gemma blinked back unexpected tears as she beat the water, milk, and flour in the saucepan with more force than necessary, causing the steel pot to skitter across the grate. From her perspective, there was no good answer.

She'd finished the *pâte à choux* in her mixer and was halfway through piping the rounds that would become her pastry shells when her phone rang from her purse in the hallway. She froze, torn between the Pavlovian impulse to answer her phone and the desire to get the shells cooked so she'd have time to cool and fill them before it got too late. The pastries won out. She finished the tray of puffs, slid them into the oven, and strode to the hallway to check her message.

Missed call from Liv Quinn.

Gemma stared at the phone, jarred by the disconcerting sensation that her two separate worlds had collided. No, her two separate selves. Here in her million-dollar house with the expensive finishes, a view of palm trees and bougainvillea through the wide plate glass windows, it was easy to believe that Gemma Van Buren, Attorney at Law, was all there was.

But Liv belonged to a different self, a Gemma who had dreamed about marrying her high school sweetheart and opening her own bakery in their tiny mountain town, who reveled in nature and the cold winter air, who had not yet learned exactly how cruel people could be and how few souls she could truly trust.

Of everyone in her two lives, Liv was the only overlap, the single gossamer thread that connected the old and the new Gemmas together.

Her finger hovered over the call button, stayed by a sudden rush of guilt. Liv might have always been there when Gemma needed her, but she couldn't say that she'd been the same kind of friend in return.

Sure, she would drop everything in an emergency, and she'd done just that a couple of years ago when tragedy had struck: Jason, Liv's husband of only two years had died in a freak plane crash over the mountains on a clear day. Gemma had immediately canceled her meetings and flown to Colorado to be with her friend in her grief, but when she had returned to California, the phone calls had turned to texts and the daily check-ins had stretched first to weeks, then to months. Now she couldn't remember the last time she'd talked to her.

But guilt or no, Liv was the one person whose call she'd always return.

Liv answered on the first ring. "Ah, there you are. I thought you might be working late. I didn't interrupt anything, did I?"

A pang struck Gemma at the words but she shrugged it off. "What's going on? Is everything okay?"

"I'm not sure," Liv said thoughtfully. "Did you mean it when you said you owed me one?"

"I don't remember who last had the favor baton, but sure. What's up?"

"Apparently, I have to go to New York next week. The publisher has called everyone into the office, even those of us who work remotely."

Even through the line, Gemma could hear the hitch in her friend's voice that meant she was worried, and Liv rarely worried. She had always possessed the sunny disposition of someone for whom life had always worked out; the bigger feat was that she'd managed to keep it after the tragedy she'd experienced in the past few years. "Any idea what that means?"

"No, but I can tell you the last time Eric called an all-hands meeting, they laid off half the editorial staff."

Gemma cringed. Liv had started her career in publishing in New York, surviving the various shifts and takeovers within her volatile industry to eventually achieve her dream position: Senior Acquisitions Editor of a youth fiction line. When she and Jason decided to move back to Colorado, her boss had agreed to let her work remotely as long as she came into the New York office once a quarter for their sales meetings. Considering most of their business was done via email and video chat anyway, it wasn't much of a stretch.

So to be called back for an emergency meeting was alarming. Still, Gemma didn't know how she was going to be of any help. When she said as much, Liv said, "It's a last-minute trip. I don't have anyone to stay with Taylor, and I'm not comfortable letting her stay with any of her friends that long."

"Ah." Now Liv's emergency made sense. Taylor was Liv's fifteen-year-old stepdaughter, her late husband's child from his previous marriage. Since Taylor hadn't had any other family to go to and they'd already lived together for several years, a judge had granted Liv guardianship.

"I don't suppose . . . I know it's a lot to ask . . ."

Gemma laughed, though there was a fragility in the sound that surprised even her. "Oddly enough, I was just advised to take some vacation time."

Now it was Liv's turn to sound cautious. "Not that I don't think it's a good idea, but . . . you never take time off. What happened?"

"I had a weird feeling that you were going to have a career crisis and figured misery loved company."

"Ha ha," Liv said. "Really, though, Gem, why?"

When Gemma had returned the call, she was sure she was going to spill out the whole story, but now that it came to it, she was too weary to put it into words. "You remember my one non-negotiable requirement when I took the job?"

"Of course. You only represent the good guys."

"Something like that. Five years in and the big boss decided he didn't like me turning down clients. They gave me an ultimatum: take on the clients they want me to take or they won't let me do pro bono work. Or, you know, quit. They gave me a week to figure out what I wanted to do."

"Oh, Gemma, I'm so sorry. I know you love it there. What are you going to do?"

"It varies by the minute. None of the options are good. Represent the sort of people who victimize my pro bono clients just so I can keep helping them or refuse and lose the reason I took the job in the first place. Or quit and be no good to anyone."

"I wish I had a good answer for you." Liv hesitated. "But if you're going to just be moping around the house . . ."

"I'm not moping," Gemma said without any real conviction. "But I do have some thinking to do . . . and while Haven Ridge is the last place I would really consider inspirational, it has been a long time since I've seen my honorary niece . . ."

Liv took the opening immediately. "If you came out, you could be my first guest in the vacation suite! I just finished the remodel. Plus . . . there's a hot tub."

"Hmm," Gemma said, pretending to consider, and Liv laughed. They both knew she was coming with or without a hot tub, but this way Liv could feel like she'd coaxed her and Gemma could pretend she'd held out. If she were being honest, it had been so long since she'd actually taken a vacation that it hardly mattered where it was, as long as there was a comfortable bed and an internet connection for her streaming services. And because Liv's house was located several miles outside of historic downtown Haven Ridge, if she played her cards right, she could pretend she was at a remote mountain retreat and never have to see anyone she knew.

"I'm in," she said finally. "When do you need me?"

CHAPTER THREE

STEPHEN OSBORNE HAD NEVER BEEN SO HAPPY to see a Friday afternoon in his life.

He'd thought he knew the meaning of tired back in Salt Lake City, working eighty-plus hours at his ad agency, sometimes sleeping on the leather sofa in his office when the fifteen-minute drive to his Capitol Hill condo either felt too dangerous or like too much effort. But that was nothing compared to this.

Teaching high school was no joke.

When the last bell rang at 3:10, he didn't even need to dismiss his final class—they were already shoving notebooks and binders into their backpacks as quickly as they could, some of them hitting the door before the peal of the bell faded from the air. Stephen chuckled to himself, not taking it personally. He remembered what it was like to be seventeen on the cusp of a weekend; heck, if he didn't know that his weekend was just as packed as the previous five days had been, he probably would have beat them all there.

"Don't forget," he called futilely after them, "you have reading this weekend! Take twenty minutes tonight to . . ."

He trailed off when it became clear that everyone was either out of earshot or not paying attention. It was up to them to check the assignment app that Haven Ridge High School—and most of the other schools around here—used, or they'd be staring down a zero in classroom participation. He'd never thought he'd be one of those teachers who gave homework over the weekend, but they'd already had three snow days this semester, and his World Lit seniors were getting dangerously close to not being able to finish the book he'd planned for this quarter's unit.

Then again, he'd never thought he'd be a teacher, period.

Stephen shoved his laptop into his battered messenger bag, grabbed a fat white binder out of the bottom drawer of his desk, and slipped on the shearling-lined bomber jacket he'd owned since he himself had been a student at this high school fourteen years ago. Nikki had always been on him to get rid of it, but he'd insisted that everything came back into fashion sometime. He'd been right, and now that they lived in separate cities nearly five hundred miles apart, at least she didn't have to look at it.

Five minutes after the last bell, the corridors of the high school already looked like a ghost town, and he made his way to the front entrance, the leather soles of his dress shoes smacking the scuffed linoleum floors. He'd no sooner gotten halfway down the hall that led to the exit before he heard his name behind him. "Stephen."

Stephen paused and turned, his heart taking a slow, downward slide into his feet when he recognized the school principal, Edgar Daughtler, poking his head out of his office. "I was just heading out," Stephen said. "Can it wait until Monday?"

"I'm afraid it can't." Daughtler's tone gave away

nothing. "Come on in and take a seat. I'll make it quick, I promise."

Stephen nodded and changed course into the small office, closing the door behind him as he entered. There was a larger office that the principal in Stephen's time had used, but apparently his boss liked this smaller one because it allowed him to "take the pulse of the school" rather than be isolated on the upper level next to the gym. Or, to translate, he liked to know what absolutely everyone in his school was doing at any given time.

Daughtler waited until Stephen was seated uncomfortably in the 1980s chair with its oak arms and faded seat and steepled his fingers together. If he hadn't known that the man had come along shortly after he'd graduated, Stephen would think that he was as much a fixture in the school as the chairs—the short-sleeved striped dress shirt, '80s glasses, and comb-over made him look like he'd intentionally combined every school principal cliché to make a point.

But Daughtler's face was genuinely concerned when he said, "It's been a little over five months now. Do you feel like you're settling in?"

Stephen's stomach found equilibrium. Maybe he wasn't actually in trouble for anything. Funny how going to the principal's office could be anxiety-inducing even as an adult. Maybe Daughtler just wanted to check in, make sure that Stephen was doing okay. After all, he was the only one here without a credential, having applied for an alternative certification so he could fill the open literature spot at the last minute. It would be difficult for even an experienced teacher to step into teaching four classes, each a different year, with only a couple of weeks of preparation.

"I think it's going well," Stephen said finally. "The spread of grades in my classes are consistent with what my colleagues are seeing in their own sections, which tells me that the curriculum isn't too hard or too easy, and I think they're really connecting with the material. As much as any teenager connects with literature, of course." He added the caveat even though the idea of not connecting with literature was as foreign to him as the terrain of the moon. He'd read his first book at the age of three and hadn't looked back, even when it made him the odd man out. Most football players didn't read Maya Angelou on the team bus.

"That's what I wanted to talk to you about," Daughtler said, and Stephen's thoughts had spun so far out that he was half-expecting a discussion of *I Know Why the Caged Bird Sings*. "There have been some concerns from the parents about your . . . choices of reading material."

Stephen blinked, slamming back into the present with a mighty jolt. "I'm sorry? What concerns exactly? In what class?"

"In every class, actually." Daughtler reached into one of his deep drawers and drew out a stack of books, which Stephen recognized immediately as a selection of his required reading this year. "This one, for example." He held up a copy of *The Color Purple*. "I've highlighted the passages that the parents find objectionable if you'd like to look at it."

"No, that's okay." Stephen blinked away his confusion. "So . . . the objection is because there are hard situations inside? Have you ever walked the halls of this high school, sir? These kids are dealing with the same sorts of issues that are printed inside that book."

The slight twitch of Daughtler's mouth showed the point hit home, and he finally gave a nod. "I agree with you, actually. Which is why I dismissed the complaints against *Catcher in the Rye* from your American Lit class. I think we all know it's a classic for a reason."

"And *The Color Purple* is a classic for a reason. It's a good book. I stand by the pick. The kids are connecting with it, and that's hard to do when you're dealing with freshmen, especially when it's not an easy read."

Daughtler just looked at him with a sad sort of smile on his face, and Stephen finally got it. "The objection isn't about the book. The objection is because I swapped in diverse books for Intro to Lit."

The principal didn't immediately answer, but Stephen knew he had hit on the problem. "You have to understand, Stephen, this is a small town that has done things the same way for a very long time. I supported you bringing in your own choices for your classes, because frankly, I thought it was time for a refresh. But there's such a thing as doing too much too fast. We took a chance on you, hiring you without a teaching credential, because we thought the students might connect with someone who had been out in the real world, who had had experience outside of Haven Ridge. But Stephen . . . teaching is not a sprint, it's a marathon. And if you want to continue with the support of the parents, not just the administration, you're going to have to understand what you're dealing with."

Stephen swallowed hard, pushing down the swell of irritation—no, anger—that was building inside him. "I do understand what I'm dealing with. I grew up here. I know how slow the town is to change, and I know that's part of the reason that it's dying around us. I chose these books for a purpose." He took a deep breath and gentled his tone, leaning forward to plead with his boss. "Mr. Daughtler—Edgar—we're a town of under a thousand. Ninety-five percent of the population is white. We're two hours from the nearest city with any sort of diversity. These books are perhaps the only exposure some of these kids are going to have to people with another perspective, another kind of experience, before they go out into the real world. Wouldn't you rather have them prepared to live in the modern world, as they inevitably will, than to leave with some sort of 1950s sensibility?"

"I would. I really would. But, most here believe that's still the role of the parents. I know you aren't a parent yourself yet, so you wouldn't understand this, but—"

"No, it's okay." Stephen slumped back against the chair. He knew when he wasn't going to win an argument. It wasn't even that he disagreed about parental rights or the role of teachers; it was just that he had been trying to do what the school had hired him to do. And now he was being taken to task for it. "They've already read the book. The 'damage,' if you'd like to call it that, has already been done. Up to you if you want me to finish out the unit. Otherwise, I'll just give them credit for it and we'll move on."

Daughtler sat back as well, seemingly relieved that this wasn't going to turn into a fight. "I'm glad you're being so reasonable about this. I'm on your side, Stephen, whether it seems like it or not. From what I've observed, you are an excellent teacher, and I'd like to keep you on after this year. But you have to work with me on this. If we get enough parental outcry, I'm not going to have any choice."

Stephen nodded. "So what now?"

Daughtler slid a piece of white paper with plain typing on it. "Here's a list of the books that we're having complaints about. I'd like you to select alternates and submit them to me by next week for approval."

Stephen reached forward and took the paper, not looking at it. He didn't have the heart. "Is that all?"

"That's all. Thanks, Stephen. Have a nice weekend."

Sure. It'll be great. I already have no time to sleep, so let's

*just add in a complete change of lesson plans for the rest of the
year. No problem.*

But he just gave a weak smile, nodded, and slipped
out the door, feeling the weight of all his choices more
heavily than he had in the last year.

* * *

"I think I made a mistake coming back here."

Stephen traced the scratches in the scarred
countertop at the Brick House Cafe, wishing for
everything that a) Haven Ridge had a bar, b) it wasn't
four o'clock on a Friday afternoon, and c) he wouldn't
somehow get fired for being a bad example if someone
saw him drinking in public.

Thomas Rivas, the proprietor of the cafe and a
somewhat recent friend, grimaced as he picked up
Stephen's cup and wiped the ring of spilled coffee from
beneath it. "Uh oh. What happened?"

"Principal Daughtler called me in to talk about my
curriculum choices."

"Ah. Let me guess. Intro to Lit?"

Stephen jerked his head up. "How did you know?"

Thomas gave a wry chuckle. "I'm half-Cuban. I'm
pretty much the only multicultural thing in this whole
town. It didn't take too much of a guess. But you grew
up here too. Shouldn't have been a big surprise."

"Yeah, but I'd kind of hoped we'd come into the
twenty-first century in the fifteen years since I left."

"Bro, we're lucky if we've made it into the 1980s
here. I'm more surprised you got to February without
any complaints."

"That's true." Stephen had gotten a good chunk of
diverse books into his ninth graders before anyone had
gotten the wiser, though what he would do next year

was anyone's guess. "I have to change half the curriculum and have a plan by next week. With the carnival. And my classes."

Thomas winced. "I can't really empathize, but you know Mallory can. She's in the thick of it too."

"Yeah, where is she? In the Springs today?" Thomas's fiancée, Mallory, had come to Haven Ridge about the same time Stephen had moved back last summer, and to hear the story told, their meeting was like a lightning strike, love at first sight leading to wedding plans later this summer. She was currently finishing up a master's degree in history at the University of Colorado in Colorado Springs, after which she was planning to continue on to a Ph.D. If there was anyone who could understand the pain of working full time and going to school simultaneously, it would be her.

Except she had Thomas to lean on, and Stephen . . . well, the once- or twice-a-week call he had with his sort-of girlfriend back in Salt Lake City wasn't exactly the kind of support he needed right now. He was suddenly glad that Mallory wasn't there, even if she could commiserate, because seeing her and Thomas together was almost painful. They were so happy and in love that the sparks between them practically burned his retinas.

But now he was starting to sound like the maudlin, emo literature nerd he'd always secretly been; it was time to summon the jock that everyone still thought he was if he was going to get through these next couple of weeks. He'd had lots of practice. Smile, act like he hadn't a care in the world, the only thing that was important was running a ball into the end zone. It was no surprise that half the town had gaped in shock when he was announced as the new literature teacher. Clearly they'd missed the fact that he'd been salutatorian—losing out on valedictorian to one of his best friends,

Liv—because they seemed downright bewildered he could even read.

Stephen ran his hands through his thick hair, grabbing it hard, as if the pain in his scalp could pull him back to reality. "It's fine. I've got this. I'll figure out my books tonight and get it out of the way, finish my grading. . . That leaves me all weekend to catch up on the classwork I didn't do this week and work on the last-minute details for the winter festival. It'll be good."

"Yeah, keep telling yourself that. You're going to give yourself an ulcer if you don't slow down."

Stephen shot his friend a reproving look. "Aren't you the one who's always 'everything happens for a reason' and 'we just have to have faith'?"

"You're mistaking me for my fiancée or grandmother. Besides, sometimes the reason is that you overextended yourself because you don't know how to say no."

There was an uncomfortable amount of truth in that. "It's a bit too late for that now."

Thomas shrugged. "What you really need is a weekend away. Fly back to Salt Lake and see Nikki. You'll feel better. Trust me."

Stephen shook his head. Thomas might be right that he needed a weekend away, but he wasn't sure that seeing Nikki would help things. Things had been strained between them for a long time, even if they hadn't yet broken up. Mostly, Stephen thought, because Nikki was too busy to date anyone else, and Stephen had no interest in diving back into the dating pool, even if he had the time. Had they not worked together at the same ad agency, he as a Creative Director and she as the VP of Finance, they probably wouldn't have gotten together in the first place.

But after their call on Monday, Stephen had been thinking that maybe even she had gotten tired of the arrangement. She'd been distant and distracted, more so than usual. He was beginning to wonder if there was someone else in her life.

No, going to see Nikki would only make things worse by complicating what was starting to feel like a much-too-complicated life. He would go home tonight, make a list, prioritize his tasks, and then he would get it done, one by one. It wasn't like there was anything to go back to in Salt Lake City, so he had to make this work. He might not like it, and it just might kill him, but there was one thing that he'd always understood.

There were too many people counting on him to fail.

CHAPTER FOUR

STEPHEN HADN'T BEEN SURE about living so far out of town, but on days like this, he was happy for the separation from Haven Ridge.

He backed out of the parking spot at the Brick House Cafe and rolled down the windows on his Ford truck to feel the cold winter air stinging his cheeks and whipping through his hair. As soon as he was clear of the residential area and signaled his turn onto the highway, he pressed a button on the stereo and cranked up the volume. Heavy metal, loud and chaotic, filled the cab, crowding out all the dark thoughts that had consumed him earlier.

He was okay. He really was. It had just been a long week after a long couple of months, and the meeting with Daughtler had been the last straw. But he wasn't really sorry that he had moved back to Haven Ridge.

He'd missed it. He'd been so eager to graduate after what had amounted to a tough two years that he swore he would never go back. But six years in Massachusetts, first getting his literature degree from Boston University and then working as a junior creative at a huge ad agency, had showed him that no matter how much he might have wanted to escape small town life, he wasn't really a city boy. When an opportunity to work for an up-and-coming ad agency in Salt Lake City had materialized, he'd jumped on it. Salt Lake was still big, but it had a kind of Midwestern feel that made it seem more like home than his previous East Coast metropolis. Even the scenery was similar to his native state— soaring mountain vistas, snow, seas of evergreens and aspens.

When it came down to it, though, there was something about this part of Southern Colorado that would always have a hold on him—lonely and beautiful, vast untouched forests and charming small towns. In the end, he had concluded that he was a small-town boy after all.

Except he'd come back with his big-city ways and not everyone knew how to deal with that, his parents foremost among them.

But that was something that he absolutely did not have the energy to think about now. He had bigger fish to fry than his dad's opinions about his life choices: namely, not getting fired from this job, too, and maintaining his sanity along the way.

The brash, loud music did the trick, shoving out all his dark thoughts with a combination of pure volume and biting social commentary. By the time he reached the turnoff that led back through the edge of the forest to his cabin, he was feeling calmer, clearer than he had all afternoon. He flipped on his signal and navigated into the center lane, waiting for an oncoming semi to pass before he turned. As soon as he hit the unpaved road with its slow speeds, he turned off the music, listening instead to the crunch of dirt and gravel beneath his tires.

When at last he pulled up in front of his place, he felt like he'd left the day behind him. He turned off the ignition, the engine dying into a silence so deep it echoed. He climbed out and took a deep breath, listening to the wind rustling through the trees, the distant call of a bird carrying on the wind.

It had been a dream, this tiny rustic house, two stories clad in cedar with a wrap-around upper porch; he'd had something like this in mind for years without knowing it actually existed. And when he had moved here for good after selling his expensive city condo and packing up all his worldly possessions, the real estate listing up on the cafe's community board had felt like a sign. A bit of imagination miraculously come to life. He'd gone out to see it the same day, put in an offer that night.

Stephen grabbed his messenger bag from the back seat of his truck, leaving the binder where it lay as punishment for existing, then walked to the lower door in a crunch of gravel. He let himself into the small paneled foyer, then took the stairs upwards to the living spaces on the top level. The house still needed some renovation, but anyone who walked into this place and looked at the decor wasn't paying attention. The real view was straight ahead.

He dropped the bag on the counter and headed to the glass doors that led to the deck. The high-desert landscape stretched out for miles, the sweeps of evergreen and piñon appearing as dots of dusty green in the otherwise brown-and-white landscape. Beyond, the mountains rose in a craggy jumble, turning purple and blue where the evening shade was already beginning to touch. Here and there he could see houses dotting the land, finished in similarly natural shades so they didn't stand out in the countryside.

It was beautiful. But more than that, it was the kind of view that made him understand how Whitman or Thoreau could have produced their works. It made him wish that he had writing talent of his own and not just an appreciation for the talents of others.

In any other season, Stephen would take his grading outside, sit in one of the brightly painted Adirondack chairs, and work until it got too dark to see. But the temperature was dropping rapidly, sign of another cold front moving through, and he could already tell that they'd be headed for a sub-freezing evening. Instead, he wandered over to the fireplace and pulled a few logs from the stack on the brick hearth, then began building a fire. If he was going to have to work on a Friday night, he was going to do it English library-style—propped in his leather club chair before a fire with an adult beverage, wearing his favorite sheepskin slippers.

He was officially the most boring man alive.

"Just born in the wrong century," Nikki had said once, dropping a kiss on his nose. He'd thought she thought it was charming, but now recalling their last conversation, he wondered if maybe that had just been an excuse, a way to make him feel better about actually being boring. After all, Nikki was a city girl—born and raised in New York before hopping around to Miami, Los Angeles, and London—and she'd only come to Salt Lake City because the offer had been too good to pass up. All it would take was a guy who would rather hit the clubs than stay in and read a book, and Stephen was long gone.

He probably already was, he just wasn't admitting it to himself.

But, like his father, Nikki was another topic he didn't have the emotional capacity for. As soon as the fire caught and was crackling merrily in the hearth, he covered it with the iron screen and moved to the bar cart to pour himself a double bourbon, neat, in a cut-crystal glass. Then he retrieved his messenger bag, pulled out his laptop, and got to work.

No one would come out and say exactly that he had to cut the diversity from Intro to Lit, so it was up to him to find the most—on the surface—unoffensive books that still had redeeming literary and academic quality. He finally found his answer on a teacher's forum, where a teacher in Texas had posted about a similar dilemma. After he sorted through all the outrage over her school district's short-sightedness, there were actually some good suggestions, most of which Stephen had already read. Slowly, he cut and pasted the books into a document, making notes on themes and how they might work into the lesson plans he'd already set out. There would be heavy changes, of course, but at least picking books within the same cultures as the ones that had been pulled would mean his research and materials on cultural context wouldn't go to waste.

It was after nine before he finished, both his glass and his stomach conspicuously empty. He was contemplating whether he wanted to drive back into town to grab some food or make something at home when his phone screen lit up.

Message from Liv Quinn.

Stephen blinked, surprised to be hearing from Liv. They'd been friends for years—they'd both been part of a tight trio until it had all imploded their junior year of high school—but he hadn't really kept in touch with her until he'd returned to Haven Ridge last summer. Talk about someone who had had some tough breaks. And yet she was always cheerful, willing to help. Sometimes he thought he could take a note from her; other times he wondered if that cheerful demeanor was as much a mask as the former-jock, hometown-hero persona he projected around the people who knew him from back-when.

He swiped off the lock screen so he could read the message. **I'm so sorry to do this to you, but I got called to New York on Tuesday. I won't be back in time for the festival. Can I do anything before I go? I know I'm leaving you in the lurch.**

He closed his eyes and dropped his head back against the leather headrest of his chair. Perfect timing. Just when he was feeling better about his prospects of getting everything done, he would have to handle the most work-intensive week of festival prep on his own. Not that Liv hadn't been a godsend when she'd volunteered to help him—anyone who did anything with the PTO knew she was the beating heart of the organization, not just for her organizational skills but for her amazing ability to talk people into anything. Stephen hadn't gotten anywhere soliciting donations and vendors for the market portion of the festival, but Liv had taken care of it within three days.

But she couldn't help the vagaries of her job any more than he could. Quickly, he tapped out a message. **No problem, I understand. I've got this.**

Do you really?

He paused, considering how to answer. They'd been close once, but a shared history didn't necessarily make for shared confidences. Not after what had happened with Gemma. He knew that Liv's loyalty would always be with her best friend, as it should be. He suspected that when Liv talked to Gemma about her life in Haven Ridge, his name was carefully omitted.

And honestly, he couldn't blame either of them.

Which meant that he would give her the expected answer and not the honest one. **It's fine. Pretty much** everything has been confirmed. I'll rope Thomas in to help with setup on Saturday.

Just let me know if I need to persuade someone to step in, Liv replied, following up with a grin emoji. Oh yeah, she knew exactly what she was doing when it came to her powers of persuasion.

"It'll be fine," he told himself, letting his own confident tone convince him it was the truth. He turned on the oven, pulled a frozen lasagna from the freezer and popped it onto the middle rack, then set the timer for an hour. Then he poured himself another drink, brought up his first student essay on his laptop, and got back to work.

CHAPTER FIVE

THE FIRST THING GEMMA ALWAYS FORGOT about Haven Ridge was that there was no good way to get there. Tucked between the Arkansas River and the eastern slope of the Sangre de Cristo mountain range, it was nowhere near a convenient airport or any sort of public transportation. Either you took one plane and drove three to four hours into the mountains or you took two planes and drove an hour back down. No matter which option she selected, it was ten hours from her house in Santa Monica to Liv's house in Haven Ridge—it would almost be faster to drive.

Gemma selected the second option, which brought her to the second thing she forgot about Haven Ridge: the area around it was absolutely gorgeous. The tiny regional jet cut southwest from Denver over the mountains, giving her a bird's-eye view of a sparkling expanse of white, the usual desert-like landscape blanketed from a recent snowfall, scrubby patches of evergreens and piñon groves punctuating the country-side like islands of gray-green in a vast white sea. Beyond rose the stunning silhouette of the Sangre de

Cristo range, home of many of the state's famous fourteeners. It wasn't the mountain view that so many associated with Colorado, but it still touched a place in her that she'd forgotten about, the part that yearned for snow days and wide-open spaces. Despite her misgivings, she felt unaccountably excited about the prospect of actual weather once more.

The jet bumped down on the single paved runway at the Gunnison-Crested Butte Regional Airport, then taxied to its resting place outside the outdated, low-slung terminal, which from the outside always reminded Gemma more of an outdoor supply superstore than an actual airport. While the crew of the tiny jet performed all its arrival procedures and a cart-mounted stairway rolled up to the door, she retrieved her backpack from beneath the seat in front of her and tried not to chew her thumbnail while she waited. She'd only been back to Colorado twice since leaving the state for good fourteen years ago. One of those times had been for a wedding, the other for a funeral.

She was already wondering if she'd made a mistake.

Fortunately, she was in the front of the plane, so she didn't have much time to dwell on the thought. She crept up the narrow aisle and broke free into the blinding sunshine, the stiff wind immediately cutting through her sweater like a knife and raising goosebumps all over her skin. She descended the stairs and followed the straggly line of passengers across the asphalt apron toward the terminal doors, huffing and puffing by the time she finally got inside.

That was the third thing she always forgot: it was hard to breathe at almost 7,700 feet when you were no longer acclimated to the altitude.

The inside of the terminal was just as rustic as the outside, with beamed wood ceilings and long stretches of pine paneling that at least distracted from the tragic 1980s patterned carpet. Despite herself, Gemma smiled as she made her way downstairs to the single baggage claim. After the barely controlled chaos of LAX, this Podunk little airport struck her as charming. If she weren't so apprehensive, she would almost say it was good to be home.

Fortunately, the baggage handlers were efficient, and before long Gemma was able to drag her bright red suitcase off the conveyor belt and break free of the other passengers in favor of the ground transportation area. She'd barely made it more than a few steps into the parking lot when she heard a squeal and a flurry of blonde enthusiasm launched itself at her.

"Gemma! You made it! I wasn't entirely sure you would!"

Gemma laughed and caught Liv in a tight hug, compressing her friend's down tech jacket between them. "I'm not sure whether to be amused or hurt by that."

"Amused, definitely." Liv pulled away with a grin. "You look great, by the way."

"Liar," Gemma threw back. She'd gotten hardly any sleep the night before, and the bags under her eyes were so big she'd worried that the check-in desk attendant was going to make her tag them as oversized luggage. Liv, on the other hand, really did look great. She was as trim and toned as ever, sheathed in leggings, sheepskin-lined snow boots, and that slim-cut jacket; without makeup, she was fresh-faced and beautiful, the messy bun on top of her head making her look more like a college student than a thirty-year-old guardian of a teenager. Two years into widowhood, that haunted look was finally leaving her eyes. Gemma let out a sigh of relief, and a bit of the guilt she'd been carrying sloughed away.

"You've got to be freezing," Liv said, taking her suitcase handle from her hand without asking and starting off across the parking lot at a quick clip. "I hope you have a jacket in there."

"Of course I do. I haven't been away that long. But it was warm when I left LA and I didn't want to wrangle it on that tiny plane."

"I told you I would pick you up in Denver!"

"And make you drive almost eight hours round-trip? I don't think so." Gemma nudged Liv's arm with her elbow. "You know, it's really good to see you."

"It's been too long," Liv said, smiling, without a hint of reproach. "And Taylor has been dying to have you stay with us. I hope you don't plan on getting any sleep because she's got every hour planned out. You're her very favorite aunt."

"It wasn't much of a competition, given I'm her only aunt, and not even a real one at that."

"Well, I'm not her real mom either, but we make do with what we have, don't we?"

Gemma grimaced, regretting touching on the topic before they'd even made it to the car. "How's that going, by the way?"

Liv stopped in front of a big blue SUV and popped the hatch. "It's been rough, to be honest. But we're getting through it. She's finally . . . come to terms with what happened."

Gemma heaved her suitcase into the back of the SUV and hit the button to close the hatch, then turned to her friend. "Liv, I'm sorry I haven't been more available. You know I—"

"Don't start." Liv waved off her apology with a manicured hand. "We're grown-ups. We have our own lives. I know where to find you if I need you. And I did."

"I know, it's just—"

"Enough." When Liv got that stern look, she meant business. "Now hop in. We've still got a drive."

Gemma always worried that when they saw each other after so long, it was going to be awkward, but every visit proved that time was no match for true friendship. For the next hour, they caught up on their lives and gossip. Liv told her about the books that she had acquired and edited for her line in the last year or so; Gemma told her about the more memorable cases she'd handled. Then they moved on to the usual small-town gossip: who had gotten married, who had had babies, who had left and moved back.

"Oh, you'll never guess who's mayor now. Doug Meinke."

"No," Gemma said, scandalized. "Didn't you all vote him most likely to go to prison?"

Liv laughed. "I'd forgotten about that. I think we did. He's all respectable and everything. Hard to believe, isn't it?"

"Not as hard to believe as the fact he married Chelsea Young." Gemma shuddered. "I hated her in high school. She was just so mean. And unnecessarily, you know? As if we had anything to do with our parents' problems."

"Time hasn't changed much," Liv said wryly. "Would you believe she's the head of the elementary school PTO? I've never been so glad that Taylor is in high school. The high school PTO is really chill by comparison."

Gemma grinned at her. "You're kidding me, right? You're a PTO member?"

"Have to be. Taylor's in speech and there are a lot of fundraisers."

Her admiration for her friend went up another notch. It would have been hard enough to lose her husband, but to be thrust into guardianship of a girl she'd only known for four years? That was a level of adulting of which Gemma could barely conceive. Then again, considering she hadn't managed to have more than a second date in the last five years, marriage itself was an achievement level she couldn't imagine.

"So are you . . . seeing anyone?" Gemma asked gently, but before she even got the words out, Liv was shaking her head.

"No, not at all. It's just still too hard. Not just for me, but for Taylor, too. I don't know how she'd react to me bringing someone home so soon after her dad died."

It was Liv's tone, so matter of fact, that allowed Gemma to continue on the line of questioning. "Are you lonely?"

"Sometimes. But honestly, I'm so busy I don't have time for dating, even if I were ready. Working full time while raising a teenager by myself? I'm lucky I sleep."

"Maybe you should extend your trip in New York a little," Gemma said slowly. "Do some sightseeing. Maybe see a show. I don't have to be back until next Monday."

Liv shot a sharp look at her. "I couldn't."

"Why not?"

"Because it's not your responsibility."

"Oh, please. Take the weekend. Taylor and I will be fine."

"Are you sure?" Liv asked again, but a little smile was playing at her lips.

"I'm positive. Check with Taylor if you're worried, but I have a feeling she's not going to complain. I am her favorite aunt, after all."

Liv gave a long exhale. "You are amazing. I haven't been to the theater since I moved back here. And I think the New York City Ballet's spring season will be in full swing . . ."

While Liv rhapsodized about Broadway and Lincoln Center, Gemma just sat back and listened with satisfaction. Her friend deserved this. She'd had difficulty upon tragedy these past few years, and if Gemma could give her back a bit of herself, it was more than worth the sacrifice, especially if her all-hands meeting turned out to be bad news. Besides, it wasn't exactly a sacrifice. She and Taylor couldn't have gotten along any better had they been blood relations. The girl often visited Gemma in LA over spring and fall breaks, with or without Liv, and she was everything that she would have wanted in her own daughter: smart, sarcastic, inquisitive. If she hadn't known better, she would have credited that to Liv; they were the same attributes that Gemma admired in her best friend.

True, it had been over a year since she saw her last, when she had invited Liv and Taylor to share a beach house in Santa Barbara for a week as a way to get them away from their grief, away from all the reminders of Jason Quinn that no doubt surrounded them. Liv claimed it was a miracle to see Taylor smile again, playing in the surf like a little girl. When they'd come inside, sandy and spent from the sun and wind, they'd curled up beneath blankets and watched stupid movies on Netflix until they couldn't keep their eyes open. Surely, they could reproduce some of that heavenly relaxation, even if they were back in Haven Ridge and not on the California coast.

Put that way, maybe Gemma needed an escape as much as Liv.

She'd been so distracted by her new plan that she hadn't paid attention to their destination. Now, as Liv stopped at the intersection of a four-lane highway, Gemma recognized where they were. Turn left and they'd go directly to Liv's house. Turn right and they'd be in Haven Ridge in five minutes. If she could help it, this was going to be the closest that Gemma would come to town the whole time she was here.

"Wait until you see it," Liv said. Apparently, she had switched subjects while Gemma's mind was wandering. "You're going to love it. The old owners were just using it as storage, but now it's a two-bedroom, one-bath with a full kitchen and a separate entrance. You'll be as close or as far from the house as you want to be."

Gemma realized Liv was talking about the remodeled rental unit atop their garage. "Will Taylor be okay in the house by herself?"

"So she says. But I wouldn't be surprised if she moves into the second bedroom while I'm gone." Liv glanced at her, the first hint of worry creasing her forehead. "I hope that's all right with you."

"Of course it is. You're sure it wouldn't be easier for me just to stay in the house?"

Liv cringed. "You probably wouldn't say that if you saw it. It's . . . a work in progress."

Gemma would have asked for more details, but Liv had turned onto an unsigned dirt road and they were bumping down the rutted track through a dense piñon grove. Widely-spaced houses lay behind gates, their conditions as varied as their architecture; brand-new modern builds sat right next to dilapidated farmhouses with rusting cars in the side yard. Liv finally turned onto a long dirt drive and paused to punch in her code on a keypad a few feet away from a wide automatic gate.

Gemma smiled as Liv pulled onto the property, as charmed now as the first time she'd seen it. When Jason and Liv had gotten married, everyone in town thought they were insane for buying this rundown property that had once been the town's one-room brick schoolhouse with a barn-garage conversion. But they'd fallen in love with it and they'd gotten the property for a song, so they'd shrugged off the naysayers and gotten to work.

The first phase to make it livable had taken almost a year, with them living in a travel trailer on the property while they did much of the work themselves. They had just been embarking on the second phase of the renovation when Jason died. Gemma had been one of their first guests, and they'd jokingly teased her that they'd make her an in-law apartment over the garage so she could come visit whenever she wanted.

It looked like Liv had finally made good on the promise.

Liv parked in the newly-cemented driveway, and Gemma hopped out, taking a deep breath of mountain air mixed with dusty piñon pine. Cold air stung her skin even as the heat from the sun warmed her. She'd missed the strange contradictions of her hometown, even if she didn't miss the people in it. There was simply nothing like high, dry Colorado air and the brilliant blue, wide-open sky.

"Come on, let me show you the place." Liv grinned at Gemma, as excited as a kid on Christmas morning, practically skipping around the side of the two-story garage to the door on the side. She punched in some numbers on the electronic keypad—"I made it your birthday so you couldn't forget"—and then opened the door on a pretty little foyer.

Gemma stepped inside with a smile. The small space had hardwood floors and creamy walls, decorated with a woven bench and two bright orange metal lockers. A flight of wooden stairs stretched halfway up to the second floor before making a steep left turn and continuing the rest of the way. She climbed them slowly, stopping to admire the view of the mountains from a window on the small landing and then continued up into a long hallway.

And then she stopped. "Liv, this is. . . ." Beautiful? Incredible? Neither of them seemed to do Liv's work justice.

"It is, isn't it?" Liv smiled proudly and brushed by her to give her the tour. Two sizable bedrooms opened from the right side of the hall, each with a queen bed covered with a fluffy comforter and an antique dresser. To the left was a bathroom that was the size of Gemma's kitchen, with a soaking tub, a walk-in shower, and an octagonal porthole window over the sink. Gemma remembered that window from the old barn. Toward the far back of the space was a comfortable living room with a turquoise sofa, leather chair, and a fluffy sheepskin rug; opposite it was a shockingly large kitchen with all the amenities of home.

"So," Liv prompted, "what do you think?"

"I think I'm never leaving," Gemma said, then impulsively hugged her friend. "You did all of this yourself?"

"Well, I hired people for some of the construction, but yeah. I did most of it myself. All the painting, the floors, the decorating. It's going to be a vacation rental, but considering what we promised you, it only makes sense for you to be the first guest."

"Thank you. I'm honored."

Liv waved off the thanks. "Let's lug your suitcase up here and get you settled before Taylor gets home from school."

"Is she driving already?"

"Not yet. Gets her license in six months. But don't worry, she rides the bus to school."

Liv led her back out, where they retrieved her suitcase and backpack from the SUV and dropped it in the downstairs vestibule. She quickly unearthed her coat and then followed Liv to the main house.

It was easy to see why Liv had been charmed by the

place. The original schoolhouse was a big rectangle of square brick with twelve-foot ceilings and expansive picture windows that had probably been added in the fifties or sixties. Two extensions in a dark-stained wood siding jutted out from either end. Liv went in the side door, which opened onto a mudroom, and then led her down a short hallway to the kitchen.

Gemma stopped short and started to laugh helplessly. "Oh, Liv."

"I know, right?" Liv turned in a full circle and let out a sigh. "It's awful."

The original kitchen hadn't exactly been anything to write home about, but at least it had . . . existed. Great bits of plaster were missing from the walls where she'd demoed the old ugly tile. The upper cabinets were completely gone. The lower cabinets appeared new, but in place of a permanent countertop were several thick slabs of particle board. Thankfully, she had a sink and new appliances, but the rest . . .

"What happened?" Gemma asked.

"I ran out of money. Or more accurately, I used the money that was earmarked for the kitchen to finish the apartment."

"But why?"

"My contractor flaked on me halfway through the project, and all the quotes that I've gotten since have been twice the amount. So I figured that I'd finish the apartment first, start generating income, and hopefully that will help me finish the kitchen. I mean, it's functional now. It's just not—"

"Finished?" Gemma suggested at the same time Liv said, "Pretty."

"The priority was finishing Taylor's room anyway. If you're lucky, she'll let you see it." Liv threw Gemma a wry smile. "I wouldn't dare invade her privacy."

"Teens, hmm?"

Liv chuckled and led her into the living room, where they flopped on the overstuffed sofa. "She's a good one, as teens go. I don't know what I would have done without her these past two years."

Gemma kicked off her shoes so she could draw her legs under her. "Anything I need to know while you're gone? About Taylor, I mean."

Liv hesitated.

"Come on, spill it. I have to know if I'm going to help."

"She's struggling in school a little right now," Liv said finally. "She's failing English."

"English? When she has an editor for a guardian?"

"I know. It's shameful. It's not that she doesn't get it, she just won't make an effort. I'd think she's having trouble adjusting to her dad being gone, but she's got As in algebra and chemistry."

"Not everyone is good at language arts, I suppose?"

"It's never been a problem before." Liv turned hopeful blue eyes toward her. "I'm hoping maybe she'll tell you something she wouldn't tell me."

"I can try, but everything I know about parenting a teenage girl comes from being one, and you know as well as I do that doesn't always translate. I mean, when we were her age, all we had was MySpace, and barely."

"Don't I know it," Liv muttered. "When did we get so old? One minute I'm debating whether I should do pink or blue streaks in my hair and the next day I'm yelling at my daughter to finish her homework."

Gemma chuckled. "I think it was the mortgage that did it."

"Probably." Liv sighed. "It's times like this that I really miss Jason. I'm sure he would find his daughter just as incomprehensible as I do, but at least I wouldn't be alone in my confusion. Now I just keep thinking, he entrusted his kid to me and I'm screwing this all up."

Gemma reached for Liv's hand and squeezed it hard. "You are not screwing it up. And you are not alone."

"Thanks, Gem." Liv smiled, and this time it reached her eyes. "I really appreciate you being here."

The keypad on the front door beeped as numbers were punched in from the outside and then it opened with a squeak. Booted footsteps clomped on the aged hardwoods, then the door slammed shut.

Liv twisted around on the sofa. "Hey, Taylor! Aunt Gem's here. Come in the living room and tell us about your day!"

"I don't want to talk about it!" Taylor snapped. All Gemma got was the impression of dyed blue hair, tall black boots, and a sullen expression as the teen blew by the living room, stomped down the hallway, and slammed the door to her room.

Liv closed her eyes, took a deep breath, and let it out slowly. When she opened them again, she gave Gemma a helpless smile. "Changed your mind about that offer yet?"

"Of course not," Gemma said automatically, but inwardly she was wondering: what on earth had she gotten herself into?

CHAPTER SIX

To Gemma's great relief, what the kitchen lacked in style—and substance—it made up for in a well-stocked pantry. It only took a few minutes of rummaging for her to realize that they had all the makings of one of Taylor's all-time favorite meals: chicken pot pie. Liv didn't complain when Gemma nudged her out of the way and started pulling out pots and appliances from the lower cabinets to begin her savory pie crust while the chicken breasts thawed for the filling.

"I have never seen any problem so great that it couldn't be fixed with some sort of pie," Gemma said in a low voice to Liv, who was still looking upset about Taylor's rude entrance. "Trust me. She'll smell this baking and she won't be able to resist coming out."

Sure enough, the pie had just gone into the oven, scenting the air with cooking vegetables and butter and a lightly sweet crust, when Taylor's door opened and soft footsteps padded down the hall. Gemma barely looked up as she cleaned—with difficulty, she might add—the particle board countertops. "Hey, Taylor. You hungry? I've got a chicken pot pie in the oven."

"That sounds good," Taylor said in a quiet voice. She moved around the island and offered a side hug to Gemma. "Thanks for coming, Aunt Gem."

Gemma squeezed her to her side a little harder before letting her go. "Wouldn't have missed it."

"Hey, Liv," Taylor said, shooting an abashed look at her stepmom. "Sorry about earlier."

"That's okay," Liv said quietly. "Anything you want to talk about yet?"

Taylor shook her head, but she didn't flee the kitchen, which Gemma took as a good sign. Now that she knew Taylor wasn't going to escape, she took a surreptitious look at her niece. What she'd initially registered as blue hair was actually an electric blue streak through her long, dark ponytail; the school clothes and boots had been swapped for baggy sweatpants and slippers. A few smudged remnants of mascara dotted the skin beneath her eyes—it looked to Gemma that she had been crying.

"So," Gemma said, trying to think of a topic that didn't involve school and the day's teen drama, "Liv tells me you made a list of things you want to bake while she's gone."

Taylor brightened considerably. "We got stuff for your famous chocolate croissants."

"That's a no-brainer. But what did you want to do for your Showstopper Challenge?"

Now that earned a grin. Gemma had introduced Taylor to her favorite BBC baking show a couple of years ago, and since then the teen had been trying to stump her with things like decorative Cornish pasties and Baked Alaska.

"I had been thinking macarons, but Liv said those are hard to make at our altitude . . ."

"They are, a bit. I only mastered them at sea level."

". . . so I say baklava."

"Ah. Homemade phyllo dough. I like a challenge." Gemma grinned at Taylor. "Did you get the ingredients for that too?"

"Of course we did. And we even got the good butter."

"The student has become the master." Gemma winked at the teen, then smiled at Liv behind her, who looked relieved. "I think we'll do that in the apartment, though. I'm afraid we'll be trying to get phyllo out of these countertops for the next week if we do it here."

"Liv said I could stay in the spare bedroom in the apartment? Just to make things easier?"

"Oh she did, did she? I suppose that would be okay. Just for the ease of baking and such."

Taylor beamed, suddenly looking like the young girl she remembered. Inwardly, Gemma gave a sigh of relief. After that entrance, she'd been wondering if the sullen teen was here to stay.

For the next several minutes, Taylor rattled off her baking wish list and demonstrated that they had, in fact, gotten all the necessary ingredients for everything. Then Gemma pulled the pot pie out of the oven, its top golden and flaky and delicious-looking, and they all moved to the dining room adjacent to the living area. They were just finishing up the last delicious creamy bites when Taylor said in a low voice, "Everyone has a date for the Valentine's Dance except me. My friends were supposed to go as a group and they all caved."

"Ohh," Liv said softly, and Gemma didn't need to know the details to understand. There was enough heartbreak contained in those words to take her back to when she was Taylor's age. There was nothing worse than being a singleton in a sea of pairs. She could tell her it got easier as you got older, but the truth was, you just got more adept at hiding it.

Once Taylor had cleared the dinner dishes, Liv pulled out a quart of rocky road ice cream from the freezer, dished out a bowl for her stepdaughter, and then poured big mugs of flavored coffee for both adults. Taylor didn't seem to want to talk, just ate her ice cream and then retreated to her room to finish homework. Liv and Gemma took their coffee back to the sofa, where Liv flicked on the TV as background noise.

"I'd tell her that boys will make more sense when she grows up, but I'd only be lying to her," Liv said wryly.

"You're telling me. I've had more first dates than a calendar."

"Nice one. Really, though, there's no one?"

Gemma shook her head. "Seems like whenever a guy I'm remotely interested in finds out I'm a divorce lawyer, it's like someone's yelled 'fire' in the restaurant. He's out of there before the appetizers hit the table."

"If you think that's really the problem, you could always say you practice family law. That sounds friendlier."

"What do you mean if that's the problem?"

Liv gave her a sympathetic look. "Did it ever occur to you that you can be a little intimidating?"

"What? No! Why—"

Liv ticked off her fingers: "You're beautiful, over six foot in heels, you make a good living, you've got an impressive education, you own your own house, you drive a nice car . . ."

"Why should that be intimidating?"

"Because a guy might look at you and wonder what he could contribute to the relationship?"

"If the only thing a guy can contribute to a relationship is money and height, why would I want him in the first place?"

Liv laughed, shaking her head. "I'm just saying."

"And I'm just saying I'd rather be alone than have to

be less for someone else. Even if that means I have to rent the apartment over your garage when I'm old so I've got someone to look after me."

Now Liv's laughter turned a little bit hysterical. "We're the same age!"

"We both know you're going to age better than me. You'll have to introduce me as your mom when we go places."

"You are insane."

Now it was Gemma's turn to grin. "I missed you, Liv. I'm sorry I haven't been there for you."

"And I said stop. You're here when I need you. I can't expect you to stop living your life to monitor me. I'm doing okay."

"You really are," Gemma said softly. "I'm so proud of you."

"You make it sound like I had a choice in the matter."

"I know, but you've made a good life for yourself and Taylor. Some people fall apart."

They both fell silent then, knowing exactly what Gemma wasn't saying. Finally, Liv asked, "How is she anyway?"

"Mom is . . Mom." Gemma shrugged. "She's okay. Still working the front office for that dentist in Phoenix. Seems happy enough."

"But . . ."

"She's never gotten over Dad. And I don't mean she hasn't forgiven him. *I* haven't forgiven him. But I've at least moved on. It feels like Mom is just passing the time. Yet she still wants to know when I'm getting hitched, even after all she went through."

"She was from a different era," Liv said. "That's just what women did."

"Which is exactly why I'm not fretting about not being married yet."

"What about your dad?"

"What about him?"

"Have you talked to him?"

Gemma shook her head. "Not since he sold the house here and called to ask if I wanted my old bedroom furniture. I have nothing to say to the man."

"Even if he's contrite?"

"The one thing I know about *Dr. Van Buren* is that nothing is ever his fault." Gemma drained her coffee mug and pushed herself off the sofa. "I'm beat. I'm going to go to bed now. What time do we need to leave for the airport?"

"Don't worry about it. I've already booked the express coach."

"No, I can—"

"I have to fly out early, and you need to get Taylor off to school. There's not enough time to drive there and back." Liv finished her own wine and stood. "You've already done enough." She paused, then pulled Gemma in for a hug. "I really appreciate this, Gem. It's nice to have someone to count on."

"That's what I'm here for." Gemma planted a kiss on Liv's cheek, then gave her one more squeeze before letting her go. "Text me when you get to New York, okay? And keep me posted with the meetings."

"You've got it. And if you need anything at all . . ."

"Don't worry about us. We'll be fine." Gemma pulled on her coat; even though it was only a short walk across the driveway to her temporary digs, the temperature had fallen into the single digits. But once she got to the door to the apartment, she paused.

So far away from the city lights, the night sky spread out in an endless sweep of inky blue, the Milky Way a lavish spill of glitter above her. It was nearly impossible to believe that this was the same sky that rode above

Los Angeles, pale from reflected light, all but the brightest stars hidden from view. She stood there, staring up, until her ears started to hurt from the cold and her fingertips began to go numb. Then she went inside, the slightest smile lingering on her lips.

CHAPTER SEVEN

GEMMA AWOKE IN A PANIC with sunlight streaming in through her uncovered windows and the bright red numbers showing 9:06 on her digital clock. She was late for work. No, she was late for—

Taylor.

She leapt out of bed, shoving her bare feet into boots and slipping her arms into the sleeves of her coat while she scrambled down the stairs of the apartment and out the door into the yard. The cold hit her like a physical force, squeezing the breath from her lungs into a cloud that froze instantly on the breeze. How could February be so cold? Or rather, how had she managed to forget that February was so cold?

She hurried across the gravel yard and let herself in the door with the key code. "Taylor? Are you still here?"

She darted down the hallway to Taylor's room. The door stood open, revealing the room just as clean as yesterday, the bed perfectly made. No backpack or coat or books. She slumped against the doorway while her heart rate returned to normal. Thank God her niece was the self-sufficient sort, or Gemma would have already failed at her first few hours in charge.

As if to punctuate that Taylor was currently the more responsible of the two of them, a note lay on the kitchen island, written in the girl's loopy script:

> *Be home from school at 4. Coffee and bagels on the counter.* — *T*

At the bottom, she'd scrawled her cell phone number. Gemma hadn't remembered to check if Taylor had her number, though knowing Liv, she probably did. Just in case, she'd text Taylor later.

But now, she poured a cup of coffee from the pot on the warmer and popped one of the bagels in the toaster. She had seven hours until her niece got home. What was she going to do with her time?

First, she should probably make up a meal plan and go grocery shopping, while she was still unlikely to run into anyone she knew. Then maybe she'd take one of the half-dozen paperback books she'd stuffed in her suitcase and spend a little time in the hot tub on Liv's back porch. After that . . .

The thought was too intimidating to consider. When she'd agreed to come back to Haven Ridge to stay with Taylor, she hadn't considered the fact her niece would be in school. How on earth was she ever going to fill her days?

She took her time getting ready in her apartment, dressing in her typical mountain uniform of jeans, long-sleeved tee, and jacket, then retrieved the keys Liv had left behind and hopped into the massive SUV. As she drove back down the rutted dirt road and pulled out onto the highway, she was struck by a sense of . . . aloneness.

Not loneliness—Gemma was far too accustomed to being on her own to be uncomfortable doing anything by herself. But after the press and the noise and the traffic and the smog of Los Angeles, the wide-open spaces left a strange, untethered sense of solitariness in her chest. The desert-like landscape stretched out on either side of the blacktop, broken only occasionally by houses or farms, signs advertising wildflower honey and fresh beef and RV storage. Even the sky above was a desert sky, a dim blue streaked with clouds, which filtered bright, milky sunshine down onto her and gave everything a strange golden haze.

The spell was broken by the big white superstore at the intersection of two rural highways, the parking lot half-filled with cars even on a Tuesday morning. Gemma parked as far out as she could and hiked into the heated building. Besides the convenience store back down the highway and a single gas station outside of Haven Ridge, this was the only retail outlet around for thirty miles.

She kept her head down as she scanned the aisles, praying that there was no one here who would recognize her and want to catch up on the old days, pretending that they'd actually missed her and that she hadn't been the topic of gossip for months after she'd left. Fortunately, the shoppers were either tourists or harried-looking moms with young children. She piled the cart high with all she'd need for breakfast, lunch, and dinner for the next several days, then took her time browsing the rest of the aisles just to kill time.

The store had the survivalist bounty that characterized Colorado mountain superstores, ranging from gluten-free baked goods and gourmet ice cream to live bait and ammo. She stopped in the book section—also boasting an impressive selection, which was helpful considering

Haven Ridge no longer had a bookstore—and chose a hardcover bestseller on a whim, then browsed comforters, stainless steel thermoses, and auto parts for no other reason than she could.

By the time Gemma left, she was smiling.

Make no mistake, she appreciated Southern California with its casual cool and perfect weather and proximity to the ocean. She enjoyed being able to grow roses in her garden year-round and get authentic *pho* for dinner from any number of shops on any number of street corners. But there was something about the mix of rustic and modern and hippie and outdoorsy in these far-flung reaches of Chaffee County that had always made her giddy with happiness. It had just taken coming back to remind her of what her family drama had almost made her forget.

She loved Colorado.

She took her time unpacking the groceries back in her apartment, arranging them just so, then borrowed a laundry basket from the main house to transport all the baking supplies Taylor had dictated for her stay. She'd planned to take her new book to the hot tub and enjoy a little mid-day soak, but the baking ingredients were calling to her and instead she found herself whipping up a batch of lemon-blueberry muffins for breakfast the next morning. That led to a batch of banana nut muffins from a bunch of black bananas she'd salvaged from the main house's pantry. It was more than they could eat in a single week, but she could stick a dozen in the freezer so Liv and Taylor would have breakfast after she left.

By the time she had the muffins cooled, her dishes washed, and the kitchen cleaned, the hands of the oversized clock on the wall were inching toward four o'clock. Gemma stepped back with mingled surprise and pleasure. Her first real day of vacation by herself, completed without even the urge to check her email. That must be some sort of a record.

But as the hand ticked past four, then four fifteen, Gemma began to worry. What if Taylor really hadn't made it to school this morning? What if something had happened and she didn't know? She pulled out her cell phone and the scrap of paper Taylor had left that morning and texted her: Everything okay? Expected you home already.

Almost immediately, a response beeped through: Fine. Had to stay after school. Missed bus. Pick me up?

Instantly, Gemma's stomach dropped to her feet. Haven Ridge High School wasn't in town exactly; it was more on the edge. But still, it was near enough that it would be almost impossible to fly under the radar. And once one person recognized her, it would be all over.

She groaned. Who would have ever thought that she'd take facing her least favorite judge in the courtroom than go pick up her niece from school?

But that's what a good aunt did, and she certainly couldn't tell Taylor to find her own way home just because she didn't want to see any of her old acquaintances. So she slipped her coat on, jumped in the SUV, and made her way down the highway to her old stomping grounds.

Haven Ridge High School was exactly as she remembered it. The main school building was still that weird post-modern mixture they'd always made fun of, a sort of Bauhaus style filtered through Colorado Rustic, with lots of black-framed glass and cantilevered roofs. The grounds, which would be in full greenery later in the year, were the yellow-brown of grass that had recently been buried under inches of snow, the trees still bare of their spring buds. The large asphalt parking lot was scattered with a handful of cars—the beaters that the kids drove and the slightly nicer beaters that the teachers drove.

She smiled as she wove up and down the aisles, guessing that since there were no kids lingering outside the front doors, she'd find Taylor hanging in the lot near someone's car.

She was right. She glimpsed Taylor's blue-streaked ponytail and Doc Martens in a clutch of girls standing next to a decrepit Plymouth and pulled into a parking spot a couple of spaces away. Apparently, the great date betrayal had been forgiven, or at least the drama was still unfolding. Taylor waved but didn't rush over to the car, so Gemma hopped out and wandered to her side.

"Hey," she said, when the conversation stopped and all eyes turned toward her. She smiled at the girls, but focused on Taylor. "Are you ready to go?"

"In just a second," she said. The girls giggled.

Gemma frowned, suspicious. "What's going on?"

"Nothing," a pretty blonde said airily, though she still wore a secretive smile. "I'm Layla, by the way." She stuck her hand out.

Surprised, Gemma shook it. "I'm Taylor's aunt, Gemma. Kind of," she added with a smile.

"Yeah, Taylor told us. Cool that you could come out and stay with her for a little while."

The girls started giggling and whispering again, and Layla nudged Taylor in the ribs. Her niece flushed beet red and hissed, "Shut up! You guys are so embarrassing."

Okay, this had to have something to do with a boy. Gemma recognized that I-want-to-sink-into-the-asphalt posture all too well. Curious, she craned her neck to see who they were looking for. An athlete, no doubt, if they were hanging out in the parking lot so late; she'd spent far too much of her high school career waiting for the football team to leave practice.

Finally, she got a glimpse of a boy coming their way, dressed in athletic gear with a duffel bag slung over his shoulder. She'd been right about that part at least. But as he came closer, she realized it wasn't a boy, but unmistakably a man. Not even football players were that well filled out in high school. Gemma stifled her grin with difficulty. Dear, sweet, prickly Taylor had a crush on a teacher.

"Here he comes," one of the girls sing-songed, while another one sighed, "He's so hot. Seriously. Why does he have to be our teacher?"

"Like that makes any difference," Layla said. "We're all still jailbait."

Gemma wasn't sure whether to be amused or horrified, and she was so focused on choosing between the two that she wasn't paying nearly enough attention when the teacher stopped at a muddy truck a few spaces away and waved at them. "Night, girls. See you tomorrow."

The blood drained from Gemma's face, her stomach taking a downward plunge to the pavement. *That voice.* She'd recognize it anywhere, even roughened and deepened in the fifteen years since she'd heard it last. Her heart instantly skipped a beat, her traitorous body responding to the sound as if she'd been waiting her whole adult life to hear it again.

Automatically, she swiveled on her heel, turning her back to him, and a word slipped out of her mouth that Liv definitely would not approve her using around her daughter.

She couldn't have done anything that would pique the girls' interest more.

Taylor frowned. "Do you know Mr. Osborne?"

Mr. Osborne. Apparently, there were things that Liv had forgotten to mention to her, or maybe purposely omitted. Slowly, Gemma turned back to the girls, but her eyes sailed right over the teens and landed on the man, who was now staring back at her.

Just get in your truck and drive away, she pleaded silently as the blood rushed back to her cheeks in a furious flush.

No such luck. He was coming their way, his eyes fixed on her. Except for Taylor, the girls spread out, making her feel suddenly, terribly exposed.

"I don't believe it," he said when he was finally standing in front of her. "Gemma, is that actually you?"

Gemma had known coming here was a bad idea. A terrible idea. She automatically straightened to her full height, something that usually made her feel powerful given she literally looked down on half her colleagues while wearing heels, but she didn't have heels today and he'd put another couple of inches on his already-tall frame. "Stephen. I had no idea you taught here."

"Yeah," he said slowly, still staring at her with an expression of confused wonder. "I teach English Lit. And I coach the track team, of course. How are you?"

"Good. I'm good." She had no idea where to look, because everywhere her eyes landed, it just reminded her why she'd fallen for him in high school and how very little had changed since then. His hazel eyes were just as beautiful as she remembered, fringed in lashes so long and dark they made every female jealous. His handsome, boyish features had instead become chiseled and rugged, particularly now, shaded by a five-o'clock shadow. And there was no way she could look anywhere else without him thinking she was ogling.

But oh, how she wanted to ogle.

And that alone made her angry. All she should feel when she looked at him was fury. Or maybe indifference. Certainly not stirrings of the old magnetism that had once made her think that he was her true love, that they were meant to be together, as if his betrayal and the ensuing fifteen years had never happened.

But he seemed to be completely oblivious to her inner turmoil, looking her up and down with bland curiosity. "What are you doing here? Last I heard, you were practicing law in California."

"Yeah. I am. I mean, I was. I . . ." Gemma shook her head to stop her babbling. "I'm just in town for the week while Liv's on a business trip."

"Ah, that's nice." His attention flicked to Taylor, who was watching the whole exchange through narrowed eyes, then back to Gemma. "We should get together for coffee while you're in town, for old times' sake. My number's in the school staff directory." He smiled at the group of girls, who were clustered around them again, not to be left out of the awkwardness. "Don't forget about your sonnets, ladies. I'm expecting some great things from you."

A chorus of "Okay, Mr. Osborne" came from the girls. He smiled at them all once more, lingering on Gemma for just a few seconds longer, then headed back to his truck with a jaunty wave. All the female eyes followed him, including hers.

Layla was the first to speak. "You knew him," she said, almost accusingly. "You have history."

Gemma shook her head to clear her thoughts and focused on Taylor's friends. "We used to date in high school."

This sparked some laughs and nudges. One of the girls, the redhead—Gemma was really going to have to learn names—asked slyly, "Was he as good-looking then as he is now?"

"Honestly?" Gemma leaned around Taylor to catch one last glimpse of Stephen Osborne as he climbed into his car. "Not really." She shrugged, but even as shell-shocked as she felt right now, she couldn't keep a wry smile off her face. "Some things get better with age."

That earned her full-on laughter and it dispelled whatever trance she'd fallen under in his presence. She glanced at Taylor. "Come on, we have to get going. I've got big plans for us tonight."

Taylor hoisted her backpack and said her goodbyes, then followed Gemma back to the SUV. But despite all her attempts to engage the teenager in conversation as they pulled out of the parking lot and back onto the highway, she only responded in vague, single-word answers.

Finally, when they were almost near the turn-off for the house, Taylor asked, "Are you going to call him? Mr. Osborne, I mean?"

Gemma glanced at her niece, who was chewing on her lower lip, a sure sign the answer mattered to her.

"No," she said slowly. "I don't think I will. Besides, I don't see where I would have the time, given this extensive list of baked goods you've left for me. Where are we starting tonight? Cookies or eclairs?"

"Eclairs, definitely." Taylor smiled at her, but the apprehension didn't leave Gemma's gut.

Crushes on teachers were inevitable, but she couldn't help but feel that Taylor was setting herself up for a fall. Inappropriate or not, teenager or full-grown man, she knew just how hard Stephen Osborne was to forget.

CHAPTER EIGHT

He and Liv were going to have a serious conversation.

Stephen climbed back into his truck on autopilot, shock wiping his mind as blank as his whiteboard at the end of the semester. There was no way that Liv just accidentally forgot to tell him that Gemma was in town. Not when she'd specifically texted him last week to say she wouldn't be making the carnival. Even if the plans hadn't been set yet, you'd think this news would have warranted a little heads-up. *Hey, just so you know, the girl you were madly in love with in high school is coming back into town for a week. You might want to prepare yourself.*

Except Gemma hadn't seemed angry. He'd imagined their reunion various times over the years, but in those fantasies—or nightmares—he'd always imagined her staring at him with something like anger or disdain or disappointment. Not. . . this complete and total indifference. It made him feel both juvenile and foolish, his expectation that she hadn't moved on from their relationship and the traumatic way it had ended. It seemed that he was the only one who was holding on to the past.

He navigated out of the school parking lot with only half his mind on his driving, the other half fixed on the image of current Gemma imprinted on his mind. She'd always been cute in an endearingly nerdy sort of way, with frizzy brown hair she had worn in a braid or some sort of knot, a wardrobe comprised of concert and message tees, and big brown eyes that made her look like a Disney character. In his imagination, he'd somehow morphed her into a grown-up attorney version with a severe bun, boring business suit, and sensible heels, which he now realized was probably based more off a sexy librarian cliché than any objective sort of reality.

The projection hadn't prepared him for the stunning woman standing before him, dressed casually and looking completely at ease in her own skin, glossy dark hair curling over the shoulders of her jacket, so beautiful without a single touch of makeup that for a moment, he'd forgotten where he was. He felt hopelessly stupid for casting her as Dido in his mind—betrayed and ruined by a man's actions—when she was really Helen, a woman who could bring cities to ruin with her beauty.

Just more proof that of the two of them, he was the *much* bigger nerd.

He couldn't spare any thought on Gemma right now anyway, especially considering how little consideration she seemed to have given him over the last decade and a half. He had too many other things to finish up tonight. Daughtler had approved his alternate lesson plans, the look he gave him when he handed back the papers saying that he knew exactly what Stephen was doing and wasn't willing to press the issue. That was fine. He'd wanted to make a point and he'd made it. For anyone else to complain when he'd complied with the letter of their objections would be to admit to darker, less pleasant motives beneath, and no one was willing to cast themselves as racist or discriminatory, least of all the town leadership. He considered that a win. It also meant he would be scrambling to rewrite the next unit's material for three of his four classes. Ironically, no one had objected to *The Yellow Wallpaper* in American Lit, even though it was a strongly feminist nineteenth-century text protesting the societal oppression of women. He took that to mean that the Powers That Be had never read it.

He wasted no time when he walked into his home twenty minutes later, locking the door behind him before he continued straight down the hall to his wood-paneled bedroom. It had been one of the things that he'd liked about the house, this unusual layout with the bedrooms on the ground floor, the living area positioned upstairs to take advantage of the view. Down here it felt private, and the walk-out patio that led from his room was choked with wildflowers and native plants during the summer, a string hammock placed for reading beneath the shade of the upper deck.

It usually felt idyllic, the isolation allowing him room for his mind to work and his soul to breathe. Today, however, it just felt lonely. He wouldn't let himself think about the reasons why, even though they hovered in the back of his mind—he'd first hatched those dreams for a tiny cabin in the middle of nowhere in high school, with Gemma's head cradled in his lap and his fingers trailing through her hair. Back then, he'd figured she would be here to share it with him. He wondered what she would think about the fact that he'd gotten the thing he'd wanted most so many years ago.

He shook the memories off and headed straight into the en suite bath, stripping off his damp workout clothes as he went. Gemma's arrival couldn't have come at a worse time, when he'd been questioning coming back to

Haven Ridge in the first place. He couldn't help but feel like he was under scrutiny now. He wasn't the same person he'd been when he'd left, even though everyone in town expected him to be. He couldn't be upset if that extended to her too.

"Enough," he told himself sternly, turning the shower as hot as it would go, counting on the stinging spray to erase his uncomfortable thoughts. When he was finished, he toweled off, pulled on a comfortably-worn pair of jeans and a heavy knit sweater and headed upstairs to start his work for the evening.

He was just finishing up a round of grading when his phone rang. He turned it over and blinked at the name on the screen. Nikki. "Hello?"

"Hey, handsome," she said, her voice as cultured and sexy as ever. He'd always been annoyed at writers who described dialogue as being *purred*, but that's exactly what Nikki's voice sounded like. "What are you doing?"

"Grading papers. I'm about to log on and work on one of my own. I'm behind with school."

"Sounds exciting," she said wryly. "I still don't understand why you moved back home to make less money for more work."

"I wouldn't say it's more work, but I've been asking myself the same question. What are you doing? Are you still at the office?"

"Oh. No. I actually escaped early tonight. I'm having dinner with some friends in the city. There's a new restaurant you would like, I think, the whole farm-to-table, nose-to-tail vibe you're so fond of."

Stephen chuckled. "You know me too well. Not that there's much opportunity here for that sort of thing. Though I will say, our diner in town is shockingly good. You'd be impressed."

"Well, maybe I'll have a chance to try it."

Stephen paused, his muscles freezing. "You're coming for a visit? Here?"

"Unless you don't want me to . . ."

"No! That's not it at all, I was just surprised. You've had me come to you the last couple of times."

"Exactly why it's my turn," she said. "This weekend?"

"Uh . . . this weekend is kind of booked. It's the winter festival, remember? I'm going to be busy. Unless you want to come help."

She laughed. "I'll pass, thanks. I had enough of the quaint small-town festivals when I was growing up. How about Monday? I have some vacation time I need to use or lose."

"I have to work," he said. "The following weekend? You can help me chaperone the Valentine's dance."

"Not exactly what I had in mind, but if it's the best you can do . . ."

"The best I can do is a weekend in Crested Butte, but I still have to be at the dance."

She laughed. "Okay. We'll make it work. I'll send you my itinerary after I book the flights."

Silence fell between them. It had never been a problem to find something to talk about before he moved, but the difference in their worlds seemed to grow greater with each passing month. What exactly was he doing with Nikki? Why was he keeping this relationship up? He'd signed a one-year contract with the school and intended to continue once he'd gotten his credential, assuming the school offered him another one. She'd made it clear, having escaped the small-town life in upstate New York, that she would never move here. Sometimes it felt like they were each waiting for the other to break, but the longer they were apart, the less likely it seemed like either of them would give in.

"What are we doing here, Nikki?" he asked quietly.

"I thought we were trying to make this relationship work," she said, that flirty, upbeat note in her voice. When he didn't respond, her voice turned quiet and serious. "I don't know, Stephen. I like you, a lot. You're the only man who has ever really looked at me and just. . . seen me for who I am. Without wanting me to change in any way."

"Except not changing you means never living in the same city again," he said softly. "You know I've had enough of Salt Lake, of advertising. I'm not coming back. And I don't see how we're ever going to make this work if neither of us are willing to compromise."

Nikki nearly whispered her response. "I know."

He waited for more, hoping she'd save him from what he had to say next, but she remained silent. He cleared his throat. "It's been six months. If neither of us has budged, I think . . . I think it's time to call it."

"I know. I just. . ." She broke off. "You're right. I'm just sorry to see it end this way. You're a great guy, Stephen."

He let out a breath, relieved that her response had been measured and mature. "And you're an amazing woman. Go have fun with your friends."

"Yeah. Sure. Goodbye, Stephen."

"Goodbye, Nikki."

Stephen hung up and let out a long breath, staring at the phone. It was the right thing to do. Dragging out the inevitable helped neither of them. Had he not left Salt Lake, had they been in the same city, maybe things would have been different.

But even as he told himself that, he knew it wasn't true. No matter how much he'd dated, regardless of his handful of steady girlfriends, he'd only really, truly loved one woman.

And she'd just come back to town.

CHAPTER NINE

GEMMA PUSHED THOUGHTS of Stephen aside when they pulled into the driveway of Liv's house. She still owed Liv a few choice words over the fact she'd conveniently "forgotten" to tell her that her ex was back in Haven Ridge, but she couldn't make more of this than what it was. He was her past. He was of no consequence to her trip here. The sooner she put him out of her head—sculpted athletic body and five-o'clock shadow and stupid rugged good looks—the better.

Taylor ran into the house to change and Gemma went upstairs to the guest apartment to put in one of the frozen pizzas she'd picked up at the store earlier that day. Even if it wasn't her favorite brand—surprisingly tasty for being frozen—she'd save her efforts for baked goods over supper any day of the week. She was just taking it out of the oven when Taylor pounded up the stairs and burst into the apartment's kitchen, her cheeks flushed and her eyes bright. She'd changed out of her school clothes into a black pinafore dress with a pair of black striped stockings and her Docs, looking like an adorable Goth schoolgirl or maybe a character out of a Tim Burton movie.

"Aunt Gem? Don't kill me . . ."

Gemma slid the pizza onto the cutting board and turned to her niece, bemused. "You've got plans."

Taylor winced. "Kind of? Amélie told Layla that Jonathan was going to ask me to the dance, but he couldn't find me at school today. So he and his friends are going to Mario's tonight—"

"Say no more. Do you need a ride?"

"No, Layla is going to pick me up." Impulsively, Taylor darted forward and gave her a hug. Then she let her go and dashed off with a squeal. "I'm so excited! I'm going to the dance!"

Gemma watched Taylor race down the stairs again, amused by her lightning-fast mood changes. Here she was worrying about how she was going to talk to her about her crush on her teacher, and before the hour was up, she'd reverted back to a boy her own age. Gemma shook her head and dug through the fully-stocked drawers, not surprised to find that Liv had thought to include a pizza wheel. There wasn't enough money in the world to make Gemma go back to high school, with all the angst and the wondering if you were ever going to get a boyfriend or obsessing over what your crush thought about you.

Except with Stephen Osborne, she'd never had to guess. From the first day of ninth grade, when she'd slid into the desk beside him, she'd just known that he was the one for her. And wonder of wonders, when their eyes met in shared commiseration over their teacher's corny jokes, she'd known he felt the same way. Even though she'd spent the next two-and-a-half years wondering when he'd come to his senses and realize that a football star like him could have any girl in school, he'd never once looked at any of the girls who threw themselves at his feet. She had been his one and only. His best girl, he used to say with a 1950s sense of irony. But he'd meant it.

So much so that when she and her mom had left Haven Ridge midway through junior year, she hadn't even thought to question if their relationship could handle the separation. He was the one for her. Why would he ever question that she was the one for him?

She smiled wryly as she slid one of the pieces of pizza to a plate and took it to the sofa in the living area. The funny thing was, his memory was so wrapped up in her feelings about Haven Ridge that she hadn't realized that somewhere along the line, her sense of betrayal had faded into a muted sense of disappointment. But that only stood to reason. It had been a high school romance, no matter how intense, and she'd moved on. She was no longer the shy, optimistic, naive girl she'd been back then. Too much had happened in the interim.

And yet the look on Stephen's face earlier had surprised her. She could understand indifference or maybe abashment, but not that look of puzzled wonderment, like he couldn't believe she was standing before him. Then again, maybe she could. The last time they'd spoken, they'd been sixteen and the words had not been friendly. Even now, the recollection brought with it the vague churn of nausea. It seems that over the years she'd forgiven him, but her body hadn't forgotten.

Gemma's phone buzzed in her pocket, interrupting her train of thought just in time. She pulled it out and checked the messages. Liv. **Finally got checked into my hotel after two-hour delays on both ends. Everything okay?**

A-ok, she typed back, awkwardly using her left hand so she didn't leave a smear of pizza grease on the screen. Taylor went out with friends for Operation Valentine. Left me with an entire pizza to myself.

The wench! You have everything you need? The apartment comfortable?

Perfect. I might never leave. And then, after a moment's consideration, Gemma added, Why didn't you tell me that Stephen had moved back?

Liv took so long to reply, Gemma thought that she had lost reception or Liv's phone had died. And then finally, the message came through. I didn't know how you'd react. I thought it would take you longer to run into him.

I'm fine, really. But seriously. . . what happened? We all got older and he just got hotter?

I know, right? UNFAIR. Can you imagine if we had an English teacher who looked like that when we were Taylor's age?

It wasn't until Liv laid it out so baldly that Gemma understood the problem. Taylor was failing the class of a teacher she had a mad crush on? Now everything was starting to make sense. She started typing out her realization, then hit the back button until the words disappeared. Liv didn't need to know the details. If Taylor wanted her to know, she would tell her. She hadn't become fun Aunt Gem by tattling on her niece.

Instead, she typed out, Gonna go have a soak in the hot tub now. Let me know how tomorrow goes.

Will do. Thanks again, Gem. Love you.

Gemma smiled and put her phone aside. Never mind the fact that it was only eighteen degrees outside. The Scandinavians did something like this, didn't they— soaked in hot springs before they flung themselves into snow drifts or some such thing? She wasn't going to be doing anything like that, but the idea of reading her new book in the spa sounded heavenly.

She hadn't done more than dig out her bikini from her suitcase, though, when her phone rang again. Gemma snatched it up as soon as she saw the name *Taylor* flash on-screen and pressed it to her ear. "Hey! What's up?"

The only response was barely audible crying on the other end of the line.

Gemma's heart plummeted into her stomach. "Taylor? Is that you? Is everything okay?"

More sniffles and then Taylor's watery voice responded, "Can you come pick me up right now?"

"Of course! What happened? Are you okay? Are you safe?"

"I—can you just come get me please? I'm outside the pet shop."

Gemma racked her brain for the location of the pet shop. It was somewhere on the main drag, but she didn't quite remember where—it had opened just before she left town. "I'll be right there. Don't move. No, scratch that. If you can wait inside somewhere, let me know where."

She hung up with Taylor and then dragged on her coat and thrust on her boots in record time before she raced out to the SUV. Dread spiraled in the pit of her stomach. Maybe it was just because of all the terrible things she heard in her job, but her mind immediately started considering the worst. She sent wordless pleas to the heavens that Taylor was okay. She'd never forgive herself if something happened to the girl on her watch.

She was so focused on her worry when she drove into Haven Ridge proper that it took longer than it should have for the state of the town to sink in, even in the dark. It had never been a bustling metropolis, but it had once been charming—it had had an old-town feel that reminded her of the black-and-white TV shows, where everyone knew each other and shop owners stood outside their doors to greet passers-by.

But even knowing that Haven Ridge wasn't a destination, that it merely caught the overflow of hikers and mountain bikers from more popular nearby towns like Salida and Buena Vista, she wasn't prepared for it to look so . . . derelict. The town center with its historic brick facades was dotted with boarded-up storefronts. Those that were occupied looked sad and unkempt, their windows streaked with dirt and grease, their wares looking limp and neglected. A secondary dread layered over the first as she navigated Dogwood Street slowly, looking for any sign of her niece. It only intensified when she passed the dark pet store without any sign of her.

And then finally, up ahead, she caught her niece's distinctive outline next to a bigger one just beyond the pool of light coming from the lone Chinese restaurant. Gemma hastily pulled into the angled parking spot and jumped out of the SUV without turning off the ignition, her heart pounding. Only when she came close enough to make out the faces did she relax; Taylor was standing with Stephen.

"There's my aunt," Taylor was saying. She buried her face into the lapels of her coat and headed straight for the passenger side without saying anything to her.

Gemma stared after her and then turned back to Stephen, who was holding a white plastic bag. If he'd looked like the hot teacher earlier in athletic wear, now in his wool peacoat and his knit beanie, he looked like every handsome small-town love interest in every Hallmark movie she'd ever seen (and hated). She carefully schooled her expression, not needing to reach far to put on the concerned-parent look. "Do you have any idea what this is all about?"

"Unfortunately, no. I just came to pick up my food and I saw her standing out here alone. She said you were on your way, but I didn't want to leave her standing here all by herself."

Why she felt a spark of surprise, she didn't know. Taken all together, Stephen had always been kind, thoughtful even. "Thank you. That was nice of you."

"Sure. Taylor's a great kid. I know it's been a rough couple of years for her. I don't like seeing her struggle."

Gemma flicked a glance at her niece through the windshield of the SUV but she couldn't make out more than a foggy outline. "Yeah. Me neither. I guess at some point we should probably discuss how she's failing your class?"

"Yeah. Maybe. But not now."

"No, not now." Gemma gave him a quick nod and turned on her heel back to the vehicle.

"Gem?" She turned, and he gave her a quick, rueful smile. "It's nice to have you back."

Her breath caught at the sincerity of his tone, an involuntary response she immediately resented. She didn't know what to say—*I'm not back* or *Thanks* or *Why do you look like this now?*—so instead she just gave a swift nod and climbed into the car. She had more important things to deal with right now than her ex-boyfriend staring at her with that hopeful look.

Inside the SUV's warmth, Taylor was slumped in her seat, her arms crossed over her chest.

"Do you want to talk about it?" Gemma asked.

Taylor just shook her head.

"Okay, then." She lifted a hand to Stephen, who was still standing with his undoubtedly cold Chinese takeout, then backed out of the parking space and turned toward home.

They were almost all the way back to Liv's place before Taylor said in a small voice, "It was all a setup."

Gemma started. "What? How? Why?"

Taylor rolled her eyes, her expression stony, but her voice still sounded vulnerable. "I walked into the pizza place and everyone was there. Jonathan's whole group and Amelie's whole group . . . and someone scooted over at their table, so I thought that meant they wanted me to join them. But when I got there, Amelie stood up and said, 'Look, it's the ugly little Goth girl. What, ugly little Goth girl, did you think Jonathan would actually ever look at *you*?' And then everyone started laughing, and Jonathan put his arm around Amelie like he was making a point . . . Ugh, it was all so humiliating."

And ridiculous and stupid and nonsensical. Gemma ground her teeth to hold back what she really wanted to say. "What did you do?"

"Nothing. I just turned around and left. I wasn't going to let them see me cry." She sniffled, her chin still tucked into her jacket.

"Well, if it makes you feel any better—"

"You think I'm pretty and he's stupid for not seeing what he's missing out on?" The sarcastic tone said she'd heard this more than once from Liv. "Thanks, but it doesn't."

"That's not what I was going to say."

Taylor jerked her head up.

"I mean, it's true. But I was just going to say that if it makes you feel any better, this is the pinnacle of their popularity and they should enjoy it before they spend the rest of their lives manning the counter at the Stop and Shop."

"Great." The sarcasm in Taylor's voice was still thick,

but now there was a tiny thread of humor beneath it. And then it was gone as quickly as it had come. "What would you know about it anyway? You were probably the homecoming queen or something. You're tall and you're gorgeous and guys were probably throwing themselves at you."

Gemma laughed. "Oh, is that what Liv told you?"

"She didn't have to."

"You couldn't be further from the truth." Gemma gripped the steering wheel harder. "If you must know, I was a total geek. Frizzy hair, bad wardrobe, chicken legs."

Taylor rolled her eyes. "Right, like I'm going to believe that. I've seen *The Princess Diaries* too, Aunt Gem."

"I'm not finished. The only reason why I didn't get picked on or made fun of was because I was friends with Liv and dating Stephen—Mr. Osborne. They were popular and so I kind of got a pass. Until my dad cheated on my mom, and he made things out to be her fault. Everyone in town sided with him. And he got everything in the divorce, including the house. He moved his mistress and her daughter in, and we had to move into this crappy little apartment on the edge of town. The rumors and lies about us got so bad we had to move to Phoenix to live with my aunt. So when I say I understand how you feel, I really do understand how you feel."

Taylor was staring at her as if seeing her anew. "I just don't understand what I did to any of them to make them hate me this much."

"Oh honey." Gemma reached blindly across the console to grab Taylor's hand. "You didn't do anything. They're so miserable and insecure that they want to make someone else feel the same. And they figure it's easier to kick someone who's already down because they won't have the strength to fight back."

"Because of my dad."

"Yeah. Because of your dad."

Taylor fell silent then, staring out the window as they left old town and headed back to the highway. Gemma figured she was licking her wounds, but then she said, "Mr. Osborne is really nice."

"Taylor—"

"Oh, don't worry. I know I'm just a kid and he's an adult and my teacher and everything. But he seems like a good person. He waited with me even though he didn't have to. Although—" Taylor slid her a sideways glance—"I wouldn't be surprised if that was because I said you were coming to get me."

Gemma groaned. "Taylor—"

"I'm just saying . . ."

"Taylor," Gemma said firmly, "I am only here for a week. I am not planning on dating anyone, let alone my high school boyfriend."

"You say that, but you didn't see the way he looked at you when you showed up at school today."

"It's because he didn't expect me to show up with good hair and boobs," Gemma said wryly. "If you're so anxious to talk about Mr. Osborne, why don't we talk about why you're failing his class? You've always been so good in literature. I don't understand. Neither does Liv."

Taylor cringed back.

"Come on. It can't be that bad."

"No, it's so embarrassing!"

"I once came back from the bathroom with my skirt tucked up in my underwear. Don't talk to me about embarrassing."

She groaned. "Okay, it's not that bad, but almost."

"Tell me. Seriously. It can't be worse than tonight."

"It is, thanks for reminding me." Her tone was acerbic but Gemma didn't think she mistook the slight lift in it. "Okay, so you know I'm in drama, and we do this dramatic reading competition every year. So I chose poetry, but I wanted something more interesting and . . . passionate . . . I guess, than like the typical Shakespeare thing. So I picked Pablo Neruda's *Love Sonnet XI*. In translation, of course."

"Of course. Which one is that?" As if she actually knew who Pablo Neruda was.

"It starts, 'I crave your mouth, your voice, your hair. Silent and starving, I prowl through the streets.'"

"Oh." Gemma's eyebrows went up. Quite a dramatic choice for a teenage girl.

"So anyway, I figured I needed the extra practice, so when we came up on this sonnet unit in literature, I chose that to read. Except when I read it, I was looking at Mr. Osborne in the back of the class, for like, encouragement or critique or whatever. But everyone saw that and thought I was reciting it *to* him . . ."

Gemma pressed her hand to her mouth, taken straight back to the humiliating days of high school.

"Right? So embarrassing. So now everyone makes like kissing noises around me when he comes in and googly eyes and things. It's just so awful."

"How does that relate to failing his class?"

"I kind of . . . cut class a few times so I didn't have to face him until things blew over. And he's really big on class participation, so when the school found out the absences weren't excused, he gave me a bunch of zeroes."

Oh. There were obviously some things that Liv had left out. Did she even know? Or had she just been trying to preserve her stepdaughter's privacy? That sounded like something that Liv would do.

"But . . . what was that deal today where you were all waiting for him?"

Taylor lifted a careless shoulder. "I mean, it was embarrassing, but all my friends kind of thought it was cool that I was going after a teacher. So I just played along."

Gemma couldn't hold back her laughter anymore. "Oh Taylor."

"I know! I know, it's so terrible." She buried her face in her hands. "But they wouldn't have believed me if I denied it. It would have just looked like me making excuses."

"So you really don't have a crush on Mr. Osborne?"

"What? No! I mean, he is *unfairly* hot for a teacher. Like, how are you supposed to concentrate when he's talking about love poetry and wearing one of those tight sweaters? Seriously?"

Gemma just continued in helpless laughter and Taylor joined her.

"Maybe I should just put around that I was *settling* for Jonathan but I really prefer older men—"

"Or maybe you should just let things lie. Taylor, it was a terrible thing that they did to you tonight, but one thing I remember about Mario's is that it's not actually big enough to fit the entire school."

"You're probably right." Taylor gave a sniffle and wiped her eyes. "Sorry I ruined our evening, Aunt Gem."

"You didn't ruin anything. What do you say we make a stop for dessert on the way home?"

"The nearest bakery is in Salida."

"What?" Gemma was truly aghast. "How can that be possible?"

Taylor shrugged. "Unless you want a cake at Wal—"

"Don't say it. I refuse to believe this town has fallen

so low." Gemma sat back against the SUV seat. "Then you'll get your homework and we'll do what girls always do when a boy starts acting stupid."

"Make a voodoo doll of Jonathan and stick pins into it?"

Gemma let out a surprised laugh. "No, silly . . . even though I'm sure that's tempting. I'm talking about sugar therapy."

CHAPTER TEN

W̲ʜɪʟᴇ T̲ᴀʏʟᴏʀ sʜᴏᴡᴇʀᴇᴅ and changed into loungewear, Gemma rummaged through Liv's baking cabinet in the kitchen, looking for inspiration. The normal level of consolation pastry—the deluxe chocolate-chip cookies she'd been planning for this evening—now seemed woefully inadequate for the evening's admissions. She was beginning to form alternate plans when she came across an unopened package of Valentine cookie cutters.

When Taylor emerged from her room again, scrubbed clean and swimming in an oversized sweatshirt over leggings, they walked back through the frigid night to the garage apartment. Gemma got her settled at the kitchen island with her algebra homework while she pulled out bowls and whisks and began to pull together her world-famous shortbread..

"What are you making?" Taylor asked, one eye surveying the growing pile of ingredients even as her thumbs flew over her phone's virtual keyboard.

"It's a surprise. Shouldn't you be doing your homework?"

Taylor shrugged. "Haven Ridge is a small town. Word travels fast."

"Yeah, about that. Where was Layla in all this? Wasn't she supposed to give you a ride home?"

"And make her leave after we went to all this trouble so she could see Robbie?" Taylor's aghast expression said how unlikely that scenario was. Then the phone beeped again and she was back to texting.

"Taylor. Homework." Gemma pointed a mixing spoon in a way that she hoped looked like she meant business. Taylor was pretty self-sufficient, but Gemma doubted that Liv would thank her if she let boy trouble get in the way of homework due dates.

"Fine." Taylor put the phone aside and picked up her pencil, but she still darted looks at the screen every few seconds. Gemma hid a smile. She'd been dealing with grownups who acted like children for so long she'd practically forgotten what actual teenagers were like.

The dough came together quickly, and she popped the plastic-wrapped disk into the freezer to chill. Once she'd cleaned up her mess, she rolled out the dough and took up a heart cookie cutter.

Taylor shot a dubious look at the tools. "Please tell me those aren't what I think they are."

"Holster the snark and give me the benefit of the doubt, will you?"

Several minutes later, when the kitchen filled with the delectable scent of butter and sugar and vanilla from the lightly-browning shortbread, Gemma caught Taylor darting looks at the window of the oven. But she kept up the disinterested facade until Gemma had frosted the cookies and was piping lettering onto them. She came up behind her and started laughing. "Oh my gosh, that's perfect!"

Gemma grinned and lifted the tip from the iced surface. On a flooded pastel field in conversation heart fashion, she'd piped a variety of snarky sayings: *Good riddance. Your loss. Boys suck. Too good for you anyway.* The last one had admittedly been a squeeze, but the sentiment was too true to pass up.

"Layla and Megan have to see these." Taylor angled her camera to snap some photos.

Gemma moved out of the way, still hiding her smile. "I can do one better. We won't be able to eat all of these ourselves. I'll pack them up and you can bring them to school tomorrow."

Mischief sparkled in Taylor's eyes. "Can we do one more saying?"

"Of course. What did you have in mind?"

* * *

The next morning, Gemma redeemed her poor showing of her first day by having breakfast—a selection of yesterday's muffins, melon, and scrambled eggs—ready for Taylor when she emerged sleepily from the guest room.

"How you feeling about everything today?" Gemma asked delicately.

"Mmrph." Taylor buried her face in a giant mug of coffee, but she looked slightly more alert when it was halfway empty. She set it aside and peeled the wrapper off a blueberry muffin before demolishing half of it in one bite. "So what are you going to do today while I'm at school?"

"I don't know." Gemma pulled up a chair across from her and helped herself to some of the eggs. "Never made it into the hot tub yesterday. Seems like a nice way to start the day."

"I could stay home with you . . ." Taylor said hopefully.

"Nice try. School first, then we can have fun."

"I have speech team after school today, so I'm going to need a ride home. Four forty?"

"Sure. Just text me if something changes."

But once Taylor was on the bus and Gemma had the house to herself again, the hot tub and hardcover no longer appealed. She kept thinking about her glimpse of Haven Ridge's historic downtown. Surely things weren't as bleak as they'd seemed when she'd picked Taylor up last night. The town had never exactly been known for its nightlife, something she and Liv had lamented as teens and which had led them to many a questionable choice of entertainment. Did you even live in a small town if you didn't drink straight from the bottle while sitting on the tailgate of an older boy's truck?

Still, she held off her desire to prove that impression true until close to eleven, when all the stores would be open. She put on jeans and a sweater, topped it with her down jacket, and took the SUV back toward town, where she parked at the very end of Dogwood Street in old historic downtown.

She'd been right about one thing at least: the stores that existed *were* already open. Unfortunately, her assumption that things couldn't be as bad as they seemed were dead wrong.

The bones of Haven Ridge were the same as they'd always been—beautiful brick buildings with crenelated tops, ornate moldings, and inset placards that announced the buildings' names and dates, anywhere between 1886 and 1920. The hills rose up behind them, still dotted with snow from the last storm, framing the wide street like an artist's depiction of a fantasy small town. But whereas almost every one of those buildings had been filled when she'd left, many of them now lay empty and deserted.

And not just the ones that were boarded up. She

passed a music shop which still had the fixtures inside but no instruments; a sign on the glass door gave a long-winded and tearful explanation that they'd had to close down and relocate to Buena Vista where they could make a living. Same for the bookstore on the corner, the pet shop, the hair salon. The historic Monarch Hotel still stood as proud as ever with its three stories of red brick, but a peek through the front window revealed it looking a bit dustier and more threadbare than she remembered it.

With every step, her heart sank lower. She hadn't lived here in a full fifteen years, but she'd been back to visit a couple of times and she didn't remember it looking so . . . sad.

The only sign of life was at the diner on the corner, aptly named the Brick House Cafe. The awnings were new and fresh, bright white letters on red vinyl, and the windows were so clean they practically sparkled. Gemma pushed through the front door with a jingle of the harness bells on top and then faltered as every head in the mostly filled cafe turned her direction. A couple of whispers broke out across the small space.

She was about to beat a hasty retreat until a woman emerged from behind the counter with a menu in hand. As if a spell was broken, everyone turned back to their meals and conversations, the noise level going back to normal.

Gemma took in the woman's dark hair and vivid green eyes, wondering if she was someone that she should know from high school, but she found no hint of familiarity in her face. Then again, she could have been anywhere from twenty-five to forty; the longer Gemma lived in LA, land of luxury skincare and plastic surgery, the harder it was to accurately gauge ages.

"Just you?" the woman inquired pleasantly.

"Uh, yeah, just me. Where's Pearl?"

She smiled. "Pearl retired a while back. My fiancé and I run the place now." She stuck out her hand. "Mallory Adams."

Gemma got over her startlement that someone had actually moved *into* town instead of running away from it and clasped the woman's hand. "Who's your fiancé?"

"Thomas Rivas?"

"Oh, Thomas! I had no idea he was back, too. He was a few years ahead of me in school, but I knew him from the cafe. I'm Gemma Van Buren."

Mallory gave her a brilliant smile. "Nice to meet you, Gemma. Booth or counter?"

There was something so welcoming to this woman that she said, "Counter" before she'd even really considered it.

"Great." Mallory placed the menu on the counter and then slipped behind it again. "Any idea what sounds good or do you need a minute?"

"I'll take a black coffee and a piece of cinnamon coffee cake."

Mallory's face fell. "Sorry, no coffee cake anymore. Sugar Dreams closed down last fall, and unfortunately, the only baking I can keep up with is Pearl's famous pecan pie." A twinkle returned to her eye. "You have no idea what I had to do to convince her to let me see the recipe, let alone make it."

Gemma chuckled. "Okay. I'll take a piece of pie then. We'll call it brunch."

Mallory swiveled away to pour the coffee and cut a piece from the pie tins displayed in the glass case at the end of the counter. When she slid the food in front of Gemma, however, she just leaned against the counter and looked at her with open curiosity. "So you grew up here? How long has it been since you left?"

"Fifteen years. I've been back a couple of times over the years, but my mom and I moved when I was a junior in high school, after my parents got divorced." Gemma caught a flicker of. . . something. . . in Mallory's eyes. "What is it?"

"Nothing. Sorry, I'm being nosy. It's just that being new to town, everyone seems to know the history of everyone else, so I'm always playing catch-up."

"How did you end up here, then? You and Thomas decided to move here?"

Mallory smiled. "We actually met here last summer. And I guess I fell in love."

"He's a good guy. At least he always was when I knew him."

"He is. But I didn't just mean him, I meant the town, too."

Gemma took a sip of the coffee—extremely good for diner drip—and shot her a wry look. "You have interesting taste."

"I think you'll find things are changing for the better. Slowly, maybe, but if you stick around, you might be surprised."

"Doubt I'll have time for that. I'm only here for the week. You know Liv Quinn?"

"Sure. She and Taylor come in here all the time."

"I'm staying with Taylor while Liv's out of town. As soon as she gets back, I'm going back to California."

"Hmm," Mallory said.

Gemma cocked her head. "You don't believe me?"

"It's not for me to believe or not. But in my experience, this town has a mind of its own." She smiled and looked past Gemma as the door opened again. "Excuse me."

Gemma twisted to watch her approach the elderly couple with a friendly smile. Mallory didn't *look* crazy, but there was a knowing undertone when she talked about the town that struck her as just a little. . .off. Especially for someone who had only come here recently.

Then again, the cafe looked to be the only place in this whole district that was thriving, like a tiny green shoot poking up in a dry brown wasteland. It wasn't so surprising—Mallory could bake a mean pie. In fact, it was as good as she ever remembered Pearl's being, sweet without becoming cloying, the pecans baked to the perfect *al dente* texture. Gemma took another bite, fished her phone out of her coat pocket, and brought up one of her social media apps, intending to kill some time with mindless scrolling. Except the little happy face icon in the corner had the tiny number *54* posted over top of it.

"What in the world?" she muttered, pressing the button to pull up the notifications. The list scrolled down, pages and pages of likes on a photo she didn't remember having posted. She clicked, and her jaw nearly came unhinged.

She'd been tagged in a post from @taylor_2fun—clearly her niece—with a photo that looked like it had been taken in study hall—an artful arrangement of cookies on top of someone's white sweater, the focus on the two cookies with Taylor's requested messages. The one that had teeth marks in the corner said *Bite me, Jonathan.* The other said *You have stupid hair.* She had tagged Gemma's personal account, adding the hashtags #pastrytherapy #consolationcookies #takesmoretobreakmethanthat #boyssuck #girlpower #brokenheartsbakery.

Gemma grinned. These girls knew how to use social media to make a point. And apparently they weren't the only ones, because dozens of comments already scrolled down the screen.

Is this a real bakery? I need some of these!
Where can I buy these? #christopheryousuck
Best Galentine's Day treat EVER.

And then the one that almost made her inhale her coffee: *@gemmabakesla what's your website?*

Mallory came back over with a pot to refill her mug. "Something wrong?"

Gemma held up the phone, still stunned. "Have you seen this?"

Mallory peered at the phone, a smiling coming to her lips. "That's clever. I could have used something like that when I was a teenager." She made a face. "As an adult too, unfortunately. Do you own a bakery?"

"Oh, no. I just bake for fun. This was for Taylor."

"Hmm," Mallory said again with that appraising tone, but she was gone before Gemma could dig further.

She sipped her coffee, barely noticing that she was burning her tongue as she read through the rest of the comments. There were, of course, the usual internet trolls calling her a man-hating feminazi, but she was used to that from her job. By and large, the internet seemed to think that the cookies were a clever way to blow off some steam. And about a third of the comments were people asking where they could buy their own, if she baked divorce cakes, if she had her own storefront.

For a second, she felt a little pang, which she pushed away as quickly as it came. Even if she had the chance to do things over, she wouldn't. The dream of having a bakery in Haven Ridge had just been a girlish fantasy. What young teen with a baking obsession wasn't seduced by the idea of being her own boss in a pretty shop surrounded by swoops of icing and silver sprinkles? It was the cold, hard reality of her parents' breakup that had shown her how little fantasies paid off, how giving up your autonomy and control could land you with nothing in the end.

Now, nearly seven years into her law practice, Gemma knew that had her mother had a half-decent lawyer, she would have gotten the house and half the money, plus child support and alimony. But she'd only had a few thousand in cash, which she'd had the foresight to squirrel away in the lining of her suitcase, and the hack lawyer she'd hired had advised her to get out of the marriage as cleanly and quickly as possible. That was the reason for Gemma's pro bono work, the reason she was considering caving to Eli's demands. Because if she wasn't helping people like her mom, what was the point of any of this anyway?

Mallory was busy elsewhere, so she tossed a ten-dollar bill on the counter next to her empty cup and hopped off the stool. But she took away the strange feeling that something odd was going on here. . . something more than just a dying town.

CHAPTER ELEVEN

GEMMA'S VALIANT PLANS to spend the day in Haven Ridge was thwarted by the fact that there were perhaps only ten shops left in all of historic downtown, and two of them—the kayak rental place and the bike repair shop—were closed for the winter. She stopped into the convenience store, which carried the usual milk and bread and potato chips alongside snowmelt and souvenir fridge magnets. She poked her head into the metaphysical book shop, which had inexplicably survived when the regular bookstore had closed, but had to duck out when the smell of incense became too much for her.

Finally, she paused at the tiny coffee stand at the end of the street—a siding-clad shack with a take-out window and a single peeling picnic bench for seating— and grabbed her fourth coffee of the day. Haven Ridge High School was probably the main reason they managed to stay in business, especially considering the diner only sold standard drip coffee and none of the syrup-heavy drinks that teenagers—and let's be real, Gemma—liked.

Paper cup in hand and sunglasses donned against the bright wash of winter sunlight, Gemma walked slowly up and down the streets of Haven Ridge, her breath making clouds around her head in the frigid air. Unlike most old towns that used a combination of lettered and numbered streets, Haven Ridge was oriented around an alphabetized assortment of nouns running east-west and state names going north-south. The far side of town started with Acorn Street, followed by Beacon, Columbine, Dogwood, and Egret, ending with Zoo (spoiler alert: there was no actual zoo). In the other direction, Alaska Avenue began a series of streets that finished at Montana Avenue, mainly because the town was only thirteen blocks deep.

As she wound around the end of Dogwood down Columbine without finding a single place to stop, she was filled with an unaccountable melancholy. With all her bad memories of the town, she never expected that the evidence of its slow decline would strike her so hard. If anything, she would have expected herself to think it served the town right—a punishment for how it had failed to be a home to her.

Still, there were signs of life even beyond the bright spot that was the Brick House Cafe. Someone had recently repainted a block of the candy-colored brick structures on the corner of Colorado and Acorn, their windows cleaned and scraped of old lettering, as if the owner—whoever it was—was expecting new businesses to move in. And despite the somewhat lonely and deserted air of the streets, there was no trash anywhere to be found—the sidewalks were clean and scrubbed free of debris. Someone in this town still took pride in it.

After that, Gemma found herself not looking for evidence of the decline, but rather evidence of a rebirth.

The art studio and supply on Columbine was empty, but hand-lettered signs in the window advertised after-school drawing and painting classes and open creator hours, where for a nominal fee people could come in and make something beautiful. An orthodontist was in the professional building at the end of Dogwood, clearly a sign there were enough teens still left in town to justify its existence. And when she came midway down Beacon Street, there was the brightest spot of them all, with its blue-painted window mullions and old-fashioned bicycle with a basket full of silk flowers out front: the Haven Ridge Gift Shop.

Gemma pulled open the door and stepped inside amid the jingle of harness bells, immediately enveloped in the aroma of vanilla and cinnamon and cedar. The walls were covered with painted pegboard sporting a variety of local arts and crafts: carved wood signs and ornaments, wind chimes, woven wall hangings. One section sported a beautiful selection of oil paintings, all of which depicted this part of Colorado, some even of the town itself. And behind a scarred wooden counter-top sat a familiar older woman wearing a bright pink sweater and several strands of colorful beads around her neck, her peekaboo blue highlights showing beneath the top layer of her silver bob.

She rose slowly when Gemma approached the back of the shop, her face splitting into a wide smile. "Well, I'll be . . . Gemma Van Buren. It is you!"

Gemma smiled. "Granny Pearl. It's been a long time. I didn't even know if you'd recognize me."

"Recognize you? Hush, child, I'd know those big green eyes anywhere." The old woman circled the counter and enfolded her into a warm hug. "It's so good to see you."

Gemma allowed herself to sink into the warmth of

the embrace for a long moment. Of all her memories of Haven Ridge, the ones involving Granny Pearl were the best. She was a fixture in town—a descendant of the town's original founder—and a figurative grandmother to anyone who was more than a decade younger than her. Back when Pearl and her husband had run the Brick House Cafe, Gemma, Stephen, and Liv had spent most afternoons after school there, sharing plates of fries and cheese sticks with the enthusiasm of youth and the carelessness of lightning metabolism. Later, when Gemma and her mother had been struggling to get by, Pearl had always found a way to accidentally discount their meals or slip them something extra to go, whether it was a slice or two of pecan pie or half a meatloaf that mysteriously hadn't sold by closing.

Gemma let herself bask in those good memories, breathing in the old lady's lavender perfume, before she pulled away and looked into that lined face. "You look good, Granny Pearl. I was surprised when I went into the Brick House and heard you weren't running it anymore."

Pearl chuckled and waved a hand. "These old bones needed something more sedate. Restaurants are a young person's game anyway. Thomas and Mallory do a good job."

"I haven't seen Thomas yet," Gemma said. "I hadn't even known he was back here." She and Pearl's only grandson had never been friends, though she'd had a massive crush on him when she was eleven or twelve and he was the handsome older boy who brought her food at the diner. Like most other Haven Ridge natives, he'd gone away to college and hadn't looked back.

"Ah, yes. Been a couple of years now." Pearl fixed Gemma with a knowing look. "Everyone comes back eventually. If they're meant to."

Gemma shifted uncomfortably, reading the implication in the statement. "I'm not back. I'm just here staying with Taylor while Liv is out of town."

The old lady hummed her disagreement as she brushed past Gemma to straighten some handmade soaps arranged artistically on an antique table.

The melancholy Gemma had been feeling earlier faded in the face of a wash of unexpected resentment. "If Haven Ridge really wanted me here, it could have tried harder to keep me all those years ago, don't you think?"

If Granny Pearl picked up on the fire beneath those words, she didn't show it. "I know, dear. And it's paying the price. Just look around you." She shrugged. "But I knew it was just a matter of time."

Gemma knew she shouldn't ask, but she did anyway. "A matter of time for what?"

"Until you came back, of course. I wasn't so sure when Liv moved here. Poor dear. What a tragedy, what happened to her husband. But Haven Ridge was what she and that sweet stepdaughter of hers needed to heal. I thought for a long time maybe that was the whole point. And then Stephen moved back . . . well, you three were so inseparable, it hardly made sense for them to be here without you."

Gemma shook her head. Pearl had always been eccentric, but this was a new level, even for her. "Like I said, I'm just here for the week. I'm going back to LA on Monday."

Pearl reached for her hand and patted the back of it. "We'll see, dear. Regardless, it's lovely to see you."

And after that, there was nothing left to say. She gave Granny Pearl one last hug and then took her leave of the gift shop, both confused and unsettled, as if she'd just had a conversation in a language in which she was only half-fluent. As if there was an entirely different subtext she hadn't caught beneath the literal words.

Gemma managed to walk off most of that feeling by the time she reached her borrowed SUV, and when she glanced at the clock and saw that it was nearly time to pick up Taylor from school, she pushed the rest of it down where it belonged, with all the other irrational feelings she suppressed on a daily basis.

Like the sudden, wild hope that she might run into Stephen again.

Stupid, stupid, stupid. Don't let Pearl get into your head.

By the time she pulled into Haven Ridge High School, she'd ruthlessly pruned all those weird soft feelings in favor of hard objectivity. The parking lot was mostly drained of cars already, and Taylor was nowhere to be seen.

She pulled out her phone and texted: I'm here. Where are you?

Almost immediately, she received a text back: Speech practice is inside the theater.

Okay. Taylor must have been running late then. She locked the vehicle and trudged across the parking lot to the boxy theater annex at the far side of the school. She'd never really been a drama kid, but she'd gone to her fair share of plays here. It looked largely unchanged.

She let herself into the theater vestibule, which was deserted but scattered with the detritus of a school day: a lunch bag, a few empty soda cans, and inexplicably, a single sneaker. She headed straight for the double doors that led to the theater itself, but before she could grasp one of the heavy handles, the door swung toward her.

"Whoa!" Gemma jumped back just in time to keep from getting smacked by the door as a petite blonde squeezed through the opening. She froze when she recognized the familiar face, shockingly unchanged by time. "Chelsea?"

Chelsea stopped as well and stared for a second before a nasty smile spread across her face. "Well. Look who dragged herself back to Haven Ridge. Gemma Van Buren."

Gemma bit back sharp words in response to her tone. Just seeing her high school nemesis brought back a flood of bad memories. The worst part was, Gemma had thought the fact that her dad was shacking up with Chelsea's mom was going to put them on the same side, embarrassed by their disgustingly indiscreet parents. Instead, Chelsea had made it her sole purpose to turn the entire school against Gemma; right before she took over her life, her house, even her beloved two-story turreted bedroom.

But that was fifteen years ago, long before Gemma had found her voice, before she learned to deal with small-minded, snipey people. Now, she simply cocked her head, a questioning smile on her face, and waited.

It had exactly the effect she was hoping. Chelsea blinked, discomfited that she hadn't jumped at the bait, and managed in a more civil tone, "What are you doing back here?"

"Just helping out Liv for the week. How have you been? I heard you got married."

More confusion flitted across the woman's face. "Yeah," she said slowly. "A few years ago. Remember Doug?"

"I do, actually. You've got kids, I hear? At least I assume you do, because Liv told me you were on the elementary PTO."

"Yeah. Twins, Cody and Etta. They're six now."

Gemma nodded and rocked back onto her heels, hands in her jacket pocket. "Congratulations. I'll see you around, okay?" She brushed past her into the theater, leaving her high school enemy standing gaping like a bass in the lobby.

"And that is how you deal with the mean girl," a low voice murmured directly to her right.

Gemma jumped now, her hand flying to her chest. "Stephen. You startled me!"

He stepped out of the shadows of the theater into the dim sliver of light still showing through the door. "Sorry. I was on my way out, but I figured you could use a couple of minutes to deal with that." He jerked his head toward the lobby, where Chelsea was striding out of the building, shaking her head like she was talking to herself.

Gemma smiled, but faced with Stephen, all her confidence seemed to flee. She studied the pattern of the dark red carpet beneath her feet.

"Listen, Gemma, I was hoping we could talk. I know it's been a long time, but . . . I have some things that I think I should say."

"Stephen, really, it's all right. I know what you're going to say. And it's been a long time. I've moved on. Can't we just leave the past in the past?"

He stared at her, his brows furrowed in a way that made her suddenly feel guilty that *she* might have hurt *his* feelings. How dare he? As if it were her obligation to accept his apology? The time to make amends would have been fifteen years ago, when she had spent two months crying herself to sleep and swearing that she would never date again. Eventually the crying had stopped, but now that she thought about it, she might have unintentionally jinxed her personal life with that vow.

"Aunt Gem!" Taylor's excited voice burst out from the front of the theater and she charged up the steps, looking far younger and more enthusiastic than today's all-black ensemble would suggest. "Can we have some friends over tonight?"

"We?"

Taylor grinned. "Well, me, but in your apartment. Maybe we could bake something?"

Stephen took a step back, his expression unreadable. "I should go. Good work today, Taylor. Gemma, I'll see you around." He gave them a little smile, ducked his head, and headed out through the doors.

Taylor looked between Gemma and her teacher's departing back and winced. "I'm sorry. I interrupted something, didn't I?"

"No, you didn't interrupt anything." She looked past Taylor at where two of the girls from yesterday were walking up the theater steps. "And yes, it's fine if you'd like to have some friends over. We still have the baklava to make, remember?"

"Thanks, Aunt Gem." She turned to her friends. "She said it's okay. I'm going to text Megan and Jada. This is Rebekah, by the way."

The pretty redhead gave her a bright smile and a little wave. "Hey. Thanks for having us over."

"Sure. You two coming home with us? Do you need to let your parents know?"

"We'll text them," they said almost in unison, and Gemma smiled wryly. There was nothing like a pack of teenagers to make her feel hopelessly old and realize how young and naive she'd really been the last time she'd been home.

And there was nothing like seeing her first love to make her realize how little she had actually changed.

* * *

Gemma called in an order to Mario's, making a mental note to find something healthier—and not pizza—for dinner tomorrow night, then sent the girls in to get the food before heading back to Liv's house. The three girls chatted enthusiastically in the back seat, using so much slang that Gemma could barely follow the conversation. Just another thing to make her feel old today.

She tuned them out until she heard Layla say, "You should come dress shopping with us in Colorado Springs this weekend. My dad's taking the big SUV so there's room."

Gemma caught Taylor's eye in the rear-view mirror. "You're going to the dance?"

Taylor actually blushed. "Dylan asked me today. He thought the cookies were sick."

"He's a drummer," Layla put in.

Gemma grinned. Apparently things hadn't changed much: musician always trumped everything except for star athlete. "And Jonathan?"

Rebekah piped up with unrestrained glee, "He tried to wear a hat all day."

"Oh no." Gemma winced, even though she couldn't help a chuckle. She actually felt a little bad about her part in crushing a teenage boy's self-esteem. Then again, he'd conspired to humiliate her niece in front of all his friends, so maybe he didn't deserve her sympathy.

When they finally pulled up to the gate, Megan and Jada were already waiting in the Plymouth she'd seen yesterday. They pulled in after Gemma, but she'd barely come to a stop before the girls burst out together in an excited, squealing huddle. Clearly Taylor's date was the talk of the night, and Gemma even caught some envy from the friends. Evidently the drummer was quite a catch.

Gemma retrieved the pizzas from the front seat and

let herself into the apartment, followed closely by the five girls, their excitement filling the tiny space to bursting. While they demolished the pizza, she texted Liv.

I'm hosting four of Taylor's friends tonight.

Which ones?

Layla, Megan, Jada, and Rebekah.

Godspeed . . .

Gemma chuckled. **Taylor got asked to the Valentine's Day dance by a boy named Dylan.**

DYLAN? He's like the sophomore class Holy Grail. He hasn't gone out with anyone this year. I can't believe I'm missing this!!!

Gemma laughed loud enough that the girls paused in their conversation to look at her. She waved them off, still grinning to herself. If there was any doubt that Liv had slipped into the role of mom, this laid them all to rest.

Jada asked if Taylor can go to CS this weekend to look for dresses.

Only if a parent drives. I've seen these girls behind the wheel. It's terrifying.

Yep. Definitely with a parent. How are things going there?

This time, it took longer for Liv to answer. **Too much via text. I'll call you tomorrow. I'm taking my team out tonight.**

That sounded ominous, but maybe that was just Gemma's pessimism talking. She waited until there was a lull in the girls' conversation and asked, "So what are we doing tonight? Baklava or eclairs?"

They looked at each other and said "Eclairs!" in unison. Good. At least that was easy. She could make *choux* in her sleep. It was hard to mess up.

This time she let Taylor take the lead, giving her the

recipe verbally while her friends measured and poured and Taylor stirred. Gemma divided the pastry into three different disposable bags so they could each pipe long dashes of batter onto their own parchment-lined baking sheets. Gemma slid all the sheets into the oven, set the timer, and began to silently clean up while the girls settled around the wooden island. She did her best to make herself invisible when the conversation inevitably turned to boys.

"I don't know what to do about Noah," Layla said in a low voice. "We've been together for . . . six weeks now? And he's getting impatient."

"Are you going to do it?" Taylor whispered, sounding scandalized.

"He used to date Angel Watkins," Rebekah put in. "You know they were screwing like rabbits. He kind of expects it now."

Gemma froze, her skin prickling at the sensation of overhearing something she really wasn't meant to and therefore couldn't weigh in on like she wanted to.

"Trust me," Taylor said. "You don't want to get a reputation like Angel. Yeah, all the guys like her, but they just want sex."

Layla sighed. "Yeah, but he's totally going to break up with me if I don't do more than—"

Gemma couldn't take it anymore. "I know no one asked my opinion, but I'm going to give it anyway."

The girls all turned to her, surprised that she had spoken. Or maybe they had forgotten she was there. But their expressions were curious, so she plowed on.

"Trying to keep someone from breaking up with you is an absolutely terrible reason to have sex. For one thing, it doesn't work. If someone's going to dump you, they'll do it regardless. You're just putting off the inevitable. And then you've done something you didn't really want to do or it's tainted because you did it for the wrong reasons."

The girls exchanged looks, debating whether they wanted to have this conversation with an adult. Apparently they decided she didn't count, because Layla said, "I think I might love him. What if this is meant to be and I screw it up because I don't trust him?"

"It has nothing to do with trust. Besides, if it's meant to be, it won't matter what you do, right? He'll understand. He'll wait. Wouldn't you rather know if he loves you or if he's just being a horny teenager?"

The girls giggled uneasily, but Taylor was watching her closely. "Is that what happened with you and Mr. Osborne?"

Darn Taylor and her perceptiveness. Gemma had been hoping she wouldn't make the connection. "Whatever happened between me and Mr. Osborne is our business, definitely not yours."

"Did you guys break up because you slept together or because you didn't?" Rebekah asked curiously.

"We broke up because I moved away. And because no one marries their high school sweetheart."

"Except my aunt," Rebekah muttered. "And they kind of prove your point."

"Yeah, how's that going?" Taylor asked sympathetically.

"Same. Uncle Doug is fine if he isn't drinking, but if he is . . . I just try to take the little kids and get out of the way."

"I don't know why your aunt stays with him," Layla said. "I don't know why she married him in the first place."

Rebekah sent Layla a significant look. "The twins were premature . . . but maybe they weren't *that* premature, if you know what I mean. Like Aunt Chelsea just decided to give up her job in the Springs and move back here for fun?"

Gemma held her breath, shocked. For one thing, she hadn't realized Rebekah was Chelsea's niece. For another, it sounded like Chelsea had gotten pregnant after college and married Doug to make the babies legitimate. Or had she been pressured to? The idea of a shotgun wedding was shocking in this day and age, but maybe not as shocking as the suggestion that Gemma's nemesis was stuck in an abusive marriage with the mayor.

"Anyway, my dad will be back from Hong Kong next month and I won't have to stay there anymore." Rebekah flicked her eyes to Gemma. "I guess that all proves your point."

The resignation in Rebekah's face spurred Gemma out of her shock. "Girls, listen to me. You never *ever* have to do anything you don't want to. Not for a boyfriend, not for a husband. There are people who will help, okay? This is why I became a lawyer, to help women out of bad situations. But the best way is to avoid them in the first place. Right? There are signs. There are always signs if we're willing to see them." She looked each girl in the eye, lingering longest on Layla and Rebekah. "And seriously, even if I'm in California, you can text me. Or Liv. And we'll find you help. Right?"

Five heads nodded, a little wide-eyed at her vehemence. She would have said more, but the timer on the oven went off and she turned away to take out the eclairs.

Like a release valve had been popped, the tension went out of the room. The girls turned to lighter topics while the eclair shells cooled and Gemma started making the pastry cream and ganache that would finish them off. She was aware of Rebekah's frequent searching looks while she filled another set of disposable bags with the filling.

She showed them how to poke a hole in the end with a chopstick and pipe the cream into the shell. And then they each got to dip their own eclairs into a chocolate ganache glaze and finish them with any topping they wanted—nuts, sprinkles, mini chocolate chips, tiny gold dragées.

At last when they finally got to eat their creations, the room fell silent. Not long afterward, the party broke up. Megan offered to drive the other girls home so Gemma didn't have to.

"Thanks for having us over," Layla said, giving Gemma an impulsive hug. The other girls echoed the sentiment, and Gemma walked them to the stairs.

Rebekah hung back. "Don't tell my aunt I said anything about all . . . that. Please?"

"Your aunt and I aren't exactly on friendly terms."

"Yeah, I know, but . . . I'll get in trouble if she finds out I said anything."

"If it comes up, I won't tell her it came from you," Gemma said carefully. "But Rebekah . . . if you need anything . . . if you feel unsafe or you think the twins or your aunt are in danger, call someone. The police, me, Liv, whoever. Okay?"

Rebekah swallowed hard. "Okay, thanks." She flicked a glance to Taylor. "Bye, Taylor. See you tomorrow."

Taylor gave Gemma a pointed glance she couldn't quite interpret and disappeared down the steps with her friends. Gemma paced the hallway a little restlessly while she waited for Taylor to come back.

As soon as the girl appeared, Gemma asked, "Can I get . . ."

Taylor held out her phone with Rebekah's name and number up on the screen. Gemma smiled and tapped out a text message to Rebekah that contained only her name, then pressed *send.*

"I hope that wasn't weird," Gemma said. "I just get really passionate about wanting you guys to make good decisions and not stick with the bad ones."

"It was a little weird." Taylor put her arms around her and squeezed. "But weird is okay sometimes." She dropped her arms. "I'm going to go do my homework now." Taylor swiped one more piece of pizza and headed for the back bedroom.

Gemma was going back to the kitchen to clean it up when Taylor called out, "Aunt Gem?"

"Yeah?"

"All that stuff you said . . . you're speaking from experience, aren't you?"

Gemma gave her a sad smile. "Yeah. Kind of."

Taylor gave her a nod and disappeared into the bedroom. Gemma thought for a long minute and then called, "Hey! Do you have the school directory?"

"It's online!"

"Can I—?"

Once more Taylor beat her to it. She came out with her cell phone extended, Stephen Osborne's number on the screen.

Gemma tapped the number into her phone. "Thanks." But before she could figure out what she planned to do with it, her screen lit up.

Stephen was calling.

CHAPTER TWELVE

STEPHEN PUSHED DOWN HIS DISAPPOINTMENT as he left the theater, thwarted once more by teenage enthusiasm in his attempts to talk to Gemma. Just knowing she was back in town had wrecked his concentration on a day when he didn't have any extra to spare. He was behind in his grading again—complicated by the change in lesson plans—and the festival loomed like a threatening storm just over the horizon. He'd been sure that his job managing million-dollar advertising projects would be more than enough preparation for arranging a school festival, but now he wasn't so sure.

That was why he had roped Liv into the project a couple of weeks ago, and she'd been a godsend. In fact, the Binder of Doom, as he was dramatically thinking of it, had been her doing . . . he'd just been working out of a bunch of files on his computer, which she rightly reminded him would not help anyone who was inclined to pitch in. Now he regretted telling her that he could handle this without her. He should have harnessed her superhuman persuasive ability to find him a replacement.

Focus, he told himself, driving back to the Brick House Cafe. He'd grab an early dinner while he finished confirming the vendors and then he would move on to calling the town members who had volunteered time, donations, and equipment for the festival on Saturday. Everyone but the retirees worked, so he could do that after office hours. He just had precious little time to get everything done before businesses closed for the evening.

Mallory was working today, and after giving him a quick, brief hug, she walked him back to a booth in the corner. "How's everything going?" she asked, nodding toward the conspicuously-labeled binder.

"I'm drowning," he answered honestly. "Between this and teaching and school . . ."

"Anything I can do to help?"

He smiled at her. "You're sweet, but I don't see how you have any more time than me. How's that last paper going?"

"Fine, I think. I'm still trying to dig up corroborating info on what I've learned from Pearl, so it's making writing about this town a little bit tricky, but it's coming along." She focused on him for a second. "What do you know about the history of this town?"

"Not much," he answered honestly. "Why?"

"Just wondering," she said, giving him a lingering look. "You want your usual?"

"Yeah, thanks. I'm going to make some calls."

Mallory swept the menu off the table in front of him, returned a minute later with a glass of ice water, and then disappeared back to the kitchen again. Stephen opened the binder, flipped to the first name on the list, and pulled out his cell phone. "Hi, this is Stephen from Haven Ridge High School. I'm just confirming your donation for this Saturday . . ."

He'd managed to make his way halfway through the corporate sponsor list by the time Mallory came back with the dinner special—Pearl's famous meatloaf, the cook Arnold's special mashed potatoes, and a side of homemade gravy. He'd hated meatloaf as a kid, but the way they made it at the Brick House Cafe in no way resembled the dense, dried-out lump of ground beef his mom used to make. That, unfortunately, reminded him that he'd been remiss in visiting his parents. He'd been back for six months and had seen them perhaps a dozen times. His mom, at least, would want to see him. His dad, however, he was never entirely sure.

He checked his watch, chewed and swallowed, and dialed the next number on the list, a company that rented snow machines for events and businesses like small sledding parks. It had actually been Liv's idea—despite the lingering patches of snow in the low spots from the last hit-and-run snowstorm, it had been a dry winter overall in this part of Colorado. And one of the highlights of the winter festival had always been a snowy, high-stakes game of Capture the Flag.

"I'm so sorry," the woman who answered told him when he asked to confirm the rental. "We'd earmarked a machine for you, but one of our regular customers had a breakdown. We had to swap out their machine, and unfortunately, we're waiting on a part before we can fix it. I know this is an inconvenience."

More than an inconvenience; it was a disaster. They were counting on the entry fees for the game to help pay for the gym repairs that the school desperately needed; the proceeds from the "farmer's market" were already earmarked for the performing arts department. There was no way they were going to meet their fundraising goals if they had to cancel the game. Not that they had to cancel the game, exactly, but part of what made Capture the Flag so fun and successful were the "add-ons" that players could purchase.

Stephen glanced at his watch, all too aware of his meal getting cold in front of him. 5:25. He had a half hour, if he was lucky, to catch one of the other vendors while they were still in the office.

But by six o'clock, he had to admit that it was probably pointless. The companies he did reach had nothing available this weekend or wanted thousands of dollars for the rental. With the others, his calls just went straight to voice mail. Which meant he would be spending precious time later this week trying to track down anyone who could help him with snow.

He took a deep breath and turned back to his now-cold meal. He needed to get a grip. He'd never thought of himself as a stress-prone person, but he was starting to feel a bit cross-eyed from all the balls he was juggling. It wasn't like he had anything else to do, he reminded himself. He didn't have a wife or a girlfriend at home waiting for him.

Mallory stopped by the table to refill his water glass, pausing to look him over with concern. "Going that well, huh?"

"Yeah. It'll be fine. I just have to . . . get organized."

"Or maybe you should ask for help." She smiled at him like she knew his protest before it even formed on his lips. "Just because you volunteered for this doesn't mean that you're the only one who has skin in the game. Delegate."

Except, he wanted to say, most of the other teachers would just shrug and tell him it was his problem. It wasn't that they were checked out—most of them still loved their jobs, at least in the classroom—it was simply that they had lives of their own, and many of them had side-hustles to make ends meet. The music teacher waited tables in Buena Vista in the evenings; the football coach was a ski instructor at Monarch on the weekends. It was why Stephen had thought he should take on some responsibility—because he was the only one who could.

But Mallory was right. He wasn't the only one who was counting on this festival being a success. And he knew someone who would probably be able to cut through all the excuses and find him someone to help. He pulled out his phone and texted Liv.

Okay, I lied. I'm drowning, and the snow machine just fell through. I need help. Who can you rope in?

Not five minutes later, Liv responded, **I'm on it. Give me an hour.**

An hour. He could do that. Rather than packing it in, he pushed back his half-eaten meal and pulled out his laptop to grade the new round of papers. If he were smart, he'd start giving more online quizzes and fewer essays. Except he didn't want his students to simply memorize facts. He wanted them to be able to articulate their thoughts and feelings on literature in a way that would make their curriculum relevant and develop those all-too-important writing skills they'd need for college and life beyond. It was a constant struggle between his integrity as a teacher and the realities of time management.

He'd managed to get through his entire junior class's essays on *The Yellow Wallpaper*, with some surprisingly good insights from some of his students—mainly his female students, but the boys pleasantly surprised him; looked like things were changing for the better. That warm feeling he got from actually seeing minds expanded carried him through until his phone notified him of a message exactly fifty-seven minutes after the last one.

So . . . I struck out. Everyone I asked is either busy, won't be there, or has some sort of good excuse.

He sighed. It was worth a try. What was a couple of night's lost sleep? If he caught up on his classwork tonight, that meant the lunch hour he usually used for doing his own schoolwork could be used for phone calls. That's okay. I understand. I'll make it work.

A long pause, then another message. Or . . . you could always ask Gemma. She's literally doing nothing but baking with Taylor this week.

Stephen stared at the phone. No. There was no way. After their brief meeting today, when she'd made it very clear that she had no interest in what he had to say— had no interest in him at all—there was no way he could go beg her for help.

Except if you did, she would have no choice but to talk to you. And then maybe she would actually let you talk. Explain. Beg forgiveness. When are you ever going to get this opportunity again? Are you going to hold onto regrets for another fifteen years until the next time you see her?

I don't like you very much right now, he texted back. Yes. Because you know I'm right.

Unfortunately, he did. But there was no way he was having that conversation in the middle of the Brick House Cafe. The second anyone caught wind that he and Gemma were even speaking, it was sure to spread through the town like wildfire. There were still people who knew all the details of what had happened and were still invested in their high school drama, all these years later. If he owed Gemma anything, it was to keep her from scrutiny.

Still, like a coward, he waited until after nine o'clock to call her, safely ensconced in his favorite chair, a bourbon in hand, the television muted. Liv, sensing that she was going to get her way, had texted him Gemma's number, and he'd stared at it in his phone for a full ten minutes before he pushed *call*. To his shock, she answered on the first ring.

"Let me guess," she said by way of answer, not even bothering with hello. "Liv?"

"You've got it."

Gemma sighed on the other end of the phone. "Honestly, Stephen, I don't have the energy for this tonight. I get that you feel bad. I really do. But like I said at the school, I've moved on. Can we please just drop the subject?"

He cleared his throat. "Actually, that wasn't why I was calling. Liv had volunteered for the school carnival this weekend, and her being gone has kind of left me in the lurch. She said you might have some free time to help?"

"Oh." The change in tone was instantaneous. Even after all these years, he could picture her sitting suddenly upright while her mind spun through the possibilities. "What do you need exactly?"

"Just someone to help me with the follow-up work. Calling local donors and confirming their donations. That sort of thing. Nothing taxing, I promise, and you won't have to solicit anyone. It's just busywork and I really have no time to do it."

"I don't know, Stephen. . . I only have so much time here with Taylor, and I—"

"I know it's a lot to ask, considering. . . everything. But part of the proceeds of the festival goes to the performing arts department. So you'd actually be helping Taylor, not me. . ."

Gemma sighed. Even through the silent phone line he could sense her weighing her annoyance with him against her love for her niece But she couldn't blame him when she'd been so quick to use Taylor as an excuse. "Okay."

"Okay?"

"Yeah, I'll do it. You want to meet tomorrow after school to do the hand-off? You can explain to me what needs to be done."

"I've got track team conditioning at the school gym until five. Let's say Brick House Cafe at six o'clock?"

"Sure. I'll be there."

He paused, his voice unconsciously taking on a lower, warmer timbre. "Thanks, Gemma. You have no idea how much I appreciate this."

"I think I do," she answered, but before he could reply, she hung up.

CHAPTER THIRTEEN

GEMMA SPENT THE ENTIRE NEXT DAY while Taylor was in school pretending not to think about her meeting with Stephen and failing miserably. The hot tub plan lasted about five minutes—the frigid air was more uncomfortable than refreshing and neither the book she'd picked up at the store when she'd arrived or any of the ones she'd packed in her suitcase managed to hold her attention. She texted Liv to check in, but when an hour passed without a reply, she had to give up on that as a distraction. She ended up scavenging lasagna noodles from the main house and turning her simple plan of pasta for dinner into a multi-hour lasagna extravaganza. . .and still managed to have half the day left over.

Taylor, conveniently, texted her that she was going to Layla's house after school and wouldn't be home until late, a transparent way of telling Gemma that she'd have the apartment all to herself. The girl was a hopeless romantic—or had been reading her stepmom's steamy romance novels—if she thought Gemma and Stephen would magically put aside the fifteen years of absence and end up back at her place after a half-hour conversation. She should probably finish that talk that had gotten aborted by the oven timer. In Liv's mind, Taylor was still the sweet ten-year-old girl she'd met when dating Jason, but overhearing the girls' conversation last night had driven home that these girls were much older and more experienced than Gemma and Liv had been at the same age. At fifteen, they had still been whispering in hushed tones about whether or not a guy would use tongue on a first kiss, not debating how long they could put off sex before they lost their boyfriends.

And then there was the revelation about Chelsea and Doug and what sounded like an abusive—or at least tense—home life. What in the world was she supposed to do with that? She'd been careful not to make any promises to Rebekah she couldn't keep, but after so many years, she was an outsider. Did she actually think she was going to intervene in a situation with her worst enemy from high school? If Chelsea was going to confide in someone, it wasn't going to be Gemma.

In short, by the time she left the house, dressed nicely but casually in a sweater and jeans with some light makeup applied, she was a ball of nerves. Driving back into town and being confronted by the sad, deserted Dogwood Street didn't help. She found a parking spot half a block down from the diner and walked to the town's single thriving business.

She entered the diner and scanned the tables, but before she could get more than a few steps in, a man circled the counter and headed straight for her. "Gemma Van Buren. Is that really you?"

Gemma blinked and took in the handsome dark-haired man in front of her. He was older than she remembered and sported a neatly-trimmed beard, but there was no mistaking the mischievous glint in his brown eyes. "Thomas?"

"None other." He grinned and pulled her into a friendly hug before stepping back to look her over. "I'd heard you were back in town, but I hardly believed it. You look good!"

She resisted the urge to say she wasn't back, focusing instead on his other words. "You look good, too. I hear congratulations are in order. I met Mallory yesterday."

His expression softened. "Yeah. She's great. We're getting married this summer."

Gemma reached out to squeeze his arm. There was no question about his feelings from the look on his face. "I'm really happy for you. Hey, have you seen—"

"Stephen's in the back corner," he said with a smile that seemed a touch too knowing. "I'll be over to get your order in a minute."

"Thanks." Gemma tilted her head down, aware that the exuberant reunion had drawn more than a few pairs of eyes in her direction. So much for making this a quick meeting and tipping off as few people as possible to her presence.

She thought she was actually going to accomplish it, until she passed an elderly couple at a table by the window. "Gemma?"

Gemma stopped, caught by the familiar voice, though it had grown thready with age. She turned in surprise. "Mrs. Walters?"

"Yes, yes it's me!" The white-haired woman beamed up at her. "Of all the people I never expected to see here again, you were right at the top of the list!"

Gemma smiled uncertainly, not sure what to make of that comment. Mrs. Walters had been her history teacher for both sophomore and junior year, and she'd been ancient back then. She had to be older than Pearl, not that you could tell from her bright eyes and nearly unlined face. Her husband watched the two of them with bemusement.

"I'm just here for the week, helping out Liv Quinn with Taylor."

"Yes, yes, terrible thing about her husband," she said, tutting. "But it was good timing to come back. She needed her community around her. The town does that, you know." Mrs. Walters fixed her with a knowing look and nodded sharply. "Brings back the people who need it when they need it most."

Was there something in the air? Had there been an industrial spill upstream and now everyone was suffering from toluene-induced dementia? Gemma had lived in Haven Ridge for sixteen years, and if the town had any sort of interest in her well-being, it certainly hadn't shown itself when it might have actually been useful.

Her skepticism must have shown on her face, because Mr. Walters gave her a crooked smile and then reached across the table to pat his wife's hand. "Let Gemma get on with her evening, Mama. She doesn't want to sit here and reminisce with us old-timers."

Gemma smiled, breaking free of her thoughts. "Not at all. It's good to see you both. I just have to . . ." She nodded toward where she could see Stephen watching the entire exchange with an amused look. "Have a nice meal. Hopefully I'll see you before I leave."

"You too, dear," Mrs. Walters said vaguely and then reached for the ketchup for her coffee before she realized she meant to grab the sugar shaker.

Not exactly a resounding endorsement for the town's interest in Gemma's well-being.

The detour did have the effect of erasing her nervousness in meeting Stephen, and by the time she slid into the booth across from him, she was just glad to be somewhat obscured from the view of the diner. "So, that was interesting."

Stephen smiled at her, crinkling the corners of those arresting hazel eyes. "Did she give you the 'Haven Ridge wants you to come back' speech?"

Gemma glanced over her shoulder. "You heard it too?"

"Only once I'd already moved back. The town likes to take credit for it." His eyes twinkled. "It does not, however, like to take credit for my three-thousand-dollar-a-month downtown Salt Lake City rent, which was the real reason I moved back here."

"Ouch," she said. "Just as bad as L.A."

"Your weather is better, though."

Thomas chose that moment to arrive at their table. "What can I get you two?"

"You hungry?" Stephen asked.

Gemma shrugged. "Not really. I'd take a cup of coffee, though."

"Same," Stephen said. "And a basket of fries to share?"

"Coming right up," Thomas said, before he headed back to the kitchen.

"I should have asked," Stephen said. "You do still eat fries?"

"Of course I eat fries. Who doesn't eat fries?"

"Well, you are a big-time California attorney now. Maybe you only consume wheat grass shots and pro-biotic smoothies."

Gemma snorted. "Thanks." She didn't protest too much, though, having actually drunk both of those in the past month. The organic juice bar downstairs from her firm was the furthest she managed to get for lunch some days.

"So, I'm sorry to spring this on you, but we're only a

couple of days away and there's still a few details to be wrapped up." Stephen pulled a thick binder off the seat next to him and placed it on the table with a thud.

"A few?"

"Don't worry, Liv documented every conversation she ever had with anyone about this festival. I'm handling all the on-site logistics of booth construction, games, entertainment, etc. I just really need you to follow up with all the businesses and individuals who have offered to donate to the festival. Make sure they're bringing what they say they're bringing, things like that."

That didn't sound so hard, and Gemma wasn't afraid of a handful of phone calls. Unfortunately, it pretty much shattered the rest of her hopes that she would be able to get out of here without engaging with the town. Flipping through the binder, it looked like Liv had solicited something from practically every person they'd ever known, and some Gemma didn't recognize.

Following her thoughts, Stephen said, "Liv can be very persuasive."

"I can see that." She closed the book. "Anything else I need to do?"

"I could use help organizing on Saturday morning. I'll be supervising the setup and we have parent volunteers, but there's always a need for another person there to help direct. Liv was kind of my right-hand man on this. I could never have gotten this far without her."

Unexpectedly, she felt a spike of jealousy at the comment. Which was stupid, because she hardly thought that Liv had any interest in Stephen beyond being an old friend and a way to volunteer her superior organization skills. His face was as guileless as ever, unaware of her thoughts.

Thomas came back and set down a basket of French

fries still steaming hot from the fryer, along with two plates. "Enjoy, guys."

Gemma reached immediately for a fry, glad for an excuse to look anywhere except in Stephen's face. He was studying her too intently for her comfort.

"You look good," he said quietly. "California agrees with you."

"Thanks. You've held up pretty well yourself."

Their eyes met, and though his expression was pleasant, he didn't smile. "Gemma, I owe you an apology."

"Oh? What for?"

"We both know what for."

"Stephen, it was fifteen years ago. We were kids."

"Yeah. But that's no excuse. I should have known better."

Gemma crammed another fry into her mouth. "Just. . . let it go."

"I don't want to let it go."

She jerked her head up and looked him in the eye. "Okay. You want to talk about it? How's this? You *should* have known better. Maybe we were just sixteen, but I was in love with you. Madly. Stupidly. I thought you were the one person in this town who would never hurt me."

He dropped his head, looking ashamed of himself. "I didn't mean for things to happen the way they did. I missed you. I was sad, and Amber was sympathetic. And *here*."

Gemma stared at him. "You think I was mad because you started dating Amber?"

He frowned. "Of course."

She folded her arms over the table and leaned in. "I was mad because we talked on the phone every single night. You told me you loved me. That you missed me so much you didn't know how you'd get through the week. I left home without telling my mom and rode a bus five hundred miles to see you, just to find out you already had a new girlfriend. And every single person in this town knew. Except me. From the moment I got off the bus, everyone was looking at me with pity.

"I could handle being the subject of whispers about my dad. That sucked, but it wasn't on me. But you . . . you made me the dumb girl who couldn't see that I was just a conquest to the football star. *You* were the one who finally made me doubt myself. It took me years to forgive myself for being taken in, to realize that I wasn't the one who should be ashamed in that situation."

Gemma swept up the binder and tucked it into the crook of her arm as she stood. "I'll get on these right away. I'll see you on Saturday."

"Gemma, wait—"

"No. You stay here." Gemma fumbled in her purse for a ten-dollar bill and then tossed it on the table. "Enjoy your fries."

And then she stalked out of the diner, heedless of the dozens of pairs of eyes following her angry progress.

Outside on the sidewalk, a stiff spring wind whipped her hair into her face and bit through the sliver of sweater exposed in the front of her jacket. She fumbled with the binder while she tried to mate the zipper halves, then finally gave up and speed-walked up the street to where she had parked, focusing on the cocoon of quiet and anonymity the SUV would provide. She was within the last final steps when someone stepped in her path.

Gemma stopped short, blinking at the man in front of her. He was several inches taller than her, a little paunchy, dressed in jeans and a sport coat over a western-style shirt. It took her a long moment to get past the outfit to realize who she was looking at. "Doug? Now is not a good time." She ducked her head and prepared to move around him.

Doug stepped into her path, and only then did Gemma note his red face and flashing eyes. The fury practically radiated off him in waves. "How dare you?"

Gemma took a step back automatically, thrown by the hostility. She and Doug Meinke had never exactly been friends, but she hardly thought her brief return to the town warranted outright hostility. "I'm sorry. What? What am I supposed to have done?"

"Apparently, you had a little talk with my wife's niece last night. Gave her your number?"

A chill of foreboding lifted the hairs on the back of her neck. She'd figured that Chelsea might find out and speak to her at some point, but she hadn't predicted it would be Doug to confront her. Still, she wasn't going to let this big bully intimidate her, town mayor or not. She straightened her shoulders and looked him directly in the eye. "So?"

"You're not part of this town anymore. You never were. You may think that your law degree and your expensive clothes give you the right to stick your nose into other people's business, but it doesn't." He stepped closer so he was only a few inches from Gemma's face, trembling. "Stay out of our lives. Do you hear me? You leave my family alone or I promise you, I will make you regret it."

Without another word, he pushed by Gemma, knocking her out of the way, and kept walking.

Gemma stared after Doug for a moment, shocked, then raced the last few steps to the car, where she jumped in and locked the door behind her, her chest heaving.

If she hadn't already convinced herself of it, she was sure now.

Coming back to Haven Ridge had been a mistake.

CHAPTER FOURTEEN

IT DIDN'T TAKE LONG for anger to replace Gemma's fear. By the time she returned to Liv's house, she was seething. If there was anything she hated, it was a bully, and now there was no doubt that Doug Meinke fit the bill. There was also no doubt that what Rebekah had said about life in the Meinke household was accurate. When faced with an accusation—or even the barest implication of abuse—most people didn't go straight to threats. They tried to explain themselves. For that matter, guilty people often tried to explain away their actions or blame it on others. The fact that Doug didn't even try and instead went straight to bullying told her everything she needed to know about the man.

And made her actually feel a little sorry for Chelsea for the first time in her life.

But that wasn't her problem either. She knew all too well that it sometimes took years for women to be willing to escape their situations and she couldn't force anyone to seek help who didn't already want to. Rebekah had her number and knew she could call her or Liv if necessary. There was nothing else she could do.

In a weird way, she was glad for the confrontation. It took the edge off her explosion at Stephen in the diner. Apparently, she wasn't as over his transgressions as she'd thought.

Gemma slammed the SUV's driver door and strode into the garage apartment, clutching the binder to her chest like some sort of protection. It was already Thursday. Her flight back to California was Sunday. All she had to do was get through the next three days without running afoul of Doug Meinke and his family or having to spend more than passing moments talking to Stephen. Forget all this nonsense and get back to her normal life.

Except her normal life might not *be* her normal life. She'd done a good job of completely putting her impending decision out of her mind since arriving in Haven Ridge, but she still hadn't figured out what she was going to do when she got back. Cave to John's demands? Walk away from everything she'd worked for? Neither option seemed like a good one. And yet it didn't feel like a coincidence that it came about at the same time she was reminded exactly why she had left this town and never came back. It was as if she was being reminded of the consequences of failing at her current path in life.

Maybe the lesson was that no one got everything they wanted. That compromises were just part of life.

Gemma shook off the gloomy thoughts and turned on the oven, popping in the lasagna as soon as the preheat timer chimed. Seemed like even her attempt to cook something healthy had ended up in another carb, tomato sauce, and cheese-fest. She was going with it. She quickly texted Taylor that dinner would be ready in an hour and she was welcome to come home to eat since she was most definitely alone.

And then she sat down at the island table and flipped open the binder. Thanks to Liv's awe-inspiring organization, it was easy to see what needed to be done—the spreadsheet in the front of the binder listed every donor with their promised items and contact phone numbers, along with columns to check off for the follow-up calls and delivery on the day of the event.

She started at the top with Christine Fischer, a name Gemma recognized but couldn't quite place. She dialed.

"Hi, Christine? This is Gemma, following up for Liv Quinn about your donation for the Haven Ridge High winter festival?"

"Gemma? Gemma Van Buren? Well, I'll be. . . that's a name that I never thought I would be hearing again."

Gemma blinked. "Pardon me?"

"It's me, Mrs. Fischer. I used to own the laundromat in town. Of course that was a long time ago. . . Don't you remember? Pearl always used to send you down to deliver my lunch from the diner."

"Of course I remember you," Gemma said, though the memories were fuzzy. She had to have been, what, six or seven when that had happened? "How are you?"

"Oh, these old bones are hanging in there. But what are you doing, calling for Liv? Have you moved back to town?"

"No, not moved back. I'm just here for the week to stay with Taylor while Liv is in New York."

Mrs. Fischer clucked her tongue in a way that immediately brought to mind Mrs. Walters, so she knew what was coming next. "Such a shame, losing her husband like that, so suddenly. It's been two years. I wish she'd get back out there. She's far too young to be alone."

"She's not alone," Gemma said. "She has Taylor."

"And Taylor will go off to school in two years just

like all young people do." Mrs. Fischer sighed heavily. "In any case, I'm glad you're back. The town has missed you."

Hardly. Gemma would be willing to bet that no one besides Liv and Stephen had even said her name aloud in the last decade.

"Yes, thank you, Mrs. Fischer. I just wanted to follow up that you're still set to donate four dozen cupcakes to the carnival for the food stands?"

"Oh, I did volunteer for that, didn't I? I'm so sorry, dear, I'm afraid I won't be able to follow through with that. You see, Mr. Fischer and I are driving to Denver tomorrow to see his cardiologist and we won't be back until Sunday. But call my daughter, Katie. I'm sure she'll be able to fill in for me."

"I understand," Gemma said, a pit starting to form in her gut. "I'll call Katie. Do you have her number?"

Katie, no surprise, didn't appreciate that her mother had volunteered her for four dozen cupcakes, and from the sound of squealing in the background, couldn't possibly have children old enough to care what the high school did. Gemma highlighted the cupcake line as something to be dealt with later and moved on to the other donations.

The rest of the calls went somewhat predictably. Almost everyone expressed amazement that she was back, after which she had to explain that she wasn't actually back. The people her age and a little older were pleasant and expressed their congratulations for her success. The older people tutted when they heard she wasn't moving home and only helping out her prematurely-widowed friend. She tried to return the conversation to the topic at hand and confirmed the loan of shade shelters, portable propane heaters, barbecues, craft items, and other random bits of equipment necessary to make what sounded like a big block party in the high school parking lot.

She couldn't help her growing surprise, tinged with a little bitterness. When she and her mother had needed help, there'd been none to be found—these same people had instead turned their backs on them, choosing to believe the ugly smear campaign against them, rather than their own experiences. But now, for the sake of some school programs, the town was determined to pull together?

Except for one thing. Without fail, everyone who had agreed to donate baked goods to the festival begged off, citing family emergencies, ill-timed colds, or sudden business meetings. And everyone *those* people suggested as possible replacements balked at the idea of throwing together two dozen cupcakes or several loaves of zucchini bread or a few pans of brownies at the last minute.

It would be laughable if the pattern weren't so obvious.

Gemma debated for a long moment with her phone in her hand, then texted Stephen. **Confirmed for everything except baked goods. You wouldn't happen to know why every single one of our donors has backed out?**

His response was almost immediate, and she was glad to see that it was on task and not a spill of apologies. **Wait, what? How could that be? They practically begged Liv to contribute, probably because it was literally the least they could do.**

Despite herself, Gemma cracked a smile at that.

Gemma, I don't suppose . . .

Don't say it.

Yeah, but you're clearly still an amazing baker. We've tapped every person in town and the bake sale

is our biggest earner. We were counting on that money
to pay for the buses to Denver for the speech meet
next month.

Gemma stared at the phone. Of course he would go
there. Tie the success of the bake sale to one of the two
people she actually cared about in this town. He might
as well have said, *If you don't help out, you'll be letting
Taylor down.*

She typed out a handful of replies, all of which she
deleted before she could send them. There was really no
other answer to this. There was one full day and a
handful of overnight hours until the festival on Saturday. She knew how hard it was to convince anyone to
donate at the last minute, let alone spend their Friday
nights baking. She bowed her head and then forced
herself to type the only possible response.

Fine, I'll do it.

His only response, a long line of praying-hand
emojis.

Gemma rubbed her nose, still a little disgruntled. If
Mallory were here . . . or Mrs. Walters for that matter . . .
they'd say something about the universe conspiring to
pull her back into Haven Ridge's weird little orbit. It
was too much coincidence otherwise. And if Gemma
was anything but strictly pragmatic, she might be
tempted to agree.

And then, seized by what she only could call
absolute insanity, she messaged, **But I'm not doing it
alone. You have to come help.**

When his response didn't come through immediately,
she let out a sigh of relief. It had been a mad impulse.
The only reason he'd asked her to help was because she
was the only person in town who didn't have something
better to do. And the only reason she'd said she needed
his help was so he didn't think she was still the pushover

she'd been in high school. The fact he was taking so
long to reply surely meant he was going to bow out. He
wouldn't have asked her if he had any extra time in his
schedule. He'd get his baked goods, she'd get to hold
onto her righteous indignation, and even if neither of
them were exactly *happy*, things would remain just as
they should.

Except her phone beeped and his reply flashed up
on the screen. **Deal. When do you want me?**

As if that wasn't a loaded question.

She took a deep breath, ignored the subtext, and
typed her response to the actual message. **Tomorrow at
6. Liv's apartment, not the house.** He'd stayed in touch
with Liv; he should know what that meant.

I'll be there.

Fine. She'd agreed to do this and she'd forced
Stephen to help, but that didn't mean she'd be happy
about it. Or that she was doing it for anyone else than
her beloved not-quite-niece.

"Did you hear that, Haven Ridge?" she called. "This
isn't for you. This is for Taylor. I'm leaving on Sunday
and I don't care what happens to you. Any of you."

With that settled, she pulled out a fresh legal pad and
began to make her shopping list.

CHAPTER FIFTEEN

As STEPHEN DRAGGED through his long, plodding Friday, he couldn't decide if he was more likely to die from lack of sleep or from anticipation. Considering how one had led to the other, the answer was probably both.

He still couldn't believe that Gemma had asked him to help her. He'd figured she'd rather do all the work herself than ask him for a single thing, and even though he suspected that she thought he'd say no, there was no way he was giving up the golden opportunity he'd been handed.

A way to hopefully, if not erase, then mitigate the high school mistakes that had haunted him for so many years.

But that also meant that the time he'd earmarked for various other things would be taken up by baking, so instead, he'd stayed up until three in the morning, catching up on asynchronous class sessions online and finishing schoolwork that was due by 11:59 pm tonight. Even pounding cup after cup of coffee this morning wasn't helping his alertness; all it was doing was putting his anticipation and nervousness on overdrive.

Somehow, he made it through the end of the day without falling asleep or saying something especially inane to his classes, and he made a point of joining in the sprints and other exercises with the track team in the gym during their optional Friday session. That left him just enough time to get home, shower, change into something other than sweaty gym clothes, and then drive the opposite direction to Liv's place. When he pulled in, he punched in the code Liv had given him last year and pulled up to the parking pad in front of the garage.

Before he could knock on the apartment door, however, it opened. "Right on time," Gemma said, stepping back. "Come in."

He'd seen the place once after Liv had finished the renovations, proud of what she'd accomplished on her own, but that meant there was no distraction from Gemma as she climbed the stairs in front of him. She was dressed even more casually than before in a pair of sweat pants, thick socks, and a long-sleeved Henley shirt, the buttons undone to show just the barest hint of cleavage. Her hair was doubled up in a rubber band, the messy ends fanned out like a peacock tail. He wasn't sure whether to be flattered by the fact that she felt no need to dress up for him or take it as a warning that she couldn't care less what he thought of her. He hoped for the former but figured it was probably the latter.

When she led him into the back of the apartment, however, his attention snapped immediately away from her fashion choices. The delectable smell of sweet things drew him toward the kitchen, where it looked like a bakery had exploded—the island countertop was scattered with flour and various baking implements, a small trash can on the side filled with empty paper flour and sugar bags. That only led his attention to the tray upon tray of baked goods sitting on the countertop near the window.

He wandered to the neatly organized foil trays and looked over what she'd managed to complete since they'd spoken last night. There were piles of individually-sized quick breads—banana and zucchini, according to the labels handwritten in her loopy script—as well as trays of uncut brownies, blondies, and lemon bars. "You've been busy."

"There were a lot of people who bailed," she shot back.

"What are these?" He moved to a covered tray of shortbread cookies, a smile forming on his face. Some of them were shaped like hearts, iced in pastel colors with non-traditional conversation hearts sayings: *You go girl. Go 4 it! U R Loved. U can do it. Believe in urself.* The others were round cookies iced in Haven Ridge High colors of silver and blue with sayings like *Go Bobcats!* The others, *Slay the Spartans!* and *Down with the Demons!* were clearly in reference to their cross-county rivals, Salida and Buena Vista.

"Down with the Demons?"

Gemma threw him a cheeky look, the sparkle in her eye making her look so much like the girl he remembered that he caught his breath. "I figured 'Go to hell, Demons' would probably get me kicked out of the festival for inappropriate language."

Stephen threw his head back and laughed. "I'd forgotten about that. You remember we used to chant that at games?"

"Remember? I'm the one who started it!"

Stephen grinned, and for a minute, Gemma grinned back, both caught up in the recollections of their less conventional and more school-spirited years. She might not have been an athlete, or really, had any sort of interest in sports at all, but the nearly three years they'd dated, she'd never missed a single one of his games. And then her smile faded, as if she was remembering the same things. Before the lightness between them could slip away, he rolled up the sleeves of his sweater. "Okay, then, tell me where to start."

That did it. Even though surprise flickered across her face, she said immediately, "If I write down the recipe, can you measure ingredients for me?"

"Of course. I can handle that."

"But be sure to—"

"Scoop the flour into the measuring cup first and then sweep it off. I know." He smiled. "I remember."

For the first time since Gemma had been back in town, the tiny smile she gave him actually felt genuine. "Perfect. I'm going to preheat the oven in the main house, and we can use both. I've got about nine dozen cupcakes that need to be baked now if we're going to have time to frost them all. I tried to plan things in a sensible way, but the day kind of got away from me . . ." She pushed a strand back from her forehead, and for the first time, he realized that she was just as stressed out as he was.

"Hey," he said, reaching to squeeze her shoulder. "We've got this. You've worked nothing short of a miracle."

"Thanks." She froze under his touch for a moment, and he found himself holding his breath while he waited for her reaction. Had he overstepped? He dropped his hand, a knot forming in his middle.

But she just gave him a weak smile, then reached for a pad and started writing out the recipe with its variations in her feminine script. "Each of these into a different bowl. I'll mix them, you fill the cups, and then you can run the first batch over to the house. I'll be right back."

Gemma thrust her feet into a pair of boots and disappeared down the hallway, the echo of her footsteps and the slam of the downstairs door telling him that he was momentarily alone. He read over the recipe, located the measuring cups and ingredients, and got to work. When Gemma came back a few minutes later, the first batch was ready to be mixed.

"That was quick work." She swiveled away to the stand mixer and began to cream the softened butter and sugar together while he started measuring the second batch. And then, to his surprise, she asked over her shoulder, "So, teaching. How did that come about?"

It wasn't exactly easy to talk over the whir of the stand mixer—probably what she'd intended—but he wasn't going to waste the first spark of genuine interest he'd had from her. "You know I always wanted to teach literature."

"I do," she said. "But you went into advertising."

"Yeah," he said. "You can probably guess why that is."

"Your dad?"

He touched his nose with a fingertip. "You know he was always on me to get out of the town and make something of myself. Of course, I'm pretty sure he meant professional football, but anything that made a good deal of money would be acceptable."

"No offense, but you're not big enough to play pro ball."

Stephen chuckled. "None taken. Besides, that was never my dream anyway. Why do you think I applied to schools that didn't have football teams? Anyway, I kind of just fell into advertising. It was fun for a while."

"What happened then?"

Stephen drummed his fingertips on the counter while he considered how much to tell her. "I guess I was already slightly uncomfortable with the job. I mean, it's not like I have anything against commerce in general. But we had *huge* clients. And I would say I didn't exactly have the same values as some of the companies I was developing ad campaigns for. So even though I was really good at it, I felt like I was . . ."

"Selling out?"

"Exactly."

"So what changed, then?" She shut off the mixer to add the flour, and the sudden silence in the room made the question seem much more intimate than he was sure she'd intended.

"I . . . finally ran up against something I absolutely would not advertise. It was a drug that had recently gotten a black box warning because of mental health risks to teenagers. So they needed a damage control campaign to help boost flagging sales . . . and their vision involved a bunch of happy young people."

Gemma's sudden, horrified look mirrored Stephen's feelings back then.

"I told my boss that I refused to work with a company whose response to teen suicides was to double down on selling it to patients under twenty-five. He said that he understood. And I'd be receiving my final check in the mail."

Gemma leaned back against the counter, her expression open for the first time. "I'm so sorry. That's horrible. For the record, I think you did the right thing."

"I think I did, too. But once I no longer had the job to worry about, I started thinking about what I really wanted to do with my life. Came back to Haven Ridge for a visit, and that's when I heard about the literature opening at the high school. Ironically, standing up for faceless teenagers made me realize that maybe I actually wanted to work with them. The rest is history. Very stressful, slightly neurotic history."

Gemma flashed him a quick smile before she turned the mixer back on. "Tough re-entry?"

"Emergency credential requiring me to finish my alternative licensing within the year. So yeah. Full-time work, part-time school, coaching—"

"And organizing the winter festival. I thought I was supposed to be the pushover here, not you."

"No," he said resolutely, "you were *never* the push-over. I remember the way you held your head high and stared everyone down who dared to disrespect you or your mom. I was not at all shocked to hear you'd become an attorney."

Gemma was quiet for a minute while the batter finished mixing, then shut off the machine and removed the bowl from the stand. She set it in front of Stephen with a big ice cream scoop. "Muffin liners in each well of the tin, then one level scoop," she instructed. "Try to be precise so they're all the same size."

"Yes, ma'am," he said, taking up the tube of cupcake liners. He wordlessly placed the fluted papers into every indentation in the pan and then carefully measured out the first scoop of batter. When Gemma was sure he was doing it to her standards, she turned away and grabbed a second mixer bowl to start the next batch.

He'd assumed the conversation was over, but when the mixer started up again, she said, "Unfortunately, I can relate to the career angst."

He continued to scoop batter, careful to keep his voice casual. "Oh? How's that?" She might have changed in superficial ways, but he still recognized that slightly hunched stance that said she was protecting herself. She wasn't sure she really wanted to tell him this.

"I took the job at my firm with the understanding I could choose my clients. One of the partners has decided not to honor that agreement. So, I'm taking some time off while I make an impossible decision. Keep my job and my pro bono clients while helping people like my father screw over their spouses, or quit and have no income that allows me to take pro bono clients in the first place."

Stephen pushed aside a filled tray of cupcakes and set an empty one in front of him. "Seems to me there's a third option."

"What's that?"

"Quit out of protest, hang out your shingle, and take whatever clients you want for whatever price you want."

Gemma laughed humorlessly. "My mortgage makes your rent in Salt Lake look like a bargain. Besides, I've spent years building up my reputation, but I'm not so sure my name could carry a firm."

"I wish I had better advice. I didn't actually love my job like you do. I might not have come back here had it not felt like an opportunity."

"For what?"

"A do-over." Stephen filled the last couple of liners and set down his scoop. "Here. This batch is done. Should I run them over to the house or do you want to?"

"You can, if you don't mind."

"How long?"

"Twenty-five minutes."

"Okay. I'll be right back."

He took a tin of cupcakes in each hand and headed for the stairs, even though he was loathe to walk away when Gemma was actually talking to him. But he sensed that she could use the time to gather herself. For that matter, so could he. He couldn't be the only one who saw how tightly wound she was, how much pain she was still holding onto. The fact that she'd gone into family law to help people just like her mother and now was faced with this agonizing choice. . . . He could see that she was pretending it wasn't tearing her up inside, that this decision was just a simple calculation of risk versus benefit.

Stephen crunched across the gravel walk to the main house and pushed through the kitchen door. The oven was already heated, so he just put the tins on two evenly spaced racks and set the timer on his watch for *twenty-four* minutes. But he didn't immediately turn back to the apartment, caught in his renewed web of regrets.

At sixteen, Gemma had just lost everything in her life—her home, her nuclear family, her boyfriend—because of her dad's cheating ways and her mom's terrible lawyer. Stephen had promised her that he would be the one solid thing she could count on. And then she'd come back to find out he was just like the man who had let her down, saying one thing to her face and doing another thing behind her back. He couldn't blame her for being furious at him for years. For being so hurt that she carried that distrust into adulthood.

It might be overstating things to say that he was the sole reason she was still single, but he knew it couldn't be because of her. She had been amazing in high school, and everything he observed at this moment and heard from Liv said that she was every bit as amazing now. No one could exactly blame her for having trust issues when she had gotten repeatedly let down.

He took a deep breath and pushed himself away from the unfinished counter in Liv's kitchen, then took his time going back to the apartment. He knew before he hit the stairs that he was potentially about to commit friendship suicide, that what he said next might make her kick him out for good. But he couldn't let her go on without knowing the truth.

She was just taking the new batch of cupcake batter—this one chocolate—off the mixer when he returned to the apartment kitchen. "Just in time for another batch." She held out the washed scoop to him, then lowered it when he didn't reach for it.

"I didn't cheat on you in high school because I didn't love you."

Her easy expression vanished, locking him out. "Stephen, don't—"

"No, please, I have to say this. And if you want to throw me out afterward, I'll go and I won't bother you anymore."

She stared at him, her green eyes wide and wary, but she gave him a single nod.

"I hated my life in Haven Ridge, Gemma. You were the only good thing about it. I was so wrapped up in being what my dad wanted me to be, what the town wanted me to be, that I always felt like I was drowning. The only time I could ever draw a full breath was when I was with you. All of those nights that we just sat and read and talked and planned for the future, they brought me out of some really dark places."

Her expression cracked into uncertainty. He held her gaze, willing her to feel the sincerity in his words. "And then you left. I knew that it was just a matter of time before some other guy saw how amazing you were. I figured once you were with someone new, you would realize how little I could offer you. I figured you would see me as I really was, the coward who wouldn't stand up to anyone for my own good. Especially when I saw how fierce you were to this town and everything they did to you.

"I had convinced myself that it was inevitable. I knew you leaving me would hurt so bad I would never recover. And with all the pressure my parents were giving me to break up with you and move on. . .I started dating Amber. It was easier to lose you immediately and make them happy than wait and lose you later."

Gemma stared at him, her expression shifting through wary to stricken. She opened her mouth and closed it without saying anything.

"That's not to guilt you into forgiving me. That's just so you understand. I've never forgiven myself for not standing up for us. I've never forgiven myself for hurting you. I am sorry."

Gemma swallowed hard, looking everywhere but his face. "You were my first, Stephen. That night at the hot springs, when we. . ."

He took a deep breath, remembering. Their farewell, how they'd undressed each other tenderly before they'd slipped into the warm water, what had come after. "I know," he said softly. "You were mine, too."

"My mom never liked you either, you know. She said that I couldn't trust guys like you. But after that night. . . and finding out you'd picked up with Amber a week or two later. . . I figured she was right." She glanced away, swiping furiously at a tear. "You'd think after all this time, I'd be over it. But. . ." She fixed a defiant stare on him. "Stephen, you asked me to *marry* you. You said you'd wait until we turned eighteen and we'd start our life together."

"I know," he said softly. "I meant it. I just. . . got scared. Scared that you didn't love me as much as I loved you."

She exhaled a long heavy breath and scrubbed her hands over her face. "Yeah. I get that. We were pretty young." When she lowered her hands, her expression was clear even if it still held sadness. "Thank you for telling me. I think that was a long time in coming."

"Gemma." He reached for her, but she gave a sharp shake of her head.

"No, don't. Let's just get back to work, okay?"

Stephen inhaled deeply and let out his breath in a

long, quiet stream. He'd said what he had to and she hadn't thrown him out. Hadn't shut down, at least not completely. That was all he had wanted anyway. A chance to say those words aloud that had been locked inside him and wrapped in guilt for his entire adult life.

But now that he'd spoken them aloud, they didn't feel like nearly enough.

CHAPTER SIXTEEN

I<small>T WAS ALL</small> G<small>EMMA COULD DO</small> to concentrate on the cupcakes after Stephen's apology. For years—well through college and law school, in fact—she had dreamed of hearing those words from him, though the variations in her head had involved a lot more groveling and had turned into fantasies of coldly turning him away, hurting him like he'd hurt her. But now, standing just a few short feet away from him in Liv's borrowed kitchen, she realized how long ago it had all actually been. How young and naive they had been to think they understood love at sixteen, that their whispered plans for the future had been anything other than imagination. It had taken bringing her grown-up, present-day self back to Haven Ridge, back into the same room with the person who had hurt her, to know that it was long past time to let it all go.

Maybe, deep down she had always known why Stephen had done what he'd done. It wasn't as if it had been any mystery how he felt about the town and their adoration of him for something that didn't much matter to him. How nothing he was truly proud of—like

winning a merit scholarship from the National English
Honor Society or having a piece of poetry published in
BU's literary magazine while he was still in high
school—ever meant even half as much as his father's
need to relive his own thwarted high-school hero
fantasies. Stephen might think now, with the benefit of
hindsight and twice the life experience, he should have
been braver, but she knew all too well how difficult it
was to swim against the status quo. Wait for a girl who
might never come back, whom the town didn't want in
the first place and who would earn him outcast status as
well? Or date the cheerleader homecoming queen who,
by the law of high school athletics, should have been his
girlfriend by right? Objectively, she couldn't blame him
for the choice.

But she hadn't known how much she needed those
words anyway.

She stole a look at him as he worked quietly at the
island, filling cupcake liners perfectly and precisely as
she'd demanded, and smiled a little to herself. This was
the incongruity she'd always loved in him, that the
broad shoulders and athletic body hid a sensitive heart
who loved people and literature and the world around
him. If anyone should be ashamed of anything, it
should be the town for making him leave long enough
to gain the courage to be who he really was. For
heaven's sake, it had been easier for a classmate to come
out as gay than it was for a football player to admit he
loved literature.

The alarm on Stephen's watch went off, making her
jump and snap her head back to her mixing bowl before
he could notice her attention on him.

"Cupcakes should be done," he said. "Do you want
me to bring them here to cool or leave them there?"

"Here please. I don't want to burn her house down."

When his brow furrowed, she added, "Particle board countertops."

"Ah, right. I'll be right back." He lifted the tins filled with chocolate batter and turned toward the hallway.

"Wait, take these." She thrust a pair of pink flowered oven mitts in his direction, and he took them with a twitch of his lips. Their eyes met briefly, and the twitch turned into a full-blown smile. Gemma turned away before she could return it, even though she couldn't stop the spread of warmth through her body. She really didn't need to lean into these sudden feelings towards him when it was just the release of long-held pain that left her feeling soft and mushy inside.

Stop it, she told herself sternly. This was the same situation her clients often found themselves in. At some point in negotiations, a spouse would decide to stop fighting and give in to Gemma's client's demands, either because they were trying to preserve goodwill for their own last request or because they'd lost the heart to destroy a person they'd once made a life with. And invariably, her client would take it as a sign the spouse was still a good person, that he or she still loved them. When really it was just a negotiation tactic. Or more likely, a way for them to justify to *themselves* that they were still good despite all the time and money they'd invested in destroying someone they once promised to honor and cherish. Over and over, she'd had to remind her clients that they were getting divorced for a reason.

Now, she had to remind herself that there was a reason she and Stephen had never gotten back together.

When he came back with a cupcake tin in each of his flowered-potholder-covered hands, she had a grip on herself. "Put them on the stove so they don't burn anything. I'm going to get started on the frosting."

"Can I help?"

"Nope, but you can start individually wrapping the brownies in plastic. They should be cool enough to cut."

And that was how they passed the rest of the night, in near silence that managed to be both companionable and heavy with unacknowledged meaning. Stephen wrapped strips of plastic wrap around brownies and blondies without complaint while Gemma made batches of blue and "silver" frosting—the school's colors. They formed an assembly line by which Gemma frosted the cooling cupcakes with a fat star tip on a pastry bag and Stephen decorated them with silver dragées and candy confetti and sparkling sanding sugar. By the time ten o'clock rolled around, they were just about finished.

The door slammed downstairs, making both of them jump, followed by Taylor's voice. "Aunt Gem? I'm home! Who else is here?" She pounded up the stairs in her boots without waiting for an answer and then came to a dead stop when she saw Stephen. "Mr. Osborne."

"Hi, Taylor. Have a good night out?"

She didn't answer, looking between the two of them with something akin to suspicion. "What's going on here? What happened?"

"Haven Ridge happened," Gemma said, though the words held far less heat than they might have earlier this evening. "Every last person who was supposed to contribute to the bake sale bailed, so guess who had to fill in?"

"Mr. Osborne?" Taylor asked with a grin, and Gemma made a face.

"No, me. Though your teacher apparently has some mad decorating skills." She waved a hand toward the rows of cupcakes that he had garnished with a surprisingly artful eye.

"Nice." Taylor looked between them as if she were

missing something, then jerked a thumb behind her. "I'm going to go. . .back there. . .and let you finish. Okay?" She turned and made to hightail it out of the room.

"Wait, Taylor. . . Are you going to come over and help me at the booth tomorrow?"

"Wouldn't miss it," Taylor said. "I made a bet with Cady Reece that we'd outsell her dad's barbecue stand by the end of the day."

"I hope you didn't bet something you can't afford to lose," Gemma said wryly. "This town certainly loves its barbecue."

"If she loses, she has to wear a unicorn onesie to the dance."

"What did you bet?"

Taylor grinned. "I have to wear combat boots with my dress. Which I'd already planned on doing."

"She didn't think this through, did she?"

Taylor shrugged, her eyes sparkling. "She's overconfident and a little stupid. Win-win." Her eyes flicked uncomfortably to Stephen again. "Can I go now?"

"Sure. Night, Taylor." As soon as the teen disappeared down the hall and into the spare room, Gemma turned to Stephen. "What was that about?"

"Cognitive dissonance. Haven't you ever run into a teacher where they weren't supposed to be?"

"Always," Gemma said. "This is Haven Ridge. The town isn't that big."

He grinned at her. "Do you remember the time we convinced our parents we were sick, then sneaked out after they left for work? And then we showed up at the diner but Mr. Cutter was there eating breakfast?"

Gemma grimaced, but a genuine smile won out. "Yeah. He told us if we were well enough to eat pancakes, we were well enough to be in his class later. I still don't know how he figured out we were cutting."

"I still don't know why he was there in the first place! Didn't he have a first period?"

Gemma laughed, recalling. She had so many bad memories of Haven Ridge, it had been a long time since she'd thought about the good ones. "I don't know, but I swear the man was psychic."

"He was just ancient. He'd probably heard every excuse in the book by then." Stephen's smile faded, but the lightness in his eyes remained. "I really should go now. Early morning."

"Yeah. Thanks for your help, Stephen. Really. There was no way I was going to finish these without you."

"No, thank you. You didn't have to do this in the first place. You saved the performing arts department. This is always our best-selling fundraiser."

"I'm happy to do it. Really. Even if it's only because Liv would kill me if I didn't."

He laughed, and then before Gemma could process what he was going to do, he leaned over and brushed his lips against her cheek. "I'll see you tomorrow."

The scent of his cologne enveloped her, mingling with his particular scent that still managed to remain familiar, and Gemma froze, unable to reply or move or make any kind of indication that she was a coherent human. He didn't seem to notice, picking up his coat and heading for the door without a backwards glance. Maybe it had been an accident. Maybe he'd shocked himself as much as he'd shocked her. Or maybe it hadn't meant anything to him at all, a reflex that one used with close friends. This had, after all, felt dangerously similar to old times.

It was the buzz of her cell phone that brought her back to reality as it jittered toward the edge of the countertop. Gemma grabbed it just before it plummeted to the floor and saw Liv's name at the top of the screen. She swiped to accept the call and pressed it to her ear. "Hey, Liv."

"Did I wake you up?"

"No, I was just finishing up in the kitchen. You owe me big time for this one. Bailing the weekend you were supposed to work on the carnival with Stephen? And then every last person backed out of the baked goods."

"Sorry about that," Liv said, her tone flat.

Gemma frowned. "What's wrong?"

It took a second for Liv to answer. "We're being sold. Again."

"What?"

"Altea has divested itself from the YA and children's book market completely. They sold us off to Tamberlane Books."

"Tamberlane. They're huge, right? Isn't that a good thing?"

"For our authors, it is. They have a lot of money and an established presence in the market. They wanted our imprint because we have a lot of good properties."

"Ones that you signed. Right?"

"Yeah. But they also have a full stable of editors already."

Gemma went cold. "They're firing you?"

Liv took a long beat before she spoke. "Not exactly. They've laid off most of the staff, but they want to bring me in as a senior acquisitions editor for YA and Middle Grade."

"That's good, though, right? Why don't you sound relieved?"

"Because anyone who wants to keep their job—and mind you, there's only three of us—has to move into the Manhattan office by July 1st."

A million thoughts spun through Gemma's head, but the one she chose was, "New York in July? Talk about adding insult to injury."

Liv snorted, but even that sounded a little weary. "Yeah. Tell me about it."

"What are you going to do?"

"I don't know. I'm going to stay with them for the time being. I need to talk things over with Taylor. And I would have to consult my lawyer to see if I can even take Taylor out of Colorado. You know as well as I do, it isn't always easy to transfer guardianships from state to state."

"I'm sorry, Liv. I mean, I'm glad you have a job at least through July, but it's not going to be an easy choice."

"No. It's not. But how on earth could I move Taylor away from all her friends, and right before her junior year of high school? Can you imagine how hard that would be?"

"I don't have to imagine," Gemma said gently.

"Oh. Right." Liv fell silent and Gemma could almost envision her pulling herself together. "But I also wonder. . . would it be better for Taylor? Her grandparents are upstate. If we lived in Manhattan—or let's face it, probably Brooklyn or Queens or God forbid, Staten Island—she'd be able to see the rest of her family more often. And it's where she and her dad lived for most of her life."

"And where her mom abandoned her."

"Yeah, there's that, too. I just don't know."

"You don't have to make a decision tonight. Take the rest of the weekend. Enjoy the ballet, your musical."

"Are you sure? I can come home if you need me. Maybe I should come home. . ."

"No, Liv, enjoy yourself. Things are fine here."

CARLA LAUREANO   157

"Really? Because that is not your fine voice."

Gemma rubbed her forehead with the back of her wrist before she flipped on the kitchen faucet. "Stephen was just over here."

"Wait. What? Why? How did that happen?"

Gemma chuckled at the scandalized tone. "He roped me into doing the baking, I demanded he come help."

"And how did that go?"

"He apologized."

The silence stretched on Liv's end. "Good," she said finally. "He should. And how do you feel about it?"

"Okay, I think." Gemma began scrubbing out the mixer bowl with a sponge, the actions allowing her to divorce herself from her actual feelings on the subject. *Okay* didn't quite cover it, but now was not the time to delve into her thoughts about her high school boyfriend, not after what Liv had found out. "At least we're on speaking terms again. I think I got over it a long time ago, but I just. . . needed to hear it from him in person."

"Good. If that's the most dramatic thing that's happened, it's a slow week in Haven Ridge."

Those words made Gemma remember that she hadn't really talked to Liv in days. "I wouldn't say that, exactly. Did you know that Taylor's friend Rebekah is Chelsea Young's niece?"

"Yeah. Of course."

"Well, Rebekah let drop the other day that Doug is. . . scary. . . when he's drinking. Hinted that things in the house might be abusive. And apparently Rebekah is staying there while her dad is out of the country."

"Yeah, he's a network specialist or something. Her mom died when she was young," Liv answered almost automatically, a sure sign she was thinking things over. "I haven't heard anything about that, but I can't say it really surprises me."

"Well, I would think maybe she was just overselling things for sympathy, but I was in town yesterday and Doug confronted me. Threatened me really. Told me if I kept nosing into his family, he'd make me regret it. Then practically knocked me off my feet as he went by."

Liv gasped. "Gem, you have to tell someone!"

"Tell who? The sheriff? I'm sure the deputy will love being called all the way out from Salida because someone was mean to me."

"Yeah, but if he's actually dangerous. . ."

"In my experience, men like that are more dangerous to their families, which trust me, is not much of a consolation. I just don't know how much I can or should get involved here."

Liv fell silent for several long moments. "Maybe you should tell Stephen."

Gemma probably should have brought it up when he was there, but her mind automatically went to other things when she was with Stephen. "I'm not sure that's a good idea. You know he'd feel compelled to get involved, and I'm sure Doug would try to make his life miserable. Besides, everyone will be at the festival tomorrow and you know Doug will be on his best behavior in front of all those people."

"You know what? I'm coming back. I'm changing my flight from Sunday to tomorrow night. I don't want you two there by yourself if this is going on."

Gemma set the bowl on a dish drainer and started on the next one. "No, Liv. Don't do that. You deserve this trip. Either you're moving to New York, in which case you'll probably feel a lot better after you remember how much you love it, or you're not, which means this is the last time you'll get to go for a while. We'll be fine. I promise. I won't let anything happen to Taylor."

"It's not Taylor I'm worried about."

"Trust me, I'm fine, too. I know how to deal with bullies like Doug Meinke. I've made my whole career off it, in fact. And if I get actually worried . . . I will call Stephen. Or the authorities. Okay?"

Liv didn't sound convinced but she relented. "You have to tell me the minute you think it's not okay. I'll come home. You two . . . you two are the only people I have left. I just want you to be safe."

"We will be safe. I promise."

"Okay." Liv's deep breath rustled over the phone line. "I'll be back in a couple days. Love you both."

"Love you too."

Gemma hung up and slumped over the kitchen counter for a moment, bracing herself on her palms. Stephen's presence and the last-minute baking rush had distracted her from the more important events at hand. Until she'd voiced it aloud, she hadn't wanted to admit that she really was worried—not just about herself and Taylor, but all the other people in Doug's household. However much she might dislike—okay, despise—Chelsea, she didn't want her to be a victim of an abusive husband. And there were three kids in the house with her.

You have made it your mission to help people like them. So help.

But how?

CHAPTER SEVENTEEN

THE DAY OF THE FESTIVAL dawned bright and clear, which boded well for a sunny day and badly for the temperature without any clouds to hold the heat in. Gemma had slept hard and soundly all night, but she still felt wrung out. Her dreams had been clouded by anxiety: Doug confronted her over and over on the street, but sometimes he wore the face of her boss, John Mercer, and other times Stephen. It didn't take a psychology degree to know that her worries centered around those three men all for different reasons.

Still, she took her time getting ready, braiding her hair into a thick plait and applying sunscreen beneath light makeup. Then she layered jeans and a sweater over thermals and slipped a hat and gloves into the pockets of her jacket. The TV weatherman had cheerily announced a high of twenty degrees today, but they wouldn't be hitting that lofty temperature until three o'clock. If she were on the PTO, she'd be moving this festival to May with a luau theme.

Taylor emerged from her room, looking both fresh-faced and exhausted like only a teenager could, dressed head to toe in black: black jeans, black boots, black hoodie with *Haven Ridge HS* printed on the front in silver. Her hair was tucked up under a black beanie, but she had yet to apply her signature eyeliner. "Coffee," she moaned.

"In the kitchen." Gemma grinned and brushed past her with the first box of baked goods she had to transfer to the back of the SUV.

Taylor didn't say a word until they were almost to the high school, curling her hands around a travel mug of coffee and slumping in the seat, her head turned away from the bright spill of gray morning sunlight. Despite the fact that Gemma's blood had most certainly thinned from living in California for the last ten years, she still loved the high-altitude Colorado mornings with their dusty shades of gray and blue, the crisp bite of the air that simultaneously invigorated and made one question why they lived someplace with seasons. She was feeling unaccountably cheery when they pulled into the school parking lot and parked in a small cluster of vehicles that could only belong to the festival volunteers.

Gemma popped the hatch on the SUV and handed a box to Taylor, balancing another on her hip as she closed the lift gate. Most of the parking lot had been sectioned off by a line of orange cones, and a number of shade shelters were already going up around the perimeter of the lot on one end. Ironically, despite the twenty-degree weather, they were necessary so the vendors didn't get sunburned—there was a lot less atmosphere between them and the sun at over a mile above sea level.

Stephen caught sight of them almost immediately and jogged over, looking cheerful and slightly harried in his heavy down jacket and thermal boots. A beanie had been pulled down over his ears, and it looked like he hadn't bothered to shave this morning. The scruffy look was good on him, she thought with a pang of appreciation, before she remembered that she wasn't supposed to be looking at him that way.

"You made it," he said. "Let me show you to your booth. Did you bring the binder, Gemma?"

"In the box." She indicated the one in her arms and followed him across the parking lot.

Setup was already in full swing. On one end of the lot, a machine hooked up to a long hose was pumping out a plume of snow, covering the landscaped areas around the lot in a blanket of white. A group of teenagers were scooping it up in gloved hands and making snowballs, which they placed in individual plastic crates. And outside, where the cement walkway usually wound through the wild grass areas beyond the school, a silver-white path glimmered.

"An ice trail?" she asked incredulously.

Stephen grinned at her. "We've been working on it all week. I'm surprised you didn't see it when you were here. Luckily, the overnight temperatures have been so cold it didn't take long to freeze up. We have a skate rental, too."

"This is . . . impressive." Gemma had expected some sort of amateurish setup, but this was downright elaborate. "This had to have cost a fortune."

"All donations, which you know because you called most of them."

"Right. But I didn't think . . ." She shook her head. "Is this all your doing?"

Stephen shrugged. "My old firm did events, too. I picked up some ideas. Your booth is over here, by the way."

The shade shelter had been placed just a stone's throw away from the Koffee Kabin stand, which was already getting up and running, its espresso machine sending wisps of condensation into the sky. It was a great location; maybe there was a reason Taylor had made the bet. No doubt the bake sale would be busy all day long thanks to the lines of people who would come for hot drinks. And then Gemma registered the big table drape across the folding table in her stand.

"What is this?"

Stephen frowned at her. "What do you mean?"

She gestured to the drape. On the same light blue as the school's colors, it proclaimed *Bake Sale,* and in smaller letters, *Courtesy of the Broken Hearts Bakery.* "That. The Broken Hearts Bakery Thing."

"Did they spell something wrong?" Stephen studied the text, as if trying to find a previously unnoticed spelling error.

"No. I mean, this is not a thing. The Broken Hearts Bakery doesn't exist. Why is it on there?"

Now Stephen was looking at her warily, as if she'd had a mental break. Carefully, he said, "You ordered it."

"No, I did not. I didn't even call the vendors about signs and drapes. It wasn't on my list."

Simultaneously, she and Stephen turned to Taylor.

"Don't look at me. I had nothing to do with this." The teen plunked her box down on the table. "It's pretty cool though."

Gemma turned back to Stephen. "If none of us did it, who did?"

"Maybe the town—"

She held up a hand. "Don't say it. I've heard enough about the town's sentience. This is someone playing a prank or who thought they were doing us a favor or something."

"No one even knew you were taking this over," Stephen said.

Gemma looked at Taylor again. "Your friend with the bet did."

Taylor snorted. "No way. You think Cady is going to spend her own money on something like this? Besides, this helps the stand, it doesn't hurt us. Every single person who saw my post—which is up to like twenty-nine thousand this morning, by the way, so thanks for that—will be stopping by to see what you have." She grinned at her teacher. "First class to Denver, baby. Er, I mean, Mr. Osborne."

Stephen laughed. "Okay, I have to get back to work. Set up your table however you want. There's an extension cord behind you for when the microwave gets here. To warm things up," he explained quickly.

"Right. Good idea." Already the brownies were feeling cold to the touch; after all day out here, they'd be almost frozen through. Gemma began unloading the items that had been individually packaged—the cookies, brownies, and quick breads—while Taylor laid out the rows of cupcakes she'd placed in foil trays and covered loosely with plastic wrap. Thank goodness for the frigid temperatures—the frosting had stayed as pristine as when she'd piped it. The leftovers remained in the box, covered by the mysterious table drape, though she was beginning to think that she'd been over-optimistic about today's traffic. If every single person in town bought something, it still wouldn't clear out the vast number of baked goods they'd brought.

Once they had their booth set up, Gemma left Taylor watching over it and went to find Stephen. She would rather just hide out beneath the shade shelter, shivering in the cold, but she'd promised that she'd help him with setup and she wasn't going to reflect badly on Taylor and Liv by bailing on him.

She found him erecting another shelter farther down the line. "Do you need help with anything?"

Stephen looked surprised. "If you wouldn't mind

going around and just making sure everyone has what they need? Tables, extension cords, that sort of thing?"

"Sure."

She only made it a few steps before Stephen called, "Gemma?"

She turned.

"Thanks. Really. Given. . . everything. . . you could have just said no."

She caught her lip between her teeth, uncomfortable with his gratitude. Then she just gave a little nod and turned away to start her survey of the vendors.

The next hour was spent fixing and tracking down petty problems: vendors in the wrong place, which resulted in her lugging boxes of crafts from one end of the line to the other; missing power cords, which brought her back into Stephen's orbit; and a collapsing shade shelter which she caught with one hand just before it could knock out Mallory Adams and obliterate her stack of pecan pies.

"It's a good thing you were here," Mallory said knowingly. The light in her eyes made Gemma uncomfortable.

"I shouldn't even be helping you! You're the competition!"

"We'll see. Care to put a wager on it? I hear there's a grudge match between Taylor and Cady."

Gemma didn't ask how she knew that; she'd have to be gone a lot longer than fifteen years to forget how the Haven Ridge telegraph worked. "You're wagering what? That you sell more or that I sell more?"

"That you sell more," Mallory said with a grin.

"Someone needs to tell you how bets work."

Mallory shrugs. "Suit yourself. I was going to offer a pie as a prize."

"So you sell less than me, and I get a pie?"

"That's what I said."

Gemma shook her head, but a smile was creeping onto her lips. She couldn't help but like this newcomer to Haven Ridge. "Okay. Taylor would never forgive me if I didn't take a chance to get a free pie. But you're going to sell more than me, so the point is moot."

"We'll see." Mallory held out her hand, and Gemma shook it. "It's a bet."

Gemma walked away, shaking her head, but her spirits had been lifted by that little bit of ridiculousness. She wove her way through the first clutch of visitors who were beginning to wander through the parking lot to the booths. At first, she thought they were headed for the Koffee Kabin stand. And while that line was indeed long and the owner, Gregory, was pulling espressos with blinding efficiency, she quickly realized that most of them were there for the bake sale.

Gemma circled around back and slipped in beside Taylor, who was holding court with the aplomb of a bazaar hawker, tallying prices on her phone and directing her customers to a big QR code on a plastic stand in the booth—Haven Ridge High had gone high tech for payments, apparently. When Gemma looked over the table, she realized that there was already a big dent in the shortbread cookies, and not just the school spirit ones. More than a few girls were holding handfuls of the conversation hearts.

"Maybe I should just go home and leave you in charge," she murmured to Taylor, who was grinning. She passed her phone to Gemma, open to a text message with at least fifty recipients.

Broken Hearts Bakery goodies at the carnival! Get here early before we sell out!

"You really want that fancy bus to the speech meet,

don't you?" The words earned a grin from Taylor, but Gemma couldn't even wait for a response, because another customer walked up to the table and began perusing the goods on offer.

She had assumed this would be like the fundraisers she remembered from high school, mostly populated by the parents of the school and relatives of the vendors, but as the morning wore on, it seemed like every single person in town had turned out and brought friends. The blinding sunshine helped, making the frigid temperature feel much warmer, and most of the teen boys walked around the festival in hoodies, athletic shorts, and plastic slides with socks, the kind of attire that would give her hypothermia. Halfway through the morning, though, even Gemma had to unzip the front of her jacket and toss off her scarf so she didn't overheat.

Just before lunch, her neck prickled with awareness of a familiar presence. She turned and found Stephen standing at her shoulder, holding two paper cups. "Mocha?"

Gemma took it gratefully. "Thanks. We've been so busy I haven't managed to step away from the booth."

Taylor craned her neck around them. "I don't suppose that other one is for me?" she asked hopefully.

He chuckled and handed it over; whether or not it actually was, Gemma couldn't begin to guess. But Taylor snatched it up and took a long drink. "Thanks, Mr. Osborne."

"So to what do we owe delivery service?" Gemma asked.

Stephen pulled up his phone and showed her an app, which listed the booths in order of sales—probably thanks to the QR codes. Broken Hearts Bakery was at the top, neck and neck with the Koffee Kabin, and just a little bit ahead of the Brick House Cafe's pie stand.

Gemma scrolled down and saw that the barbecue stand was in a distant sixth.

"Don't get too confident though," Stephen said to Taylor, who was already grinning. "It's still too early for lunch. The barbecue stand will start picking up now that people have their sugar and caffeine fixes for the morning."

"Should you really be encouraging this kind of behavior?" Gemma murmured. "Betting on a school event?"

"When it raises a lot of money for the school? I can look the other way." He winked at Gemma and then smiled at Taylor. "Keep it up, ladies. Show 'em how it's done."

He squeezed Gemma's shoulder briefly before he moved on, but the warm imprint of his palm on her shoulder lingered long after he was gone. It sparked a little quiver in the pit of her stomach, which she quelled ruthlessly. It was one thing to decide she was no longer mad at him. It was another to think that she actually liked him. Again. Still.

Even so, she couldn't help seeking him out in the crowd as he made his rounds through the vendors—he hadn't brought anyone else coffee, she noticed—and watching how everyone else responded to him. He was part of this town in a way that Gemma never had been, would never be. He focused intently when he spoke to people, and they lit up beneath his attention, as if his very presence made them feel better about themselves. It was no wonder half his female students had mad crushes on him; that kind of focused attention was enough to turn heads. He'd always had that quality, she realized, but in high school, it had been reserved for a select few like Liv and Gemma. But mostly Gemma.

Too late, she realized that Taylor was watching her thoughtfully. She jerked her eyes away from Stephen and gave her niece a warning look. To Taylor's credit, she didn't say anything, just plopped into the chair behind the table with a knowing smile.

Despite the fact that it went directly against Taylor's bet, Gemma took a break halfway through the day to go grab a plate of barbecue, which she and Taylor shared during the rare lulls at their booth.

And then an announcement came over the PA, unmistakably Stephen's voice. "School versus Town Capture the Flag begins in 15 minutes. Report to the ice trail to register and join your team!"

Gemma flicked a look at Taylor, who instantly caught her train of thought. "Go," Taylor said. "I'll hold down the fort."

"You sure?"

"Oh yeah. Liv has told me about your epic Capture the Flag games. Go show them how it's done, Aunt Gem."

Gemma zipped up her jacket and grinned at her niece. "Aye-aye, Captain." She shoved her phone into her handbag and set it under the table, then marched out of the booth.

It was almost as if they'd organized this just for her. And she had one particular teacher in her sights.

CHAPTER EIGHTEEN

A CLUSTER OF PEOPLE already stood around the skate rental at the start of the ice trail, many of whom Gemma recognized. Stephen was standing at the front with a clipboard. She waited patiently as the line moved forward. When he looked up, amusement flashed in his eyes. "I should have guessed. School or town?"

"Presumably you're school?"

He nodded.

"Then town. Naturally."

Stephen grinned. "Ten bucks for entry, five dollars per crate."

Gemma didn't need to ask *crate of what?*—this had been a Haven Ridge tradition since long before she was born. She traded two ten-dollar bills from her pocket for two paper tickets and a silver arm band, which she tied around her left biceps over her jacket. "You can pick up your snowballs to the left. Good luck."

"I could say the same for you. You'll need it." Gemma followed the flow of silver bands to where the crates the students had been filling earlier that day stood. She smiled at the teenage boy in charge and picked through the stacks until she found the snowballs that were getting firm and icy from sitting in the sun. Not that she wanted them to sting, but she also didn't want them to blow apart when she lobbed them. She'd been known for her aim in high school; the girls' softball coach had hounded her for three years after seeing her throw snowballs her freshman year.

"Hey," she said to the silver arm bands standing around, their crates of snowballs claimed. Most of them were adults, some of whom she knew and others she didn't, but she was surprised by the handful of teenagers who had opted for town instead of school.

"Gemma Van Buren?"

Gemma turned, shading her eyes against the bright sunshine to focus on the slender guy standing a few feet away. "Benji Balden?"

He smiled, his brown hair flopping into his eyes just as it always had. "One and the same. Nice to see you."

"Yeah, you too." She hadn't thought about Benji in years—he'd been two years ahead of her and as sweet as he had been shy. She only knew him because they'd been on Model UN together her sophomore year. "What have you been up to?"

"I'm a Chaffee County Combined Court judge," he said with a grin. "And an ultra-marathoner."

Gemma laughed, surprised that the unassuming boy who'd had to dig deep just to debate had ended up on the bench. The runner thing didn't surprise her—he'd run track-and-field and had been lightning fast in the 800. She leaned forward to give him a fist bump. "Congrats then. It's nice to see you." She was going to ask him more questions, but a familiar voice behind her interrupted her.

"Am I late?" Gemma turned to find Mallory behind her, wearing a silver arm band and grinning broadly.

"Not at all. They haven't even explained the rules."

On cue, a whistle pierced the air. All heads turned toward Stephen, who was holding up his clipboard for attention, the whistle hanging around his neck. "Players, gather 'round!"

Members of both teams meandered toward him, leaving a little circle of space around him. Stephen's eyes immediately sought Gemma's and then flitted away. "Okay, for any of you who haven't played Capture the Flag before, your goal is to, obviously, capture the opposing team's flag. It will be hidden somewhere in their territory. Silver team has from the skate rental back around to the theater building. Blue team has from the skate rental toward the administration building. Any snowy or grassy area is within limits. Any concrete or asphalt is out of bounds. Game ends when one team captures the other's flag. If you get hit by a snowball, you must freeze in place until you're tagged by a member of your team—which becomes increasingly difficult the farther into enemy territory you get. If you are tagged by a member of the opposite team, you're out and you should go wait by the skate rental. Any questions?"

Surprisingly, it was Benji that raised a hand and called out in a strong voice, "Tackle or no tackle?"

Stephen laughed, probably as amused by the change in their schoolmate as Gemma was. "No tackle. I don't need to remind you that we're not teenagers anymore. We don't need broken bones."

Benji shrugged in a way that felt like *Speak for yourself*, and Gemma clapped him on the shoulder and sent him a wink. He grinned.

"You have fifteen minutes to devise a strategy and hide your flag. Three short bursts of the whistle signals the beginning of the game. Elect your captains, make your plan, and let's do this!"

Gemma's group drifted away from their opponents for privacy. Almost immediately, Benji spoke up. "I nominate Gemma as team captain. She was legendary at Haven Ridge High."

"I second that," Mallory called out, sending her a grin, even though she was a newcomer and couldn't possibly know if that were true or not.

"Anyone else want to volunteer?" Gemma asked. Various heads shook, happy for her to take the lead. "Okay, then, huddle up."

Gemma began to lay out her strategy for their territory, which involved planting their flag at a protected junction between a fence and the school building. Then she started talking about tactics for infiltrating enemy territory.

"I can almost guarantee that they'll elect Stephen team captain, and we've known each other forever, so he knows all my tricks. So here's what we're going to do . . ."

As she laid out her plan, heads nodded and little laughs rang out; there was nothing like a good old-fashioned war game to put everyone in a good mood, especially when for many of them it meant playing against people they'd known since childhood. Catching Gemma's enthusiasm, players began throwing out their own ideas until they had a fully-formed battle plan.

When it looked like they'd exhausted their ingenuity and there was only seven minutes on the countdown clock according to Gemma's watch, she asked, "Everyone got it? Anyone have any other ideas?"

No one spoke up, so she said, "Okay, everyone. Hands in. Silver on three. One, two, three!"

"*Silver!*"

Benji and Mallory jogged off with half a dozen other people who would be planting and guarding the flag with as much stealth as they could, clustering in other areas as decoys while their flag remained protected by a duo with crates of snowballs in the corner. Gemma and another four grabbed their crates and went off to find protected spots where they could act as snipers and freeze opposing team members as they tried to penetrate their territory.

It wasn't until she was crouched behind concealment of some scrub pines just on the opposing territory's border that she recognized the unfamiliar lift in her heart—she was actually enjoying herself. And more than that, she was glad to be in Haven Ridge. It was such a shock that she almost missed the three blasts on the whistle that signaled the beginning of the game.

And then there wasn't any time to think about anything else. She peered around the bushes, waiting for the first of the opposing team to breach their borders. After a couple of minutes, she heard the distinctive crunch of boots in the snow and reached for her snowballs. Then the sound stopped. Too late, Gemma realized she'd forgotten the cardinal rule of ambush— she hadn't smoothed out her tracks, which led directly to her hiding place. Speed then. She popped up, drew back her arm, and lobbed a snowball at a woman about ten feet away.

"Oof." The woman let out a soft sound as the snowball collided with her chest and broke apart. Gemma looked around for other enemies and, seeing none, darted out to tag her.

"Sorry, you're out," Gemma said with a laugh. The woman just shook her head and trudged away, back toward the skate rental, before Gemma recognized her as a girl who had been a year behind her in school.

She smoothed out her tracks, took concealment behind the bushes again, and waited. Shouts went up on the field, signs that little skirmishes were going on elsewhere too. Minutes stretched into what felt like a half-hour, bringing only four people within her range, two of whom she hit and tagged, two others who were too fast and got past her deeper into silver territory. But she hadn't yet seen Stephen.

He was probably doing the same thing as she was—playing the opposite of their favorite high school strategy. Stephen had always been one of the infiltrators, going deep into enemy territory while Gemma stayed behind and guarded the flag with piles of snowballs and impeccable aim. Which meant that he was probably guarding his flag, just as she'd hoped.

When no more opponents came into view for several minutes, Gemma slipped around the bushes and started her stealthy approach into the blue team's territory, leaving her snowballs behind. They wouldn't do her any good on the offense now.

It took her a good while, creeping from tree to tree, hiding behind bushes and boulders while she tried to figure out where they might have hidden their flag. Stephen always hated her corner trick but loved the decoy, so it would be somewhere in the open in the middle of their territory, probably guarded by only one person. Most likely him. She'd told her teammates specifically to look out for him and signal if they found him.

She was making a crouching run through open ground to her next hiding place when she saw a flash of silver and a quick wave—one of her teammates trying to get her attention. Mallory, in fact. She was signaling and pointing, and although Gemma had absolutely no idea what the series of raised fingers was supposed to mean, she did gather from the pointing that Stephen was somewhere straight ahead.

Gemma signaled back, hoping Mallory understood that she was telling her to go for the flag. She crept closer until she caught sight of Stephen squatting beside an electrical box as if he were playing ambush. A likely story. She caught Mallory's eye across the field, nodded, and made her play.

As if she didn't see Stephen, she made a break through the bushes and across open ground. Just as she'd hoped, he clocked her and jumped up from his spot. Gemma veered left to draw him off, but she'd underestimated how quick he was. She should have paid attention when he mentioned coaching track. He was gaining on her fast, so she pushed herself as fast as she dared in the slippery terrain, their boots crunching in the patchy snow. And then he reached out to tag her at the very moment they hit a slick patch of ice, leftovers from the last storm.

His body collided with hers, driving her to the ground and knocking the breath out of her. Gemma groaned and rolled over to see Stephen kneeling over her, his eyes wide and worried.

"Gemma, I'm so sorry. That was an accident."

She looked past him as her first breath shuddered back into her lungs. Mallory was so close to the flag, now visible against the green-painted electrical box. There was another blue player only ten yards away now, but his focus was on Gemma and Stephen and not Mallory's progress toward the flag. Stephen twisted and followed her gaze, and she could practically see the moment he registered their tactic.

He opened his mouth to shout a warning to his teammate, so Gemma did the only thing she could think of.

She reached up, pulled his head down, and kissed him.

Stephen stiffened, taken so off guard that his first reaction was to pull away. And then he softened over her, arm curling around her to pillow her head under his hand, and kissed her for real.

It was just the brush of lips, warm and sweet and still achingly familiar, but the touch lit her up like a shooting star, blazing through her body with a heat far out of proportion to the touch. Automatically, Gemma reached up and tunneled her fingers through his hair, arching into the kiss as she forgot this was supposed to be a cheap ploy to win a game and not something she'd been longing for all her adult life.

A single long whistle blast split the air, piercing their quiet, heated cocoon, and Stephen jerked his head toward where Mallory was waving the blue flag triumphantly overhead, the attached whistle dangling from her lips.

"We win," Gemma said, her voice breathless and shaky, hardly the triumphant tone she'd imagined. She tried to grin, but her body felt too heavy and languid with desire to comply. She settled for pushing him back a few inches and trying to slide out from beneath him.

Stephen stared hard into her face, then growled, "Not yet."

This time his kiss was neither sweet nor gentle, carrying what felt like years of pent-up longing and fury, all lips and teeth and tongue until her head was swimming so much she lost track of where she began and he ended.

Until someone cleared their voice nearby. "I hate to interrupt, but in about two minutes, you're going to have a bigger audience than just me."

Stephen broke the kiss first, shock and something suspiciously like horror on his face. He shoved himself back on his heels and looked up to where Mallory was standing over them, a huge grin on her face.

Gemma pushed herself up on her elbows, knowing there was nothing that she could say that was going to explain away what had just happened. "Good job, Mallory," she croaked.

Mallory winked at her. "Way to take one for the team, Gemma." Her eyes slid to Stephen, then back to Gemma. "Not much of a hardship, though, if you ask me." And then without another word, she walked away.

Stephen held out a hand to help Gemma up, though he wasn't quite meeting her eye. Only now did she become conscious of the sting of scrapes and bruises on her hands, hips, and knees where she had hit the ground from the inadvertent tackle.

"Are you okay?" he asked softly, brushing pine needles out of her hair. "That was an accident, I assure you."

Gemma wasn't sure whether he meant the tackle or the kiss, so she just nodded. "I'm fine. The ground was soft."

They automatically put some distance between themselves as they walked back to the skate rental, carefully not looking at each other. Blue team members passed them, appearing on a spectrum of wry to dejected, and other silver team members shot by, hooting with their good fortune and calling congratulations to Gemma as they passed.

"Gemma . . ." Stephen began in a low voice.

She shook her head, even though her body hummed at the sound of his voice. She could still feel the impression of his lips on hers, his big hand cradling her head. She staved off an inadvertent shiver at the recollection. "I'm sorry. That wasn't fair. I got a little caught up in the game."

"In the game?" he said incredulously.

She straightened and made her expression impassive,

even though inside she felt anything but. "Yeah. In the game. I'm going home tomorrow, Stephen. I didn't mean to give you any impression otherwise."

"You're avoiding. Just like you always do."

The trace of bitterness stopped her in her tracks, dulled the leftover glow from the kiss. Was he really blaming her for the fact she'd cut off communication after that ill-fated prom night? If he thought she'd been so unreasonable, then why had he gone to so much trouble to apologize? What was he playing at here?

Anger bubbled up at the idea this had all been some sort of game to him, some way to make himself out to be the good guy. She rounded on him, hurt making her voice hard. "What exactly do you think is going to happen here? Are you going to take me home tonight? Sleep with me the night before I leave and then move on to someone else before my plane even lands? I think we've already covered that one, don't you?"

And without another word, she marched away, past the skate rental where her team waited, bypassing the people who tried to congratulate her, praying that no one could see the tears that were already swelling in her eyes.

CHAPTER NINETEEN

ONLY WHEN GEMMA HAD HERSELF TOGETHER did she return to the booth. But apparently, she did a poor job of it, because Taylor took one look at her and asked, "What's wrong?"

"Nothing's wrong." Gemma slipped behind the table and retrieved her purse from beneath it, then pulled out a compact mirror. No wonder Taylor thought something was wrong. Her lips were still swollen from Stephen's kiss, but her eyes had that red-rimmed watery look that signaled tears were immediately past or imminent. She snapped it closed and shoved it back into her purse, then plopped into the chair. "My team won at least."

"Okaaaay," Taylor said, clearly not believing her. "How long are we going to stay anyway? I only sold a couple of things while you were gone and the place is starting to clear out."

"You can go if you want. Is that Layla and Jada over there?" Gemma squinted to the far corner of the parking lot where a cluster of girls stood.

"Yeah. You don't mind?"

Gemma shook her head. "No, you went above and beyond today. Good job."

Taylor stood and picked up her little black backpack, which was emblazoned with pins and patches of anime and bands that Gemma had never heard of. "I had a bet to win. I think we did it, but it might have been close. If you see Mr. Osborne, will you ask him?"

"I doubt I'm going to see him," Gemma said, but at Taylor's disappointed look, she added, "But I'll ask him if I do."

"Great, thanks. I'll text you when I know where we're going. I won't be back too late. You're leaving tomorrow, right?"

"Right. Liv gets in at noon and I leave at two, so we're going to swap the car at the airport."

"Cool." Taylor hesitated and then slid an arm around Gemma's shoulders for a hug. "Thanks for coming. This has been really fun."

"I'm glad. For me, too."

Taylor smiled, the expression lighting up her face, and then she was running off to her friends.

Gemma leaned back in her chair and sighed. She'd meant it. She'd truly enjoyed spending the week here with Taylor, though she'd seen her honorary niece far less than she'd expected. Then again, when she and Liv had been that age, they'd barely ever been home, just cruising by for food, clothes, and sleep. However, she didn't want to think of the number of times that Liv had covered for her, when Gemma said she was going out with her and instead she was with Stephen. Now she couldn't even remember why. Her mom hadn't been overly strict, so there hadn't been any compelling reason to lie. At least not until that last night in Haven Ridge, which she'd thrown in Stephen's face.

She pressed her fingertips to her eyes, sighing.

Stephen. What had she been thinking? She'd gone from trying to avoid anyone she knew to kissing her ex-boyfriend in a handful of days. And she couldn't even use the game as an excuse, not when she could have feigned injury or distracted him in some other way. She'd wanted to kiss him. And now she was paying the price for that ill-advised impulse.

That didn't mean she still had feelings for him, but even she wasn't delusional enough to insist she wasn't still attracted to him. The fact that he lit her up like a Christmas tree with a single kiss—okay, two—seemed to prove a point that even she couldn't argue against.

Which was why she needed to avoid him until she left tomorrow. She'd get back to her life in LA and forget that this little interlude in Haven Ridge ever happened.

And your life in LA would be what? You still haven't decided what to tell John. She was beginning to think she might not know what she wanted to do until she stepped into the office again on Monday morning.

Gemma sat there as the sun dipped toward the mountains behind her, but the carnival traffic was only a trickle as the sun went down and the temperature dropped precipitously. Once she saw Gregory from the Koffee Kabin packing up for the day, she knew she'd done her full duty and started loading the few remaining baked goods into one of the cardboard boxes.

All things considered, the "Broken Hearts Bakery" had had a great inaugural day, and the speech team was guaranteed to have their cushy bus ride to the meet in Denver. Taylor would be thrilled. That alone made the whole thing worthwhile.

Gemma was walking back to her car among the drift of departing vendors and visitors when she noticed a familiar figure pacing in front of her, lost in thought.

Before she could consider the wisdom of the action, she called, "Chelsea!"

The woman stopped short and turned, surprise registering on her face. "Gemma."

Gemma crossed the few feet between them. "Hey. I just wanted to say I'm sorry if I caused trouble for you. I didn't mean to butt in. I just wanted to make sure Rebekah knew she had someone to talk to if she needed it. Sometimes it's hard to discuss things with a family member. Trust me, I know."

Chelsea stared at her as if she was speaking gibberish. "I'm sorry. What are you talking about?"

Gemma froze. "I . . . I gave Rebekah my cell phone number in case she needed something. Doug confronted me on the street the other day. I assumed . . ." She shook her head. "I don't know what I assumed, but I figured it had caused some sort of problem at home."

Chelsea's gaze flickered, landing anywhere but on Gemma's face. "No. I . . ." She cleared her voice. "This is the first I'm hearing of it."

"Oh. Okay then." Gemma frowned, but just as Chelsea made to move away, Gemma reached out and took her by the wrist. The woman flinched. "Chelsea, if you need help . . . if you or your kids don't feel safe at home . . . there are people you can go to. We may have a lot of stuff in our past, but *I* would help you. It's kind of what I do. You don't have to stay with him."

This time when Chelsea looked at her, there was a clear flicker of fear in her expression before it shuttered, as stony and belligerent as ever. "I have no idea what you're talking about. Just leave us alone. We were fine before you came and we'll be fine after you leave." Without another word, she turned and strode off toward her car, her determined walk at odds with the protective way she wrapped her arms around her midsection. If Gemma had had any doubt before, she had none now.

Chelsea was living in an abusive marriage, an abusive household. And she wasn't nearly ready to get help. Gemma's confident words aside, this was no longer her town. She couldn't be the one to catch Chelsea when she decided she was worth more than how she was being treated. But unfortunately, there were always more Chelseas, more than Gemma could possibly help alone. There were dozens more who would be waiting for her back home, who had to sneak out for meetings, who didn't have the funds to pay her.

Which should make her decision easy. It was too bad that it didn't.

* * *

Stephen watched Gemma stride away from him, hurt blossoming where her words had struck. The worst part was, he couldn't even be mad at her. He'd baited her by telling her she always avoided talking about things, and she had taken him at his word and unloaded. There was no mistaking what she thought of him.

And he deserved it.

He'd been fooling himself if he thought that his apology and explanation the night before was going to magically erase his betrayal. He'd been even stupider to think that her kissing him meant that she'd forgotten the past. Attraction had never been their problem. It was trust that was at issue here, and now he wasn't sure that he would ever be able to prove to her that one thoughtless betrayal didn't define who he was as a person. As much as he wished it to be otherwise, it felt like he'd simply helped prove that was what men did.

Why did he care so much anyway? By any objective

measure, he'd done everything within his power to make amends. Sure, Gemma had been his best friend, not just his girlfriend, but that was a long time ago. People grew apart. They didn't stew over it for fifteen years.

Maybe it was the lack of closure. His sixteen-year-old self had been sure they were destined to be together. His brain simply had never gotten the message that fate didn't exist and what he'd felt was the product of wishful thinking and hormones.

Stephen sighed and trudged back toward the school parking lot, nodding and waving to the shouts of regrets and encouragement that came his way for his team's loss. Let them think that his dejected stance was because of Capture the Flag. Better not to know the truth. Thank heavens it had just been Mallory to witness their impromptu make-out session—despite her intense interest in all things Haven Ridge, she was scrupulously discreet.

By the time he made it back to the festival proper, Gemma was nowhere to be seen. He went through the rest of the afternoon by rote, awarding the ribbons to the silvers—sans Gemma, who should have been accepting them for her team—and doing his final rounds through all the booths as the sun slipped toward the mountains and the festival wound down to its end. By the time he made it back around to Gemma's booth, it was empty; the remaining baked goods had been packed up and removed, leaving only the little QR code sign and the mysterious banner rippling in the breeze.

"Not exactly Cinderella's slipper, is it?"

Granny Pearl's voice made Stephen turn, but he had to force himself to put on a smile. "Have you been here this whole time? I've been so busy I haven't seen you."

"So I've heard," the old lady said with a sparkle in her

eye. Maybe Mallory wasn't as discreet as he'd thought after all. Or maybe all the legends about the Strong family's abilities were actually rooted in fact. She looked him over carefully. "You look like someone sat on your birthday cake."

"It's been a long day."

"So long you're just standing here staring at an empty booth?" She fixed him with a significant stare. "It's taken fifteen years to get her back here to talk to you. Don't tell me you're just going to let her walk away that easily."

He selected his words carefully. "I think I lost the right to demand anything from her a long time ago."

Pearl narrowed her eyes. "Who said anything about demanding? I was thinking more along the lines of begging. Pleading maybe. After all, this town has a lot to make up for. So who else is going to do it but you?"

Now that didn't make any sense. Stephen had been gone for almost as long as Gemma. Since when did he become the actual spokesperson for this town?

As if reading his mind, Pearl patted his arm. "If a journey always begins with a single step, then change begins with a single person. Don't let another fifteen years go by without fixing this."

I thought I already had! he thought, but it wasn't as if Pearl was going to accept any arguments from him. It didn't matter that she was Thomas's grandmother and not his—anyone younger than her was fair game for her advice. So even though he had no idea how he would ever fix things with Gemma, he nodded. "I understand."

"Good." She patted his arm once more. "Now I'm going to see if I can go track down my grandson." She was already ten feet away when she called back over her shoulder, "If you're interested, I think I saw Gemma in the parking lot."

It was as close to an order as he was ever going to get from the old woman, but somehow he knew if he didn't take the advice, he'd be in big trouble. He glanced around, making sure that his volunteer clean-up crew was on-site and getting to work, then hurried off to the area that had been designated for parking.

And sure enough, he found Gemma loading a single box of leftover pastries into the back of Liv's SUV, exactly where Pearl had said he would find her. He stood off a few paces and called out, "Hey."

Gemma started and whipped her head in his direction, then closed the hatch. "Hey."

"Where's Taylor?"

"Off with her friends."

"Good." He took a step closer. "I was hoping to talk to you alone. About what you said."

Gemma stared hard at the cracked asphalt. "Yeah. About that. I'm sorry—"

"Wait, what?" Stephen blinked, startled. "Why?"

"Because you've already apologized. And I accepted your apology. It's not right to keep throwing it back in your face." Gemma swallowed hard, but she still wasn't meeting his gaze. "It's just really difficult for me to trust you. We don't know each other, not anymore. And I've spent the last decade and a half thinking of you as the guy who broke my heart."

She couldn't have gutted him more thoroughly if she'd tried. He'd spent the last decade and a half thinking of her as the one who got away, wishing he hadn't screwed things up so badly as a teenager that they'd never gotten to see what might happen when they grew up. Any sort of breakup would have been preferable to the way they'd ended it, but he largely only remembered the good things about their high school romance. And here she only remembered the bad.

Except she was talking to him now. Which was more than he would have ever expected before today.

"I don't blame you," he said finally. "You have no way of knowing how much I regret not being better back then. Would you give me a shot? Could we just...I don't know. Talk?"

Finally, she lifted her gaze to meet his straight on. "What would be the point, Stephen? I'm going home tomorrow. I really didn't mean to give you the wrong idea with that kiss. I thought it would be funny and then it got out of hand."

No matter how much time had passed, he still knew her well enough to recognize a lie. "Then call it old friends catching up. Come over to my house when we're done here. I'll cook you dinner and we can talk."

"I don't know . . ."

He flashed her a grin. "I promise. No more kissing . . . unless you want to."

She rolled her eyes in response. "You think a lot of yourself, don't you?"

"Not at all. I just want to make sure all bases are covered. Seriously, though. I want to hear everything. I want to hear about school and work and how you got to where you are now." He paused and let his words sink in. "I just want to be the friend to you that I should have been back then."

Somehow, that seemed to have done it. After a moment's consideration, she gave a little nod. "Okay. Text me your address. I'll come over a little later."

He pulled out his phone and quickly typed in his address. Her phone gave a muffled beep in reply.

"Seven o'clock?" he suggested. That would give him enough time to finish up here, take a shower, and defrost the steaks he'd been saving in his freezer for a special occasion.

"Okay." She reached for the vehicle door and gave him a tentative smile. "I'll see you then."

He waited until she put the SUV into gear and pulled away before he turned to go back to the dwindling festival. This is what he should have done all along, before he had the ill-advised idea of kissing her within an inch of her life. Of course, she'd started it; he'd just been more than happy to take advantage of it. He was lucky that she was willing to even speak to him now.

It's not a date, he reminded himself as he went back to the market area, but his steps were considerably lighter than they'd been just a few minutes ago. This was just two friends, catching up, mending the hurt and misunderstandings of the past. Jokes about kissing aside, he was beginning to think that he wanted Gemma Van Buren back in his life, whatever way he could have her.

CHAPTER TWENTY

SHE MUST BE CRAZY.

That was the only way of explaining why, after a full day at the winter festival, she was putting on makeup and slipping into a slinky sweater in preparation to go to Stephen's house for dinner, instead of wrapping herself up in sweatpants and fuzzy socks and watching Netflix while eating her unsold products. The Broken Hearts Bakery, indeed.

But Stephen had seemed so sincere and earnest when he caught her at her vehicle, apologizing for something that, frankly, he really didn't need to apologize for. Gemma had been the one who had been out of line. Not because she hadn't deserved to feel her betrayal all these years; she had learned enough from working with her clients to know that wasn't a healthy perspective. But simply because he had done all he could. He'd apologized. He'd explained. Whether or not she was able to forgive him and move on had nothing to do with him and everything to do with her.

Which was why she still wasn't sure why she'd agreed

to dinner, and even less sure why she was making an effort to look appealing.

It was that kiss and you know it, her conscience needled her, not allowing her to get away with lies, even to herself.

Okay, it had been the kiss, but not just. It had been the way that even when she had intended it as a distraction, he had cradled her head to protect it from the ground, his touch so tender and sweet that she'd forgotten all the time that had passed between them and all the feelings of betrayal that she had nurtured.

And the second. . . it had been filled with pure, raw need. There had been nothing juvenile or innocent about that kiss. The very thought of it sent heat spreading through her body and sped her heartbeat as if she was crouched on a starting block.

It was probably not the wisest way to prepare for what was supposed to be a friendly, innocuous dinner.

And if you believe that's either of your motivations, you're kidding yourself, that inner voice taunted. She shut it down with utter ruthlessness. Because if she truly believed that, she wouldn't go, and right now she wanted to see Stephen with an eagerness that bordered on foolishness.

After texting Taylor to tell her to be home by ten—thus ensuring Gemma's own curfew—she gave her hair one last fluff, swiped on a coat of lip gloss, and made her way downstairs to Liv's SUV. The map on her phone told her Stephen lived only twenty minutes away, which gave her twenty minutes longer than she wanted to debate the wisdom of going there in the first place.

But her doubts were forgotten when exactly nineteen minutes later she pulled up in front of a two-story A-frame. She climbed out of the SUV and looked up at the brightly lit structure, her breath puffing out around her, a smile spreading over her face. He'd done it. He'd actually found the house of his dreams, the one they'd constructed in their imagination all those years ago.

She had no sooner taken two steps across the gravel than the door on the lower floor beside the garage opened, revealing Stephen. He had to have been waiting for her in order to get there so quickly. He gave her a smile but stayed where he was, stepping back so she could enter the wood-paneled foyer.

"You came." A smile spread over his handsome face. His choice of career really was unfair to the girls of Haven Ridge High School. Even Gemma felt her heart skip a beat this close to him, enveloped in his scent of clean cotton and well-groomed man, and she had reason to keep her distance. Those teenage girls with their raging hormones stood no chance.

"I almost didn't," she admitted. "But tell me the truth . . . did you build this place?"

"No. Hard to believe it existed like this already, isn't it? I always think we must have somehow seen or heard about it."

"No kidding." She shrugged off her jacket and passed it into Stephen's waiting hands, where he hung it on a hook by the door. "Give me a tour?"

"Sure. This level is the bedrooms—as you've probably guessed—so let's go upstairs."

Gemma followed Stephen up the knotty pine-planked stairs into a wide-open great room, lit comfortably but dimly, with a fire already crackling on the hearth. The house was furnished in a comfortable blend of contemporary and rustic that looked like he'd decorated it himself—it was in good taste but not something out of a magazine, simple neutrals with the occasional splash of color in the form of a woven rug or pillow. The kitchen itself was old, with rustic pine cabinets and a slate tile countertop, but what struck her was that it was almost obsessively clean. Apparently some things never changed. She and Liv used to tease Stephen about how meticulous he was, especially considering how at odds it was with his football player persona.

On the other end of the kitchen, French doors opened to a wide deck, which she suspected would have a panoramic view of the surrounding area, but now just showed a great expanse of darkness. Stephen headed for the kitchen, calling over his shoulder, "Wine, sparkling water, or coffee?"

Before she could think better of it, Gemma said, "I'll take a glass of wine."

Stephen took down two shimmery blown-glass wine stems from one of the cabinets and carefully filled them halfway from an open bottle of red. "Blaufränkisch," he said, handing one to her.

Gemma looked at him blankly. "Bless you?"

Stephen chuckled. "The wine. It's a Blaufränkisch, from Germany."

"When did you get to be such a wine connoisseur?"

He blushed . . . actually blushed. "I'm not really. I went to the liquor store in Salida and asked their wine guy what went best with what I'm serving, and they suggested this."

Gemma smiled at him and took a sip, nodding at the fruity undertones and smoky finish. "It's nice. Good choice."

"I was about to put the steaks on." He gestured toward a baking sheet that had two beautiful New York strips waiting, already seasoned. "You can pull up a stool at the island if you want."

Gemma did as he suggested and watched as he took out a cast iron pan and set it on the cooktop in the center of the island, cranking up the flame beneath it. "When did you learn how to cook?"

"Somewhere between college and moving back here, I guess." He threw her a smile. "Got tired of eating out all the time, gave up on finding a wife to cook for me." He winked at her so she knew he was kidding about the wife part. "Don't be too impressed. Steak is my only specialty, and if it weren't sixteen degrees outside, I would be putting these on the grill."

Gemma took another sip of the wine, not sure if the pleasant warmth she was feeling was from the alcohol or from Stephen's presence. It was easy to say that he was another figure best left in her past when they were passing in public, but in person, she felt the same magnetic draw to him as she always had. It was equal parts reassuring and irritating.

"So tell me about your journey from literature student to ad man," she said, watching him drop a sizable pat of butter into the hot pan.

He swiveled away to get the steaks and carefully put them into the skillet. "Not much to tell. You know my parents were opposed to me studying something frivolous like literature."

"As opposed to doing something really practical like majoring in football."

He laughed. "Exactly. They certainly weren't going to pay for a master's degree or a doctorate, and I wasn't keen on the idea of going into debt for a career that might not ever pay off my student loans. I had taken some business classes, and my advertising professor suggested that I apply for a copywriter position at Arnold." He glanced at her. "You know who they are, right?"

She didn't, but she figured they were probably a pretty big deal in the ad world, so she just nodded so he would continue.

"Anyway, I got it. Turned out to be quite a good copywriter, which the literature background helped with. No one had any idea that I was stealing story ideas from the great works. That got me promoted to creative director, but I kind of got stagnant. When it came time to move on, I put out some feelers and Smithson + Bosch in Salt Lake City was pretty keen on hiring and relocating me, so I left Boston."

"Where it went well until they wanted you to do an ad campaign for a drug company."

"It was all more complicated than that, but yeah, that was the last straw. Came back here not knowing what I wanted to do, and it felt like . . . destiny." He threw her a wry glance. "Which is how you know I never lost my English major mentality, because I thought the fact that the literature slot opened the very month I came home was some sort of sign."

"Was it?"

He studied the meat for a second, poking it with a fingertip to check for doneness. "I don't know. I thought so at the time."

"But you don't anymore?"

He bit his lower lip thoughtfully, then stabbed the steaks and flipped them over. "Are you sure you really want to hear this? It's going to make you uncomfortable."

"Try me."

He lifted his eyes and locked his gaze on hers. "I realized pretty quickly that the love I had for Haven Ridge had more to do with my old feelings for you than my actual enthusiasm about the town."

Gemma's heart practically leaped into her throat and she had to swallow down the lump. "I see."

"I told you it would make you uncomfortable, but now that it's too late, let me just say that it's felt more like home since you've been here than it has the entire time since I moved back."

"Stephen . . ."

He glanced at her quickly before turning his attention back to the steak. "You don't have to say anything. It doesn't require a response, and I'm not trying to pressure you into anything. I actually really like the job. The kids are great. They're so open and ready to see different points of view. The administration, not so much."

"Is Mr. Carter still there?" Gemma asked, glad that he'd moved on so quickly.

"No, he retired a long time ago, I guess. Edgar Daughtler is the new principal, and while he's trying hard, I think he has his hands tied by the more influential members of town. Can you believe that they objected to virtually all of my second-semester books?"

"I can believe it," Gemma said. "Who's pulling his strings though?"

"Best guess? Chelsea Meinke. Her kids are still young, but she's in tight with some of the high school parents because of Rebekah. Which means . . ."

"It's really Doug Meinke making a fuss." Gemma made a face. "He's got her twisted in knots, afraid to say a word to anyone without his approval."

Stephen blinked at her. "You're the last person I would expect to be defending Chelsea. After all the stuff she pulled when we were in high school?"

"Yeah, that was before I realized what was going on in her house." Gemma detailed a little of what she'd learned from Rebekah, and Stephen nodded along.

"I wish I could say that surprised me. I thought maybe he was kind of authoritarian—I've noticed a difference in Rebekah since her dad left on his trip and she moved in there—but I didn't realize it was so bad."

"I realize this is all hearsay, but the way he confronted me and told me to stay away from his family a couple of days ago—"

Stephen dropped his utensils with a clatter. "He what?"

Gemma allowed herself to enjoy the furious look on his face for a second—a very cave-woman-like reaction, she admitted—before she said, "Chelsea didn't even know about it. I apologized for causing problems at home when I saw her at the festival and she had no idea what I was talking about. So he's clearly afraid that I'm going to make trouble for him."

"Which you are," Stephen prompted.

"Which I would, if it were any of my business. If I actually lived here. If Chelsea didn't still hate my guts. Let's face it, she's not ready to get out from under his thumb. I can tell. I know the signs."

Stephen sighed and shook his head. "You're probably right. I just can't believe I didn't know about it."

"Guys like him keep it quiet. Need to keep their standing in town, keep their wives in line. I see it all the time. Trust me, if I were staying here and Chelsea were ready, I'd be his worst nightmare. There's nothing I love more than taking away an abuser's power."

Stephen studied her face for a long moment, something akin to admiration coloring his expression. "You're something else."

Now it was her turn to blush, though she couldn't say why. "I'm just doing my job."

"No, you aren't. You're really passionate about helping women."

"Not just women."

He inclined his head in acknowledgment. "No, but probably mostly women. Women like your mom."

She shouldn't be surprised that he'd guessed her motivations so easily. It didn't exactly take a degree in psychology to know what had shaped her career aspirations. "And women like your mom too."

Now it was his turn to be shocked. "My mom?"

"Oh please, don't think I didn't see how much control your dad exerted. It might not be abusive, exactly, but she was never allowed to have an opinion when it came to you. You might not know it, but your mom was always really proud of you. You weren't sitting with her in the audience when you won that essay thing. She looked at you like the sun rose and set on you."

He nodded, but he wouldn't meet her eye. "Now these need to sit." He shifted the pan off to a burner and put a mismatched lid on top of it. Just in time for a distraction, the oven timer beeped, and he swept over to the wall oven with a towel to take out a sheet pan.

"Roasted potatoes and tomatoes with rosemary and garlic," he said with a flourish, winking at her.

Gemma sensed that he wanted to shift the conversation from the serious turn it had taken, and she was more than happy to let him do it. "That looks amazing. That's a lot more than steak."

"Yes, I am amazing at tossing whole vegetables with oil and seasoning," he said seriously. "Bow down before my culinary prowess."

She laughed and reached for the bottle so she could refill their glasses. She'd only been here for a few minutes, but she was already glad she'd come. She'd expected Stephen to have matured, but there was a wry edge to him now that was unexpected. As if he'd seen all the bad and difficult things life had to offer and chosen to smile into the darkness rather than let it overtake him. It was undeniably appealing.

Now who's being poetic? her inner critic flung at her.

"I think we might be ready to eat," he said, checking on the steak. "Would you mind grabbing a couple of plates from the cabinet to the right of the fridge?"

Gemma hopped off her stool and moved to the cabinet he indicated, taking out two pieces of a rather nice porcelain dinner set, then set them down on the island beside him. He transferred the steaks to the plates, garnishing them with a smear of butter, and then added the potatoes and tomatoes beside them. It was a very manly sort of meal and it looked delicious.

"Over there," Stephen said, indicating the small kitchen table situated by the sliding doors. She noticed for the first time that there was a trio of small candles burning there.

Her heart gave another little hiccup when she realized how much thought he'd put into this. If he wasn't being so open and laid back, she would think there was a seduction scene at play here.

Except he hardly needed it. Who he was was enough. Had always been enough.

How many women do you think he's had up here since he moved back? How many women would look at you knowingly if they heard that he'd had you over for dinner?

But that wasn't fair to him. She had no right to be jealous, for one thing. For another, she didn't get the sense that was his style. At least she hoped it wasn't. Because if this was studied, planned, it cast him in an entirely different light.

Her mind spun as they took their plates and wine glasses to the table and seated themselves. As she looked at him across the flickering candles, she couldn't help herself. "Do you do this often?"

"Make steak?" Stephen asked innocently.

"Cook for women."

A smile lifted the corner of his lips. "Are you jealous?"

She was about to demur, but then she just said, "Yes."

He hadn't been expecting that, and the shift in his expression from lightness to intensity jolted her. She swallowed, but she didn't break the gaze.

"No," he said quietly. "I haven't cooked for anyone here."

Gemma just gave a little nod, finally breaking his gaze, even though her chest felt strange now, her stomach a little too jumpy. She picked up her knife and fork but found she couldn't make herself eat.

"Gemma," Stephen said quietly, reaching to rest his fingertips on her wrist. "Relax. You asked. I didn't invite you here for any other reason than to catch up. I hated the way we left things. I just want to be your friend."

They both knew it was a lie, but it was a good answer, and it relaxed her enough that her muscles unlocked. "I'm sorry. Occupational hazard. I find I'm suspicious of everyone these days. You deal with abusers and narcissists and you start seeing red flags everywhere."

"Must make dating hard."

"You have no idea." Gemma cut a piece of her steak and forked it into her mouth, then sighed in pleasure. "This is amazing."

"Coming from you, that's a compliment."

"Oh no, I'm a terrible cook. I'm just an excellent baker."

"Then we make a great pair."

The words were tossed off casually enough for her to ignore them, but they stuck anyway, put her straight back into her head. Made her analyze what she was really doing here, having a romantic meal with the man who had once broken her heart, however she might try to justify his youthful indiscretions. But it wasn't his motivations that she was worried about. It was her own.

She'd been in his presence a sum total of six times this week, and she was already falling for him. Again.

CHAPTER TWENTY-ONE

STEPHEN HAD DONE HIS BEST to keep things light and friendly. Yes, he'd perhaps made his house look a little more romantic than he'd intended, but that was simply because he'd been suddenly aware of how threadbare and masculine everything looked, how conspicuously lacking a woman's touch. He hadn't wanted to draw attention to it, hence the fire and the low light and the candles.

But sitting across from Gemma, the flickering tea lights between them, he couldn't help but feel like it was inevitable. He'd told her that coming back to Haven Ridge felt like destiny, but no more so than the time he'd slid into the seat beside her in biology class and thought that she was the most beautiful girl he'd ever seen. The fact she'd had her hair tied into a knot, wearing no makeup and dressed in a faded Van Halen T-shirt with Timberland boots and ripped jeans, and he still couldn't look away from her . . . however youthful the fantasy might have been, it had felt like love.

It felt no less the same after a fifteen-year absence.

But he locked away those thoughts. They would not

help them here. Not when he'd been aching to touch Gemma ever since they'd kissed. Not since the idea that she was about to turn around and leave for the second time felt like it might kill him again. And he could not give a single hint of that or she would go running so fast and so far that he'd never see her again.

"What about you?" he said finally. "Tell me all about college and law school."

"Oh trust me, you don't want to hear all about college."

"I do, though. What did you study for your under-grad? Prelaw isn't a major, is it?"

She looked abashed for a moment, though he couldn't guess why. "You'll laugh."

"I did a degree in literature. Why would I laugh?"

Her lips twisted into a smile. "Humanities."

He laughed. Not because he had any particular opinion on the subject, but she certainly had. He dis-tinctly remembered scrolling through course catalogs and reading the descriptions of the majors and classes, Gemma ranting the whole time. She'd been particularly vocal about Humanities. *Humanities? Why don't you call it Undeclared Major for People Who Hate Math? Or even My Parents Made Me Go Here So I'm Going to Waste All Their Money?*

Gemma narrowed her eyes at him. "You said you wouldn't laugh."

"That's before you said you studied Humanities. What happened to all those high-minded ideals about picking a major?"

"I didn't know what to study," she admitted, then fixed him with a glare. "Don't you dare say it. I wanted to go to law school, and like you said, prelaw isn't a major. There was no way a science degree was going to help me, business and accounting were boring, and I didn't love literature the way you did. This way I could read books on interesting topics with a lot of free choice."

"You don't have to convince me," Stephen said, still grinning. "It's just simply fascinating to see how the mighty have fallen."

"Oh shut up," she snapped good-naturedly, and like that, the tension between them was broken. They might as well have been sixteen again, bickering over pointless minutia. "I actually was right about the purpose of the major, it just wasn't as useless as I originally thought."

Stephen held up his hands. "I will concede the point."

"Anyway, law school was law school. While all my friends were vying for Supreme Court clerkships, I clerked for a family court judge in an impoverished district. I wanted to see the worst cases I might face as a lawyer before I fully committed to that path." Her eyes went distant for a moment. "I did. And I vowed that's what I was going to do with my life. Unfortunately, I realized that LA is not very friendly to lawyers who want to help people with no money, and I wanted to work on the civil side, not criminal, so there just weren't that many good options."

"So you went the other way. Wealthy clients to help pay for the pro bono work."

"Exactly."

"Seems like a good compromise."

Gemma leaned back in her chair. "Is it though? I just don't know. Not if I don't get to choose those clients. Does a rich woman being abused by her husband matter less than a poor one?"

Stephen thought for a second. "Matter less? Of course not. But she has opportunities. Privilege."

"You'd be surprised. The power imbalance is still

there, maybe even greater. Because people might not be rushing to help when a poor guy is beating on his family, but everyone believes it's happening. But when a guy who runs a Fortune 500 company does it? It must have been her fault. Surely no one with that much money and influence could be a creep."

Just like everyone in Haven Ridge had sided with Gemma's physician dad when she and her mom were the actual victims. Just like now, when everyone looked the other way over what was going on in the Meinke household, despite the signs. Stephen couldn't deny that Gemma was right.

"So what are you going to do?"

"I have no idea. Earlier I thought maybe I knew, but now . . . even with your third option, it's not a simple equation."

The mood was getting dark, which was not how he wanted to leave it the night before she went back to California. He sought to lighten it. "Maybe there's a fourth option."

She reached for her glass and took a sip. "Oh? What's that?"

"Quit the firm, move to Haven Ridge, and open the Broken Hearts Bakery."

Gemma let out a surprised laugh. "Oh yes, that seems like a very good use of my education."

"Well, you could always do both. The Broken Hearts Bakery and Legal Advice. Given what you do, it feels appropriate."

Gemma made a face. "Come in for a divorce, get a dozen cookies free?"

"Well, it would soften the whole process. Legal documents and tea prepared while you wait. Don't look at me like that! I really think I'm on to something here."

She rolled her eyes, but at least she was laughing. "I

didn't go into law to draft corporate documents and wills. I hardly think there's enough work for my specialty here."

"Unfortunately, you'd be surprised," Stephen said softly, before he went back to his jovial tone. "Besides, that's why you'd have the bakery. For the slow seasons."

"Nice try." Gemma smiled at him over the rim of her wine glass, her eyes sparkling. "But really, there's absolutely no reason to stay."

"Liv and Taylor would disagree. And so would I." He held her gaze, knowing that he was risking cutting their time together short, that she would run the minute he voiced his thoughts. But he had to do it. "It's really good to have you back, Gemma. I've missed you."

To his shock, her expression didn't shutter. If anything, a look of yearning crossed her face as she held his gaze. "Yeah. Me too. I'm glad we did this. I . . . I hated being angry at you."

"Probably not as much as *I* hated you being angry at me."

"I wouldn't be so sure about that," she said, but now she was smiling and eating again. "So tell me about this whole curriculum debate."

So he did. He told her the inane mandate that he'd been given, and how he'd planned to get around it. "It's a lot of extra effort, given the fact I'm already behind on my schoolwork . . ."

The conversation meandered after that, but the odd tension was gone and they'd fallen back into the comfortable space that they'd once inhabited, when it had felt like they were the only two people on earth, Gemma and Stephen against the world. She helped him wash the dishes and set them into the dish drainer, seemingly oblivious to the sparks of electricity that shot through him every time her arm brushed his. And even when he brought out the tiramisu that he'd purchased at the store that day—warning her that it wouldn't be as good as hers—he was happy that things had stayed light and comfortable, the very friendship that he had claimed to want. Even if it was a flat-out lie.

Every minute he spent with her only intensified that feeling of inevitability, of rightness. Like the gap in his life he'd tried to fill with every kind of pursuit was only complete when she was near him.

And if it terrified him, it would most definitely terrify her.

Still, she lingered, as if she too was reluctant to let the night end. He made coffee and they took it to the living room where the leather sofa and chair were angled to the fireplace. He waited for her to choose the chair, a clear signal to keep his distance.

She chose the sofa.

It took exactly three minutes of sipping their coffee in awkward silence before she set her cup and saucer down on the table and he followed suit. It took less than ten seconds after that to close the gap between them.

Stephen threaded his hand through her hair at the nape of her neck, feeling the silky weight of it between his fingers while he looked into her eyes. Her lips parted, her breath turning shallow at his touch, but he didn't want to rush this. He had no idea when she would decide this was a bad idea, as she inevitably would, and he wanted to savor every moment. He pressed his lips to her temple, her cheek, the line of her jaw. And when she couldn't stand it any longer and tipped her face to his, the meeting of their lips was the sweetest thing he could remember in the fifteen years they'd been apart.

Her lips went pliant beneath his, an invitation, but he took his time, brushing them gently with his own, teasing. Her hands found the front of his shirt, skimming his chest, then sliding around his middle and up his back as if she was exploring every bit of him she could reach. His head spun as past and present merged: they were different and yet the same; they brought with them so much experience from their time apart and yet they shared a past that no one else could understand. Having her in his arms felt right in a way that he couldn't explain.

And then her lips parted beneath his, the touch of her tongue igniting a longing in him that had been long stoked, and they were crashing into each other, drinking each other in, devouring. She moaned against his mouth, her fingernails digging into his back through the thin fabric, and he shifted her so that she was straddling him, giving his hands more access to her. If he had thought he wanted her as a teenager, it was nothing compared to what he felt now as she hovered above him with her hungry mouth and soft body.

It was this that he'd been missing. Not sex, not desire, but the feeling of rightness. The sense that he'd found the person that had been made for him, and he in return. All he could think of was how he had wasted the last fifteen years searching for the love of his life, and he could have had her all along. If only he'd waited, if only she hadn't left, if only he hadn't been so foolish . . .

Memory crashed over him like a bucket of cold water. Had he learned nothing from his past mistakes?

Gemma sensed the instant she lost him and pulled back, flushed and mussed and so gorgeous it made his heart hurt. "What's wrong?" she whispered.

"It's beginning to feel a bit too familiar," he said, aware of how breathless he sounded and how little he actually wanted to stop.

But the awareness slid over her face too, and she

shifted off him, drawing her knees up to her chest instead. Stephen took heart in the fact she didn't scoot to the opposite end of the sofa but instead nestled against his arm. "You're right. I'm leaving tomorrow. And this . . . whatever this has been . . . will be over."

It was no less than he expected from her, and yet he hated how easily she had come to that conclusion. He suddenly felt desperate to make her, if not change her mind, at least treat it like a difficult decision. "Does it have to be over?"

"What do you mean? You live here, I live in LA . . ."

"That's just geography. Why would you let something like dots on a map get in the way of this for a second time?"

"And what is *this* exactly?" Her green eyes narrowed, a calculating light in her eyes. He got the distinct sense of what it would be like to face her in a courtroom or across a conference table. She would be weighing the truthfulness of his answer. He would have no choice but to lay it out plainly and let her decide.

"I miss you," he said finally. "You're the best friend I've ever had, and I've never wanted another woman as much as I've *always* wanted you. Maybe we just reconnected, but can you really tell me you don't feel the same way?"

He was sure she was set to deny it; he could read it all in the sudden stiffness in her posture, the hard set of her mouth. And then she softened and rubbed the back of her neck ruefully. "No. I can't tell you that. But Stephen, it's insane. Fifteen years. We were kids. Whatever we said back then, we didn't really mean it."

"Didn't we?" Stephen reached out to trail his fingertips down her cheek, and almost against her will, she leaned into him. He dared her to tell him that she didn't feel the same as he did—that being together felt like getting a piece of himself back that he didn't know he'd missed. "When I said I wanted to marry you, I meant it."

"And then I came back to see you and you were with another girl." She held up a hand before he could protest. "I'm not trying to start a fight. I'm just pointing out that we're not the star-crossed lovers you want to believe we are. We are people who made decisions and those decisions took us apart. We should accept it."

"Even if it was a mistake?"

Her eyes widened, almost shocked by the words. "Stephen . . ."

"I'm not saying we run down to the courthouse. I'm just rejecting the idea that teenage love can't be real."

Her mouth twisted with wry humor. "You mean like Romeo and Juliet?"

"Yeah, well, neither of us went and committed suicide, did we?" He reached for her hand, laced his fingers with hers, and met her eyes again. "I'm just saying that I never stopped caring about you, and I'm hoping you'd be willing to start over. Give us another shot."

Gemma gently pulled her hand from his and pushed herself up off the sofa to stand before the fire, hands out to absorb its warmth. He'd meant every word he'd said, and letting her walk away without a fight felt like giving up his best chance for happiness. When she turned back, he held his breath, hoping against hope that it would be enough to convince her. But she just gave him a sad smile.

"Stephen, I'm sorry. I can't."

CHAPTER TWENTY-TWO

GEMMA HAD TO GET AWAY from Stephen. If she wanted to think rationally, objectively, she couldn't be within arm's reach of him. Because every time he touched her—God forbid, kissed her—it was like everything else in her orbit ceased to matter. All she wanted was him. And that was one thing that she couldn't allow to happen. She'd seen it far too often in her practice— brilliant, capable women who gave up everything for a man only to be shattered when he didn't return the same trust.

Which is why the only thing Gemma could find to say to his plea was, "I'm sorry, I can't."

She averted her eyes, but she still caught the hurt look on his face. How could she possibly resist him? Forget the fact that tonight he'd stepped out of a J. Crew catalog, looking so appealing she'd begun day-dreaming about getting snowed in with him here and having to invent ways to keep each other warm. Forget the fact that every time he touched her, it was like he'd set off fireworks in all the best places. It was his stupid sincerity, his complete lack of guile. What guy would

say that geography was just dots on a map when it came
to true love?

Because even if he didn't say the words, that's what
he meant. Stephen was a romantic, always had been.
She'd been the practical one, hedging her bets, planning
for the future. He'd never made any bones about the
fact he didn't care about any future without her in it.

And it looked like that hadn't changed.

Even now, he was shaking his head. "I don't believe
you."

"Why? What makes you think I even believe in love
anymore?"

He pushed himself off the sofa and approached her
slowly. "Because you wouldn't fight so hard for your
clients if you didn't think their spouses had broken a
sacred trust. If they hadn't twisted something special."

It was true. He knew her too well to deny it. She
couldn't even come up with an argument; when she
opened her mouth, all that emerged was his name.

He took her face in his hands and kissed her again,
gently but thoroughly, until her head was swimming and
her knees went weak. She gathered enough presence of
mind to push against him, even though her voice came
out hoarse and uncertain when she spoke. "Stop. Wanting you isn't the same as loving you."

"No," he said with that twist of a smile that always
caused her heart to leap. "But I'm really glad to know
that it's not one-sided."

"No," Gemma whispered. "It's not one-sided. Which
is why I have to go."

Stephen stepped back and dropped his hands immediately. "Okay. Just. . . consider it. Consider not saying
goodbye forever."

"I'll consider it."

He nodded and shoved his hands in his pockets,

even though that glint of intensity still shone in his eyes. "I'll walk you out."

Stephen was a true gentleman. Now that she'd put a halt to things, he kept his hands to himself, helped her on with her coat downstairs, walked her to her car, even though he wasn't wearing a jacket and the temperature had dropped another several degrees since she'd arrived. The most he did was take her hand and lift it to his lips.

"Call me tomorrow?" he asked. "Let's talk again before you go."

"Okay," she whispered. She didn't trust herself with any more. As much as she wanted to sit here and gather herself before she drove back to Liv's place, it was clear he wasn't going to go inside until she was safely off. So she started the engine, made a quick three-point turn in his wide driveway, and left the way she'd come.

If she'd intended to stay impartial, she'd made a huge mistake coming here tonight. But deep down, she'd known that impartiality had been the last thing on her mind. She'd wanted to be convinced. She'd wanted to know that he felt that draw between them just as strongly as she did. She just hadn't expected to have the last vestiges of her anger and caution shredded.

She was every bit of a fool when it came to love as any one of her clients.

When Gemma finally reached Liv's house, she was no more settled than she'd been when she'd left; even more restless, if that was possible. It wasn't quite ten, and she fully expected Taylor to creep in three minutes after curfew, but just in case, she remained in the car with the heater running on full blast. She couldn't vouch for what might be written all over her face right now. After a moment's consideration, she pulled out her cell phone and opened a message to Liv.

I think I may have made a big mistake.

Almost immediately, the response came back. **Oh no. How?**

I went to dinner at Stephen's tonight.

A longer pause, as if Liv was being cautious about her response. **How big of a mistake? Like, a naked mistake?**

Gemma laughed out loud, even though her cheeks heated at the thought. If Stephen hadn't put the brakes on when he had, she might have convinced herself to make a very naked mistake. The fact she wasn't even sure it would have been a mistake . . . nope, wasn't going to go there right now. **No, nothing like that. But, Liv . . . he doesn't want to say goodbye.**

I could have told you that. The boy has been in love with you for almost two decades. You think he's going to let you get away now?

Gemma dropped the phone into her lap with suddenly nerveless fingers and it took her a full minute to pick it back up. **You didn't just say that.**

Sweetie, the man doesn't do casual. Never did as a kid. You really think a guy like that would have a problem finding a wife if he wasn't already hung up on someone in his past? He's practically a freaking Disney prince.

That made Gemma laugh out loud, a call-back to their high school days. Liv had always teased her and Stephen about their instant connection, saying that insta-love only happened to them and Disney characters. Gemma had brushed it off as a joke, but now that she thought back, it was true. One look in biology class and she'd been done for. They'd been inseparable for two-and-a-half years, and she'd really, truly believed that she would marry him someday.

The fact that it hadn't worked out that way had been

the one reason she stopped believing in love and happily-ever-afters and miracles.

Gem, you still there? Or are you in a lust coma?

Yes to both? Gemma laughed out loud again as she typed it, knowing what Liv's reaction would be.

Sure enough, the phone rang immediately and Liv didn't even wait for her to answer. "Dude, you're a goner. I knew it!"

"Which was why you didn't tell me he was back!"

"Well, yeah. I thought it would be better for you two to discover each other on your own again. Without any preconceptions."

"Ugh." Gemma rubbed her eyes wearily. "I don't even know what to do."

"Move back to Haven Ridge. Easy."

"It's not that easy and you know it."

Liv waited a beat. "Maybe not, but tell me the truth. Are you or are you not the happiest right now that you can remember being in your adult life?"

Gemma thought back to how nice it had been to sit across the table with Stephen at dinner, talking about everything and nothing. How settled and safe she felt in his presence even when it didn't make any sense. How just the thought of his fingers in her hair and his lips on her skin made her feel like she was one step away from bursting into flame. She groaned. "Yes."

"There you have it."

"Yeah, but falling hopelessly in lust over a weekend is not falling in love. You think all those unhappy marriages started unhappy? I guarantee my mom and Chelsea and all my clients felt the same way I do right now."

"You're right," Liv said reasonably. "The big difference is, they didn't marry Stephen."

It shouldn't have been a revelation, but it was, that idea that she couldn't paint all men with the same brush.

That maybe her problem finding someone had less to do with them and more to do with the fact she was always waiting for the other shoe to drop. How much chance had she ever given anyone to prove himself to her? And how much did that have to do with the fact she knew she'd already found her perfect match and lost him?

Liv was going on. "The bigger question is whether you trust him or not. Forget what happened in the past. He made a big mistake, and if you can't allow someone one big mistake, you're just going to go through life being disappointed. Do you trust him now?"

Gemma drew in a big breath and let it out slowly. Did she? He seemed sincere. Clearly, he'd matured in the past decade and a half, just as she had. But to take that leap . . . "I don't know. Maybe?"

"That's the question you have to answer then. Because if you can't trust him enough now to give him a second chance, you should walk away without a second thought. Clean break. But if you can . . . do you really want to spend any more of your life wondering *what if?*"

Liv was annoyingly wise in things of the heart; but then again, she'd found her true love and lost him. No doubt she had a totally different perspective on taking chances. No matter how painful losing Jason had been—still was—Gemma knew Liv would never trade their years together for anything, and not just because it had put Taylor in her life.

"Think about it," Liv said. "I gotta go. I'm meeting some of my colleagues—well, ex-colleagues—at Serendipity for frozen hot chocolate. Love you!"

"Yeah, love you too," Gemma murmured, but the line was already dead.

She had a big, big decision to make—two of them now, actually, one of which made the other one easy. And very little time in which to do it.

CHAPTER TWENTY-THREE

GEMMA DREAMED that she was trudging through a snowstorm, shivering while the wind lashed snow into her face and pricked her bare arms with frost. If only she could reach the house ahead of her. . . there was warmth and safety inside. . . and Stephen.

Her eyes snapped open to the dim gray light of morning, as if even in sleep her mind wouldn't automatically accept that anywhere Stephen was could mean warmth and safety. Normally, her stress dreams had to do with walking into court wearing nothing but lingerie or being late to the bar exam. Snow was a new one. What had triggered that?

The thought had barely surfaced in her mind before she registered the chill bite of cold on her cheeks and ears, the only body parts that weren't covered by her down duvet. What was going on? Had the heater broken down?

Gemma fumbled for the switch on the bedside lamp and flicked it several times before she realized it wasn't doing anything. The digital alarm clock, which should be proclaiming the hour in its impossible-to-miss red numbers, was still and blank. The power was out. Gemma slipped out of bed, stumbled across the wood floor, and parted the blinds so she could peer out.

And was met with a swirl of white.

"What the heck?" Gemma dropped the blinds closed, now fully awake. She'd checked the weather last night, and there hadn't been any kind of snow in the forecast for this part of Colorado. Maybe some showers up north, but not here. But still, the light covering of snow on the ground outside didn't explain the lack of power. This was Colorado. It would take a lot more than a dusting to affect power lines.

She crept out into the hallway and convulsed into a full-body shiver. It was even colder out here. She went to the window in the living room and peered out to see if the neighbors had power. Not that it was easy to tell at six thirty in the morning, but the nearest neighbor's obnoxiously bright security light was out, and if she was right, so was the streetlight that illuminated the turn off the highway to Liv's neighborhood, though the actual highway lights were on thanks to their solar-powered batteries.

She found her phone and dialed Liv, who picked up immediately. "It's snowing," Gemma said without preamble.

"I know. I'm watching the news now. My flight was delayed."

Gemma hadn't even thought of her flight yet. Right now, she had a bigger problem, and that was the fact her toes were beginning to go numb against the wood floor.

"The power is out here, though I'm not sure why. It doesn't look that bad out."

"You can go to the house if you need to. There's a wood-burning fireplace in the living room and the woodshed is filled."

"Thanks. I'm going to see what I can figure out. I'll call you back."

"Stay safe and warm. Tell Taylor I said hello and I'll be back as soon as I can."

"You've got it on both counts. Love you, Liv." Gemma clicked off the phone and lowered her hand to her side. Now that the shock of the rude awakening had passed, dread was beginning to creep into her stomach. She had to get back to LA tonight. John was expecting an answer from her tomorrow, and preferably in person.

She realized belatedly that she should check her flight status, but before she could even pull up the app, she saw the push alert on the screen: *Flight delay. Check your departures page for more information.*

She sighed and pushed a hand through her messy hair. That was Colorado for you. Fifty-degree temperature swings in the summer weren't unusual, so why should a snowstorm in the dead of winter come as a surprise?

She and Taylor probably would have to move back to the house, but the teenager was still asleep in her room, so there was no reason to rob her of a few extra hours if the cold didn't wake her up. Gemma went back to her room where she threw on a sweatshirt and sweatpants, then padded out in her heavy socks to put a kettle on the stove. After fumbling in the drawer for matches, she lit the gas burner and put the water on to heat for coffee. Or tea, since she had no real way to make coffee besides the electric coffee maker.

The whistle had just barely pierced the air when a sleepy voice asked, "Aunt Gem, why is it so cold in here?"

"Power is out. Do you want tea?"

"Sure." Taylor moved into the kitchen, her hair wild, remnants of eyeliner beneath her lashes. She didn't even bother to poke her hands out of the cuffs of her oversized sweater when Gemma handed her the cup, just took it in wool-swaddled fingers and hopped onto one of the stools.

Gemma rifled through the cardboard box of baked goods they'd brought back from the carnival yesterday and came up with a mini zucchini bread and two chocolate cupcakes. "Breakfast of champions. Pick your poison."

Predictably, Taylor took a cupcake, and Gemma claimed the zucchini bread, knowing her niece would never stop at just one cupcake. After a minute, the girl grinned at her. "This is kind of fun. They get power outages in town a lot, but almost never here."

"Really?"

"Yeah, it's because we're on a different line or something out here."

Huh. That was strange. But then the storm had to be much worse elsewhere if there were airport delays. There'd been a scant inch on the ground the last time she'd peeked.

Taylor shrugged. "I like it though. Feels like pioneer days or something."

"If the pioneers had a reliable source of chocolate," Gemma said with a grin.

A sharp rap downstairs at the door made both of them whip their heads around.

"Probably a neighbor checking on us," Taylor said. "The guy next door brings us wood and stuff."

Hence the filled woodshed. Gemma was pretty sure that Liv had never handled an ax in her life. She took her time climbing down the stairs and opened the door, preparing herself to tell the neighbor thanks, but they were fine.

Instead, it was Stephen standing there.

Gemma looked him up and down, not comprehending his presence. He was wearing heavy snow boots, a thick parka, and a beanie pulled down over his ears, looking every inch the catalog model she'd dubbed him last night. Most importantly, he was holding two steaming to-go cups. "Hey."

Gemma's heart made a little leap, not in small part from the implied promise of coffee, before she realized she was standing in a hot pink sweatsuit with the word *Love* emblazoned across the boobs. Not to mention whatever strange things her hair was doing straight out of bed. "What are you doing here?"

"I thought you might need coffee. Power's off here too, isn't it?"

A gust of wind blew in a swirl of snowflakes, and she stepped back to let him into the foyer, closing the door behind him. "It is. Your house too?"

"No, my house is on solar. One thing the old owner did right. Batteries." He handed her one of the cups and bent to kiss her cheek, which sent her heart into sudden overdrive. "Is Taylor awake?"

"Define awake."

Stephen grinned and held up the other cup. "I see her every third period. I well know the difference between caffeinated Taylor and *un*caffeinated Taylor."

"In that case, thanks from both of us." She took the other cup. "That was thoughtful of you."

Stephen smiled a little sheepishly. "I had ulterior motives."

"Oh?"

"We're opening up the high school as a shelter since we still have power over there. The market and the cafe have donated a bunch of breakfast supplies and we're firing up the portable griddles we use for football games."

Gemma's lips twitched. "But you need help cooking?"

"Yeah. Mallory is already getting started, but we could use some extra hands." He shrugged a little bashfully. "And I wanted to see you before you left."

"Well, good news then. My flight out was delayed, and so was Liv's flight in."

"That's too bad," he said, but neither his voice nor his face looked very sorry. An undeniable warmth began to bloom in her middle. "Do you want me to take you and Taylor over? I'll wait."

"Trust me, they'll send out a search party for you if you wait. We'll be fine. I know I've been away from Colorado for a long time, but I think I remember how to drive in snow." She smiled to soften her words. "I promise, I'll come help as soon as I can."

"Thanks, Gem." He smiled warmly at her, then let himself out the door. "Sorry again about your flight."

"No, you're not."

"No, I'm not," he agreed with a wink.

"Good*bye*," she said and she nudged the door shut with her foot. But she was smiling.

She climbed the stairs and returned to the kitchen, to find Taylor grinning at her. "Mr. Osborne and Gemma, sitting in a tree—"

"Zip it," she said with a mock-angry glare, but she passed her the coffee.

Taylor took a sip and sighed in relief. "Oh sweet caffeinated nectar of the gods . . ."

"You're weird, do you know that?"

"All I know is it's a beautiful thing to have my English teacher in love with my aunt. Maybe I'll actually pass that class after all."

"Or maybe you'll actually start doing your homework now that you don't have to maintain the teacher-crush fiction." Gemma fixed her with a stern look and only received a look of wide-eyed innocence in return. "Anyway, get dressed. We're going to go be of service to the community."

Taylor hopped off the stool and headed back to her room, coffee cup in one hand and tea mug in the other. The girl really did love her hot beverages. "Now I know it's love. From what I hear, you wouldn't spit in the town's direction if it were on fire."

Gemma stared after her, not sure which she was more taken aback by—the fact that Taylor knew such an old-timey saying or the fact that Gemma's disdain for Haven Ridge was so well known.

Well, why wouldn't it be? You've made it clear that you turned your back on the place when it turned its back on you. Only a death of a loved one's loved one could get you here, and then only for the weekend.

But even now, she couldn't believe that it hadn't been justified. For heaven's sake, she and her mom had practically been run out of town. Rumors that her mother was mentally unstable and drove her father away; hints that Gemma had inherited that same instability. And worst of all, whispers that Stephen's parents were pressuring him to break up with her because they didn't want mentally ill grandchildren. That didn't even include the suggestion that her mom was having an affair with any number of single or divorced men in town. Probably started by her dad and without a single shred of truth. Just because she'd made her peace with Stephen—more than her peace with Stephen—didn't mean she'd changed her mind about the town.

Thinking about now through the lens of four years in Boulder and eleven in Los Angeles, it seemed ridiculous that the opinions of a handful of small-town folk could have made such an impact. But these were people who had known her her entire life. People who had invited her mom for coffee, whose kids she had babysat. People who turned out to be so concerned with their own images and reputations that they couldn't stretch a hand out to a woman and teenager who were broken and suffering. They'd prized self-sufficiency so much that the idea anyone might need help was seen as a personal affront.

They would never have set up a shelter at the high school for those who had lost power. Maybe that small fact showed that the town was changing, ever so imperceptibly. And maybe it made sense that of all people, Gemma was here to witness it.

CHAPTER TWENTY-FOUR

GEMMA AND TAYLOR made it out of the house in record time—if record time meant thirty minutes of Taylor second-guessing her wardrobe choices and Gemma debating whether putting on makeup was overkill. In the end, Taylor went with her first choice and Gemma split the difference with tinted moisturizer and a swipe of mascara. She was not spiffing herself up for the townspeople, because that would be silly. But if she wasn't, that meant she was trying to look good for Stephen, which was just as unsettling.

Despite her insistence that she hadn't forgotten her snow-driving skills, she still white-knuckled it back to the highway, bracing herself for the heart-stopping, gut-dropping moment where the tires spun and the car slid. But Liv's SUV had four-wheel drive and there was barely an inch of accumulation on the road.

Taylor slid her an amused look. "You okay, Aunt Gem?"

"I'm fine. It's just been a while." Gemma fell quiet for a second. "Kind of weird about the snowstorm, though."

"Yeah, but stuff like that happens here."

Gemma glanced at her before she snapped her eyes back to the road. "Surprise snowstorms in Colorado?"

"In Haven Ridge."

"Not this again. I think three people have made some sort of comment about the town wanting me back."

"I don't know about the town. I think it's probably God, but pretty much everyone has a theory." Taylor grinned. "Mr. Kozlowski thinks it's aliens."

Gemma laughed. Mr. Kozlowski was legendary for having called in UFO sightings since the eighties, so much that he'd been featured on one of those cable shows. But that still didn't explain what the heck Taylor was talking about. When she said as much, the girl shrugged.

"I don't know. You should ask Mallory. She wrote this whole article about the town before she moved here, how the founder was this young widow who started it for people who needed a safe home or were running away from things. Mallory was only supposed to be in Haven Ridge for like a weekend and she never left."

"Taylor, I'm pretty sure you just described a horror movie."

Taylor laughed. "I'm just saying. The last time we asked you to come stay, you said something like 'when the mother ship lands on Mr. Kozlowski's driveway.' And now, you're going to cook for the whole town with your estranged high school boyfriend, thanks to a totally unforecasted snowstorm. Haven Ridge strikes again."

Gemma just shook her head as she turned off the highway toward the high school. That was ridiculous. She'd lived here all her life and she'd never heard anything of the sort. If Haven Ridge wanted her to be here so badly, why hadn't it intervened before she'd been driven off by the entire town with their gossip and unkindness?

She could imagine what Taylor and Mallory would say—that this was a way to make up for that. And she could admit that with the sole exception of Chelsea and Doug, the town wasn't what she remembered. Maybe all those people had grown up or moved out or just realized that she wasn't important enough to deserve their efforts to be mean. And that didn't mean that they were good people, just that they weren't directing the unkindness toward her.

They had had fun during Capture the Flag yesterday, though. And almost every single person who had come by her booth had offered congratulations on her success, complimented her baking, and told her how happy they were to see her back. She'd been so shocked that she'd barely been able to stutter out a proper response.

When they finally pulled into the school parking lot, which had been cleared of its shade shelters and equipment and dusted in a blanket of white, she was surprised to see a couple dozen cars parked as near the gym as they could get. Looked like the outage was pretty widespread if this many families had come to the shelter in a town that prized independence and self-sufficiency. For every one here, there were probably four more hunkered down with generators and wood-burning stoves and heavy blankets.

Snow swirled around them as Gemma and Taylor moved across the parking lot to the bank of glass doors that fronted the gym. She didn't know what she expected when she walked in, but it was not the festival atmosphere that greeted them.

Clusters of people with blankets and sleeping bags dotted the perimeter of the polished gym floor, while over-excited children ran circles in impromptu games of tag. The big projection screen had been lowered in front of one of the basketball hoops and was currently showing a Disney movie to a group of kids and a few parents. On the opposite side, Stephen presided over a long row of tables holding portable griddles and waffle irons, capped off with a big outdoor grill/griddle upon which Mallory was currently frying a wide array of breakfast meats.

"Gemma!" Stephen called, his expression brightening. "I'm so glad you're here. Can you take over the waffle station?"

"I think I can manage that." She exchanged a smile with Mallory and then slipped behind the table, which had six mismatched waffle makers preheating. Beside a sports cooler beneath the table was a crate holding several large boxes of waffle mix and an assortment of measuring cups.

Stephen looked at Taylor. "Can I put you in charge of the coffee?"

Taylor grinned. "Absolutely." She made a beeline to the commercial coffee maker at the opposite end, probably purloined from the high school's staff room.

Gemma found a large bowl in a second crate beneath the table and measured out a quadruple batch of waffle mix, then the appropriate amount of water from the sports cooler. She was vaguely aware that a line was starting to form a few feet in front of them, no doubt drawn by the tempting smell of bacon and sausage.

"Thanks for coming, Gemma," Stephen murmured over her shoulder as he passed. "I really appreciate it."

His breath stirred the little hairs that had escaped from her clip and she gave an involuntary shiver. "I'm not sure I'm doing anything that no one else could do, but you're welcome." She studiously kept her gaze on her batter, not wanting to see whatever she might read in his expression, but she still felt the slightest sense of regret when he moved away.

He'd disappeared from the gym when she looked up from pouring the batter into the waffle irons, but a few minutes later, he returned leading a group of men who were rolling folding cafeteria tables and stacks of chairs in front of them. Quickly, they got them all set up in the center of the space, a convenient buffer between the rambunctious children and the hot cooking surfaces, leading a gradual migration of the townsfolk from the outer edges of the gym to the tables.

Gemma smiled. If she hadn't known better, she'd think that Stephen had never left Haven Ridge. First organizing the carnival, and now it seemed, leading the charge with the shelter for the power outage.

When they'd finally built up enough food to give them a head start on the cooking, Stephen went to the sound booth and turned on the microphone with a hair-raising squeal.

"Sorry, sorry," he said, his deep voice bouncing off the gym walls. "You can begin lining up for food now! Parents, please accompany your small children."

Gemma kept making waffles as the hungry line filed past, spearing them out of a foil tray with their plastic forks. Some of them met her eye and smiled, others shuffled through uncomfortably, darting glances at her—a sure sign that they knew exactly who she was and probably had reason to be ashamed of themselves. But she still fixed the smile on her face, nodded to people as they went past, pretended as if she had no reason to feel anything besides one hundred percent at home.

And then she looked up, straight into the unmistakable face of Amber Keyes. The girl who had helped Stephen break her sixteen-year-old heart.

"Hey Gemma," she said tentatively, pausing in front of the table.

"Amber. How are you?"

Amber gave her a quick, shy smile. "I'm okay, thanks. Would be better if I didn't have to drag a toddler and an infant out of our freezing apartment this morning, but this is all really nice. Thanks for helping out."

Gemma blinked. "Sure. It's my pleasure. I didn't know you had kids. You're married?"

Amber cleared her throat. "Uh, not anymore. But that's okay. We're doing okay."

Something in Amber's tone made Gemma think that she was anything but okay, but she didn't press. Somehow she'd always expected to run into her and feel the same antipathy she had in high school, but now the only thing she felt was mild curiosity. Before she could say anything else, Amber continued.

"Listen, Gemma, I've wanted to say something to you for . . . years, really. I just wanted you to know that I'm really sorry about high school. I didn't mean to . . . you know, steal Stephen." She winced at the impression of teen angst in her word choice. "And for all the rumors. I didn't start them or anything, but I definitely spread them. And that was wrong." She threw her a sheepish smile. "Quite frankly, I feel like I should apologize for all of high school. I was a pretty horrible person. Life wasn't great for me, but that's no excuse."

Gemma looked at her for a long moment, then dipped her head. "Thank you. I appreciate the apology. I think we can let high school stay in the past, don't you?"

Amber almost slumped in relief, her face slackening. "Yeah, I would really like that."

"Waffles?"

Amber laughed and speared a stack. "Yes, please."

Amber moved on and Gemma greeted the next person in line—an older couple she didn't recognize—but when she looked back down the line, she saw Mallory smiling at her. Reluctantly, she smiled and shook her head. Whatever the other woman might think, there was no magic to this, just people who had finally grown up enough to regret their bad teenage impulses.

And yet she felt her own heart lift just the slightest bit. In all her years in Haven Ridge, she'd seen people help each other out of necessity, but there had never been this . . . lightness about it. This sense of community. Like everyone was glad to be here, appreciative of the help, ready to pitch in where necessary.

Over in one corner, a grandmotherly-looking woman was reading a picture book to a group of rapt toddlers. A teenage boy about Taylor's age—actually, from the description it could be Drummer Dylan, which would explain her niece's wardrobe angst—was leading a group of preteens in some card battle game. A woman bouncing a baby in her lap was presiding over a board game on one of the cafeteria tables.

If she didn't know better, she would wonder if she was even in Haven Ridge.

When the line had dwindled and the griddle had been shut off, Mallory wandered over to stand next to Gemma. "Quite a sight, isn't it?"

"Yeah. I wouldn't have believed it if I hadn't seen it."

"People can change," she observed quietly. "Sometimes they just need a catalyst. One person showing kindness can be contagious."

Gemma threw her a look. "From what I heard, you were the butterfly whose wings caused a hurricane."

Mallory laughed, looking delighted at the description. "Not a hurricane. Maybe just a small thunderstorm.

Sometimes people need to be jolted out of their apathy. Realize that when they think they have nothing, they still have each other."

"Okay, Hallmark, I'll remember that."

Mallory winked. "I wish you would." Her gaze traveled to the end of the tables, where Stephen was stacking dirty mixing bowls and utensils. "Looks like he could use a little help. Do you mind?"

As transparent as the prompt was, Gemma gathered her own dirty bowls and trays and followed Stephen out of the gym.

CHAPTER TWENTY-FIVE

STEPHEN HAD A HEAD START, but before Gemma got more than a few feet into the long corridor, he called back, "You know it's rude to follow someone, right?"

"I'm not following you," she shot back. "I just happen to be going in the same direction as you."

Stephen slowed his stride and smiled at her over his shoulder. "Thanks for helping this morning. You know, only the west side of town is without power, but that also happens to be all the apartments and multi-family units. The people who are least likely to have emergency supplies or someone they can go stay with. It gets cold in those old buildings pretty fast."

Gemma hadn't thought about it, but she should have guessed. The majority of the people who had come to the school today were young families with small children or older people by themselves. It was conspicuous, though, how few others had showed up to help. The mayor, for example. Wouldn't this be the sort of thing for which it was his duty to make an appearance? Even if just for the optics, to be seen to care about the town?

Then again, why would he care about being seen as long as he still has all the power? He probably thinks his position exempts *him from having to help out.*

"Well, I can't say that I was happy to drive in snow again, but I'm glad I could be here."

Stephen sent her a searching look. "Not quite the place you remember, is it?"

She avoided his eyes, not sure what he would read there. "It was . . . unexpected," she admitted. "Amber Keyes apologized to me."

Stephen's eyebrows rose. "Really? I mean, it doesn't surprise me that she's sorry, just that she got up the nerve to apologize."

"What do you mean? Amber always was the brashest person we knew. Besides Chelsea, that is."

"She's had a rough time of it the past few years, too."

Stephen didn't elaborate, but Gemma could guess it had something to do with two young children and no husband. She didn't pry, though. If Stephen hadn't volunteered the information, he probably wouldn't tell her if she asked. He'd always been like that—he would take a secret to the grave. It was one of the things she had loved about him, even when it frustrated her because he withheld things that she thought she had a right to know . . . like what his parents were saying about her when she wasn't around. He couldn't stand the idea of hurting anyone unnecessarily.

He turned toward a set of double doors, one of which was propped open, and led her into the cafeteria. She followed him behind the lunch counter into the small kitchen, marveling at how small it looked. Filled with kids—even the mere hundred and ten of them across all four grades when she'd been here—it had always seemed so cavernous and intimidating. Now, it just looked like a small institutional space at a slightly faded high school.

Stephen went to the dishwashing sink and piled his dishes in, then gestured for her to add hers. He turned on the water and grabbed a scrubber and bottle of soap and set to work on the dirty dishes. He didn't make any indication that he wanted help, so she just leaned against the stainless-steel counter beside the sink and watched him work.

He focused on scrubbing, his ridiculously handsome face creased in concentration. She watched the muscles flex beneath his sweater, once more trying to reconcile the boy she'd known with the man beside her, a strange overlay of observation and memory. Just before the silence began to feel awkward, he asked, "Any closer to knowing what you're going to tell your boss when you get home?"

"No," she said. "If anything, I'm more confused than before."

He didn't look at her, just kept scrubbing, but she saw the sudden tension in his body. "Oh? Why is that?"

"Because of you," she said.

He shut off the water and dried his hands on a towel, but he didn't turn to her immediately. When he did, she almost couldn't bear to see the hope written on his face. "Why do you say that?"

"You know why."

He swallowed. "Tell me."

Gemma's heart jolted at the sudden rush of adrenaline through her body. Her voice came out in a ragged whisper. "Because I've never forgotten you. Because some part of me never stopped loving you, even when it was stupid and ill-advised. I mean, who stays in love with their high school sweetheart into their thirties, for heaven's sake?"

"I do," he said simply, and it felt like the floor had dropped out beneath her. It was one thing to hint about it, to think it, to hope for it, but another when it was laid out that baldly in front of them. She reached for the counter for support but found his hand instead.

He drew her close to him, his hands settling on her waist. "So what I want to know is, what's so confusing about that?"

She shook her head, unable to think clearly when he was looking at her with that focused intensity, like the answer was so simple that all she needed to do was accept it. "You're asking me to give up my whole life."

"I'm not asking you for anything but a chance, Gemma," he said. "If you asked me to, I would drop everything and start over. But. . .I don't think that's why this decision is hard for you."

"I would be giving up everything I've worked for until this point. For a guy."

"That's not at all true," he said, his fingers on her hips tugging her a little closer, almost as if he wasn't aware of what he was doing. "But we'll return to that in a minute. What do you love about your life? It's probably the nice house and the fancy car and the high-end office. And the shoes. It's most definitely the shoes."

Gemma rolled her eyes. "You know it's not. Those are all. . .perks. Ways of making all the drawbacks worthwhile."

"So if it's not the glamorous LA lifestyle—" his lips twitched at the words—"what is it that you love?"

She closed her eyes, forcing herself to really consider the question. "That moment when my clients realize there's a way out. That even though things are terrible right now, they don't have to stay that way. They have options. They have the right to hope for a future where they're safe and loved."

When she opened her eyes, he was smiling at her. "Those people aren't just in LA, Gemma. They're here too. You've met two of them this week alone. I know Haven Ridge isn't perfect . . . it never has been . . . but some of us want to make it better. Wouldn't you have wanted your mom to have someone like you?"

It made so much sense when he put it that way. Sounded so right. "But what if I move back and I hate it? What if we . . . don't work out? We barely know each other anymore. It sounds so romantic to think about getting back with your first love, but in reality . . . what if we don't fit? Then I've torched my entire life for no reason."

Stephen laughed. "And you say I'm the dramatic one. Gemma, moving back to Haven Ridge doesn't make you a different person. You're intelligent and bold and determined. So what if it doesn't work out? What if you decide you hate living here? So you move. You start over somewhere else. But if you only make decisions out of fear instead of hope . . . how are you any different from the people you're trying to help?"

She stared up at him in wonder, though she shouldn't be surprised. He'd always been wise beyond his years, but the way he spoke now reached into the heart of everything she hadn't realized she feared, everything she'd been running away from. She had built her life like it was a castle, with high walls and a moat to buffer her from the possibility of heartbreak, but it had kept out all the good things, too. No one had ever been able to breach it, until now.

No, that wasn't true either. He'd walked right in because he had the key.

And yet . . . "What if we work out, but the town doesn't?"

"Then we make the next decision together. Gemma, a town is only as good as the people in it. And I don't want Haven Ridge if I can't have you."

She stared up at him wonderingly. How could they now be having these big discussions—about life changes, about each other? She'd forced herself to put him soundly behind her a long time ago. She'd even dated, though nothing had ever stuck longer than a couple of months.

And maybe not because she'd been pining over someone lost to her, but because she was waiting for someone who made her feel the way Stephen always had, even at the tender age of sixteen. Not just the butterflies, the constant yearning to be near him, the irresistible desire to touch him. But the certainty he always made her feel, that she was exactly where she was supposed to be, with someone who would love her no matter how awful the rest of the world got. Even his betrayal hadn't wiped that away. Once you knew that sort of love existed, you could never settle for anything less.

And yet it had proved so nearly impossible to find again that she'd practically given up.

She realized she was still holding his gaze, frozen by the unmistakable conviction in his hazel eyes. She stopped resisting and let her eyes roam over his face, down the strong shoulders and taut body. She could still remember how he felt against her yesterday, the way they just seemed to mesh without effort, fitting like puzzle pieces. To say he'd grown into a beautiful man was an understatement, but it was the memory of the boy she'd loved, still lurking beneath the surface, that drew her in. That made her wonder if things hadn't changed all that much after all.

It felt like the most natural thing in the world when he took a step forward and brushed his fingertips along her cheek, pausing to tuck an errant strand of hair behind her ear before he lowered his mouth to hers. It was just the lightest touch, but it woke something in her that she'd despaired of ever feeling again.

Every brush of his mouth, every taste of his lips inflamed her senses, setting her nerve endings alight, his patience as arousing as it was infuriating, leaving her wanting ever more of him. Longing for him to deepen the kiss, to crush her to him. Somewhere in the back of her mind, she knew that was by design, but she couldn't bring herself to resent how skillfully he played her when she was wrapped in his scent, intoxicated by his taste. She sighed in surrender against his mouth, felt rather than heard his answering groan as he pressed her closer and the kiss grew ever more urgent.

"Can't leave you two alone for a moment, can I?" came an amused female voice from the door. Mallory.

Gemma snapped back to herself, heat rushing to her cheeks as she realized that once again she'd caught them in a passionate clinch in a semi-public place. But Stephen held her fast against him, still looking into her eyes even as he spoke to Mallory in a shockingly calm voice. "Give us a minute, will you?"

"Sure," Mallory said, amusement tracing her voice. "But someone's looking for Gemma, and it sounds important."

Gemma cleared her throat, unable to tear her gaze away from Stephen's. "I'll be right out."

As soon as Mallory's footsteps disappeared from the kitchen, Stephen bent and kissed her again, but it was disappointingly brief.

"I should get out there," she whispered.

"Think about what I said," he murmured, pressing a kiss to the top of her head. "Don't run away this time. Please."

Gemma swallowed hard, then nodded. She threw a look over her shoulder at the empty kitchen doorway. "I should go out before Mallory comes back and lectures us."

"She wouldn't dare. I was here when she started dating Thomas. They couldn't keep their hands off each other."

"Yeah, even so." Gemma peered at her reflection in the highly polished steel refrigerator door, trying to figure out if it looked like she'd been doing exactly what she'd been doing, and finally gave up. Who cared if anyone guessed she'd been kissing her ex-boyfriend in the kitchen? They were both adults.

Except he taught teenagers and needed to be a good example.

"How do I look? Are we going to cause a scandal?"

"Breathtaking," he said softly, causing her flush to break out once more. "But no, you just look . . . rosy."

Gemma chuckled. "Okay. Coming?"

"I'll be right behind you," he said wryly, and she let out a short, self-conscious laugh as she slipped out of the kitchen.

But her amusement faded as soon as she stepped out into the corridor outside the cafeteria, where Mallory waited with a woman. Two children and a familiar teenager sat slumped against the wall, backpacks resting in their laps.

"Chelsea?" Gemma said in surprise.

The woman turned, but it was a shrunken version of her childhood nemesis, rumpled and tearstained.

And sporting the beginning of a bruise across her jaw.

CHAPTER TWENTY-SIX

GEMMA STARED AT CHELSEA in almost uncomprehending surprise. "Hi. What are you doing here?"

As soon as the question left her mouth, she knew how stupid it was. She could make a pretty good guess about what she was doing here, considering the kids' backpacks and Chelsea's roller bag sitting against the wall behind her.

Chelsea glanced at Rebekah, almost as if she needed reassurance. "Tell her," the teenager said softly. "She'll know what to do."

Chelsea cleared her throat and stared at the ground. "I left Doug and took the kids with me. What do I . . . what do I have to do to be safe?" Her voice broke on the last word, all her fear and humiliation laced into that single syllable.

And despite the fact that Gemma had spent most of her teen years hating Chelsea with a passion, it didn't take recent experience to know that this was not the same woman who had tormented her. Without hesitation, she opened her arms and enfolded her in them.

It was all the permission Chelsea needed. She poured out a torrent of tears into Gemma's shoulder, back heaving with sobs, her fingers clutching at Gemma's for support. She rubbed her back soothingly and met Stephen's eyes over her shoulder as he came through the cafeteria doors, silently pleading for some sort of clue on how she should proceed. He just gave a helpless shrug, as taken aback as she was. Gemma had never seen Chelsea cry a single day in her life, even when she broke her ankle in gym class. She could guess what it had cost her to come to her for help.

When her tears subsided and Chelsea pulled away with an embarrassed expression, wiping her face with the back of her coat sleeve, Gemma kicked into professional mode. It didn't matter that this woman used to be an enemy or that Gemma was eleven hundred miles away from her law office. Here was a battered woman like any other, and *that* she knew how to deal with.

First things first. "Chelsea," she asked gently, "can you tell me what happened?"

Chelsea seemed to pull herself together then, glancing at the twins, who were clutching their backpacks so hard their fingers were white. They were even more scared now that they'd seen their mom fall apart. "Not here," she murmured.

Gemma looked beyond her to Rebekah. "Can you watch the kids while I talk to your aunt?"

Rebekah nodded mutely. She was being brave for all concerned, but she looked no less scared than the children.

"Stephen, will you come with us?" Gemma indicated the cafeteria's double doors behind her. Even though she wasn't licensed in the state, she was still a lawyer, and it would be helpful to have a second person as a witness if they needed to take this to court or go before a judge.

Stephen nodded and opened the door for them. Gemma ushered Chelsea to one of the remaining cafeteria tables and sat down across from her. Stephen chose the seat beside Chelsea, a subtle show of support. It made her like him just a little bit more in that moment.

"So," Gemma began softly. "Tell me what happened."

Chelsea took a shuddering breath, but she squared her shoulders and looked Gemma directly in the eye. "After you mentioned Doug had confronted you on the street, I went home to ask him about it. I wanted to believe he was going to tell me that you were lying, but I waited until the kids were already in bed, so that should tell you that I already knew it was true. I asked him if he had threatened you, and he accused me of spreading our private problems and telling lies all over town. I was afraid that he would punish Rebekah if he knew she was the one who had been talking, so I. . ." Chelsea shook her head. "It got heated and he hit me. I fell down and hit my head. Rebekah came running out and he made a move toward her. . . he only stopped because I told him that my brother would kill him if he laid a finger on her. And if you knew my brother, you'd know why that stopped Doug."

And why she hadn't said anything to her brother about how Doug treated her, Gemma thought. It wasn't unusual for women in abusive relationships to protect the abuser, especially if they thought it meant keeping their families together.

"What happened then?" she prompted gently.

"Nothing. Doug went to bed. I slept in the twins' room. He was gone this morning when I woke up."

"Do you have any idea where he is now?"

Chelsea shook her head. "No."

Which meant he could be waiting for her if she went back home. Gemma's preference was to send a Chaffee County Sheriff's deputy back with her if she needed to get anything from the house. But that was all moot if Chelsea wasn't ready to take a big step. Gemma kept her tone quiet, non-confrontational. "What do you want to do, Chelsea? Do you want to leave him?"

Chelsea swallowed and traced a set of carved initials on the tabletop with her fingertip. "I just want . . . to be safe. To not worry about him around my children."

"Are you willing to file a police report?"

Chelsea flinched at the word police, but she nodded.

"Okay, then. Give us just a minute."

Gemma stood and gestured with her head for Stephen to join her. They moved a few steps away, out of Chelsea's earshot. "Do you know anyone at the sheriff's department?"

"No. Unfortunately not. But Benji's a judge. I can guarantee he'd sign off on a restraining order, with or without a police report."

"I thought the same thing. My experience with these little police departments hasn't been all that positive, so it would help to have a friendly deputy on our side." Gemma had been so young when she left Colorado that she hadn't had any contact with this particular one, but she knew all too well that how a department treated assault victims, especially when the abuser was a spouse, depended on the temperament of the sheriff himself—and yes, it was nearly always a man.

Stephen seemed to be thinking. "Let me go check on something, okay?"

Gemma nodded. "Call me. I'm going to take them to Liv's place right now and we'll go from there."

Stephen shook his head. "No. Wait for me. That's

the first place Doug will go when he realizes you're gone and I don't want you there alone."

She hadn't thought about that. Most of her clients— and that's how she was thinking of Chelsea now—had no idea where she lived. Another drawback of living in a small town that she'd completely forgotten. When Stephen disappeared back out into the hall, she sat down across from Chelsea again.

"Okay, this is what I think we should do."

As Gemma ran through the process from police report to restraining order to temporary housing, she could see Chelsea start to turn within herself again, no doubt realizing the enormity of the decision, the potential displacement of her children. Gemma reached across the table and grabbed Chelsea's hand, squeezing it hard until the other woman looked at her. "Chelsea, you're doing the right thing. You know this is what I do for a living, right? I help people get out of bad, dangerous marriages. And no matter how charming or kind he can be on his good days, if he hits you or controls you or makes you feel like you have no choices, it's a bad, dangerous marriage. None of this is your fault."

A flicker of something surfaced in Chelsea's brown eyes, as if it was the first time she'd considered the idea that she wasn't responsible for what was happening to her. Only now did it occur to Gemma that maybe the reason Chelsea had been so cruel to her in high school was because she was unhappy, as Gemma had been.

Almost as if she was thinking the same thing, Chelsea said in a tiny voice, "I'm really sorry, you know. About all that high school stuff. It wasn't a good time for me."

Gemma threw her a wry look. "Tell me about it."

Chelsea gave a little laugh. "I deserved that."

Gemma sighed. "Yeah, maybe. But you don't deserve *this*. I wouldn't wish it on my worst enemy, which to be fair, I always thought you were."

"I was jealous," Chelsea admitted. "You and your mom were so close, even after your dad left. My mom and I never were, and when she and your dad got together, she had even less time for me. It was like I didn't exist. And in that very logical teenage way, I figured that made it your fault."

"Yeah, I mean, why would we blame our parents for their own decisions when we could take responsibility ourselves?"

Chelsea let out a little laugh. "Right."

"Or our husbands . . ."

Chelsea straightened a little then. "Yeah. You're right."

That bit of spine sparked hope in Gemma. "You're going to be okay, Chelsea. We're going to help you, Stephen and I."

"That's nice to say, Gemma, but you're going home."

"Not immediately. My flight's been delayed."

"Why would you do that for me? After how awful I was to you in high school?"

"Because it's what I do. And after a while it starts to feel silly to hold what someone did when they were sixteen against them for the rest of their lives."

Gemma's phone buzzed in her pocket, and she pulled it out. Message from Liv: **Airport is apparently open but my flight from Denver got canceled. Can't get rebooked until tomorrow. Sending new itinerary.**

Gemma should feel stressed over the fact that Liv wasn't coming home, which meant she too would have to change her flight, but all she felt was relief. She had to stay for Chelsea, at least help her through the process of getting her restraining order. Despite the fact that she was the last person on the planet Gemma ever thought she'd change her plans for, this was exactly the reason she'd become an attorney in the first place. If she turned her back on this woman now, what exactly was she going back to California for?

Stephen appeared in the doorway now. "Okay, it took some digging, but Thomas Rivas's uncle is a sheriff's deputy and he's on duty tonight. He's going to come by Liv's house later this evening."

"Good. I guess I should go get Taylor and we can head back to the house."

"I'll come with you. I still don't like the idea of you all being alone there."

Now Chelsea balked in a way that she hadn't even with Gemma. Sadly typical behavior for someone who had spent her adult life desperately placating her husband. "I can't ask you to do that! I don't want to cause any trouble."

"You're not causing any trouble." Stephen threw her a crooked smile. "Haven Ridge takes care of its own, remember?"

When Gemma had arrived in Haven Ridge, she would have laughed dismissively at that. But now, considering what she'd experienced in the past few days? She truly wanted to believe it.

Apparently, while Gemma had been kissing Stephen in the cafeteria kitchen, the power had gone back on throughout town, so the crowd in the gym had dwindled down to a handful of people who were helping to clean up. Stephen went and spoke to a few of the other teachers, no doubt giving them an update on where he was going and making sure they closed up properly, then rejoined their small huddled group near the door.

Gemma collected Taylor and then ushered Chelsea, Rebekah, and the twins out of the gym into the parking lot. She almost felt guilty that she was relieved to use her professional skills right now. Gemma Van Buren, Attorney at Law, had taken over again after a week's absence, and this self didn't have to think about whether she should get back with her high school boyfriend or move back to her hometown or what any of that meant for her future. At this moment, the only important thing was getting Chelsea away from the school, filing a police report, and taking the necessary steps to keep her and the kids safe.

Stephen trailed them, his presence strangely comforting, and not just because she knew that Doug would still be intimidated by the high school quarter-back. But as they crossed the parking lot to where Gemma and Chelsea were parked a few spaces away from each other, she sensed his steps falter. She cast a look over her shoulder and paused when she saw the look on his face. It was an expression she'd only seen once before, though she'd gone over it many times in her memory.

It was the one that said he'd been caught at something.

Gemma followed his glance to the blonde picking her way across the snowy parking lot, dressed in a brilliant white, fur-trimmed coat and matching snow boots, slim and pretty. She didn't look at all familiar, though given how much some of them had changed since high school, that shouldn't be much of a surprise.

But she truly didn't understand what she was seeing until the blonde closed the gap between her and Stephen, took both his hands, and stretched to kiss him full on the mouth. "Surprise!"

Gemma's heart plummeted to the asphalt beneath her feet, blood rushing in her ears, her eyes suddenly blurring from the surge of sickness that washed through her. Stephen was still standing there stiffly, his arms at his sides, but he wasn't pushing her away. Wasn't looking shocked by the greeting, like someone who had just been accosted by an acquaintance. And even though her mind was searching for a plausible explanation the whole time, in her heart she knew the truth.

Stephen had a girlfriend.

This time, she, Gemma, was the other woman.

CHAPTER TWENTY-SEVEN

IF NIKKI HAD WANTED to blow up his life, she couldn't have found a more effective way.

Stephen stared at her in frozen horror, his mind going blank as it tried to reconcile the fact that she was supposed to be in Salt Lake City with the fact that she was actually standing here before him. He couldn't even form a sentence before she took his hands and planted a possessive kiss straight on his lips.

It was the smell of her expensive perfume in the cold air that finally broke through his shock. "What are you doing here? How did you even find me?"

She pulled back, an uncertain smile on her face. "The guy at the cafe told me. I've been thinking a lot about what you said, about compromise. And . . . I didn't want to leave things the way we did, not over the phone." She studied him for a long moment. "This was not a good surprise."

"No, it's not that," he said, automatically seeking Gemma in the small group. But she'd already turned away, ushering Chelsea, the twins, and the two teens toward the waiting cars. It was too much to hope that she hadn't noticed Nikki or her greeting; besides, he could see in the tight line of her shoulders and back that she knew exactly what was going on but had chosen to focus on Chelsea at the moment.

"It's actually not a good time," he said. "A little bit of a town crisis at the moment."

"Oh." Nikki dropped her hands and followed his gaze to the group of women and children. "Okay. Well, if you give me your keys, I can wait at your place until you're done. That's okay, right? I know there's really not anyplace to stay here, so I just assumed."

"No, that's fine." He reached into his pocket, prepared to hand over the keys before he realized what he was doing. Was he really going to follow Gemma back and expect her not to have questions that he wouldn't be able to answer? As far as he had been concerned, the relationship with Nikki was over, a clean break. But looking at her now, chewing her lip with tentative hope in her eyes, it seemed she had a totally different understanding.

"You know what? Let's go there now. We do need to talk."

Nikki followed him back to his truck, thankfully parked at the opposite end of the row. He barely kept himself from looking over his shoulder to see if Gemma was watching. The damage had already been done; he didn't need to hurt Nikki's feelings by shaking her off in public. He opened the passenger door for her and waited until she climbed in before he circled around to the driver's seat. But once he was there, he didn't reach for the ignition. He didn't want to take Nikki back to his place. She didn't belong there. *Gemma* belonged there, and her presence last night had left an indelible imprint that he wasn't willing to erase with another woman.

"What's going on, Nikki?" he asked quietly.

"I'm getting the feeling you aren't happy to see me."

"I'm getting the feeling that we had two entirely different understandings of our relationship status," Stephen said gently. "We broke up."

"Yeah, but. . . we both know that was just logistics." She reached for him, her cold hand wrapping around his forearm. "I came here to ask you what you thought about me taking a job in Colorado Springs."

He blinked at her. "What?"

"I thought about what you said. You were right, about one of us needing to compromise. I know you were never happy in Salt Lake City, and I know you love what you do here, even if it makes you a little crazy." She threw him a wry look. "And as little as I can understand it, I would never ask you to change. So I started looking. There's a small tech startup about two hours from here that needs a CFO. It's a cut in pay, but the benefits are good, and cost of living is less here than in Salt Lake. I have an interview with them on Wednesday. I thought if it worked out, I could live down there during the week and come up here on the weekends."

"But you love your job. Wasn't that part of the issue?"

Her mouth twisted. "I *loved* my job, past tense. They hired a CFO."

Now he understood. That should have been Nikki's job; they'd been dangling it in front of her for years, all but promising her they'd move her into the position when the old CFO retired. No wonder she was keen to make a big change.

Stephen rubbed his forehead wearily. He hardly knew what to say. A week ago, he would have jumped at this prospect. Not ideal, maybe, but he and Nikki had never been ideal. He'd long since given up on ideal.

But now that he'd found Gemma again, now that he knew his feelings hadn't gone away, maybe never would, he regretted implying that distance was the problem, when the real barrier had been him.

"Nikki," he began slowly, "I'm so sorry—"

"Don't." She sat back against the seat and let out a long, quiet sigh. "It's her, isn't it? Was that her? The girl?"

"What do you mean? What girl?" Stephen knew exactly what she meant, but not how she knew it.

"The girl who broke your heart. The woman you've been hung up on all this time." She threw him a pitying look. "I'm not stupid, Stephen. I've always known we're not soul mates or whatever romantic nonsense you've held onto. But I thought maybe it would be enough. If maybe I was the one to compromise . . ." She shook her head, and he saw the sheen of tears glimmer in her eyes as she stared straight through the windshield of his truck. "I made a mistake. I'm sorry. I didn't mean to come here and . . . mess things up for you."

"You didn't," he said, even though that's exactly what she had done. He couldn't blame her for it, though. He'd been so worried about hurting her feelings that he hadn't been honest. "I'm sorry if I led you to believe it was only a matter of geography. Maybe I even believed it myself."

"Until you realized that you really were still in love with her," she said flatly.

He couldn't even deny it, however little he wanted to hurt her. "Yes."

"Well, then," Nikki said stiffly, hands folded in her lap, "I guess I should be going then. I'll find somewhere else to stay."

"I'm so sorry. I wish . . . I wish things were different."

"Yeah, me too." She leaned over and kissed his cheek. "I hope you're happy. Both of you together, I guess."

That's a long shot now, he thought, but he'd never say

the words aloud. "Thanks. I hope you're happy with whatever's next."

"Right." She threw him a twist of a smile. "Maybe I'll stick around and do that interview anyway. Who knows? Maybe a change of scenery would do me some good. It did for you."

She pulled the door lever and hopped out of the truck, then slammed the door shut and trudged toward the rental SUV waiting a few spaces away. He watched her as she climbed in, put the car in gear, and pulled away. Never once did she look in his direction.

He slumped back against the seat and dug his hands into his hair. He'd somehow screwed this up. Again. He'd hurt Nikki in an attempt to spare her feelings, which had led to hurting Gemma a second time through the misunderstanding. The situation looked so bad from the outside. Given their history, he'd be lucky if she even let him explain.

But he still had to try.

* * *

Gemma drove back to Liv's property on autopilot, even though it hurt to breathe, as if the physical shards of her broken heart were ripping through her lungs. Every time she focused her mind on the road, it wandered back to the look of guilt on Stephen's face, the familiar way the woman had greeted him. And every time, the recollection gutted her so thoroughly that she was surprised not to find her sweater awash in blood when she looked down. It wasn't just the death of whatever they'd been rebuilding in the past week. It was the death of hope. The only man she'd ever loved had now betrayed her twice.

How would she ever come back from that?

The only saving grace was that Chelsea had missed the exchange while refereeing an argument between the six-year-old twins. Even with her current sympathy for the woman, Gemma didn't think she could bear for her old nemesis to be the sole witness to her heartbreak.

No, not sole witness. When Gemma turned farther, she realized Taylor was staring at her teacher and his girlfriend, shock on her face. She shifted her stricken gaze to her aunt, and all Gemma could do was give a quick shake of her head. Not now. Not when there were more important things at stake than her own happiness.

Gemma had seized control and decided that Taylor and Rebekah would join her in the SUV while Chelsea drove the twins to Liv's house in her minivan. The recollection that they'd chosen Liv's place for its gates as much as its convenience finally snapped her out of her spiraling thoughts about Stephen. She wasn't sure if there was a real reason to believe that Doug was dangerous to anyone but his wife, but the fury in the mayor's face when he had confronted Gemma on the street made her wonder if he wasn't one of those people who confined his violence to his family.

In the ten minutes it took to navigate the snowy road from the high school to Liv's property, it seemed that all hell had broken loose. When Chelsea pulled up, both twins were sobbing in their booster seats in the back of Chelsea's minivan, and she looked like she was about on the verge of collapse. Taylor and Rebekah swooped in without being asked, each scooping up a tearful six-year-old and bouncing them across the yard to the garage apartment's entry until they got watery smiles in return.

"I'm ruining their lives," Chelsea whispered, watching the teens take Cody and Etta upstairs. "They're going to grow up without a father now."

"Better they live with a mother who knows her own worth than learn to give and take abuse when they grow up and get married," Gemma said, her own pain making her voice harsh. She softened at the woman's startled expression—until now Chelsea obviously hadn't put words to her own situation—and slid an arm around her shoulders. "Come on. Let's go in and find a distraction for them. I promise you, they'll be okay. Kids are a lot more resilient than we give them credit for."

And still, as she led her former nemesis into her borrowed digs, Gemma couldn't help but feel a twinge of vicarious heartache for the twins. Yes, it was best for Chelsea to separate from her husband and get them out of the house—she knew all too well how children internalized the unrest in their homes—but she also knew how it felt to one day have a father and the next day not. And they were young enough that they might actually blame their mother for it. They had a long road of healing—and probably therapy—ahead of them if everyone was going to come out of this relatively unscathed.

Upstairs, Gemma did the thing she always did in response to broken hearts, whether hers or someone else's—she pulled out the baking ingredients. "It's snowing right now," she said to the kids in a low, excited voice, "so what do you think about baking snowballs?"

Etta eyed her with suspicion. Clearly she was the sassy one out of the twins. "How can you bake snowballs? They'd melt."

"Because these are special snowballs, my own secret, and I'm going to show you guys how to make them. But you have to promise not to tell."

Cody lit up at the hint of a secret. "We promise!"

They were really just Mexican wedding cookies, but when they were baked and dusted in powdered sugar, they looked exactly like snowballs. And if you put different sizes together, you could bake them into snowmen, which was what finally won over Etta's suspicions. Once they mixed the dough together and Gemma had the twins settled at the counter, rolling it into various-size balls, she went over to Chelsea. "Need some coffee?"

"Yes," she said gratefully. "Even better if you can make it Irish."

Gemma laughed. "If we were at my house, it would be no problem, but Liv doesn't drink."

Chelsea waved a hand. "It's fine. I probably need my wits about me anyway."

With everyone finally squared away, Gemma took out her phone and slipped downstairs to the patio to dial Liv.

"I'm so sorry," Liv said in a rush without even saying hello. "I know this has completely messed up your travel plans."

"It's fine," Gemma said. "I have to stay for an extra day anyway. Something. . .weird has happened." More than one something, but it was most important that Liv knew what was going on at her house. It would take exactly five minutes after the deputy showed up before word started flying around town.

"Weird?" Liv asked cautiously.

Gemma gave her the run-down of the day's developments. "We're at your apartment right now, waiting for the sheriff's deputy to come take her statement. The kids are making cookies. Tomorrow we're going to go to the courthouse and fill out an application for a temporary restraining order. Benji said he'd sign it."

The other end of the line got quiet. Finally, Liv said, "Wow. I'm not sure what surprises me more. That Chelsea left him or that you two are actually speaking."

"Worse," Gemma said wryly. "I legitimately hugged her."

"Now I know the world has come to an end."

"Yeah. Tell me about it. Anyway, I don't know what's going to happen afterward. We need to find Chelsea and the kids somewhere to stay—"

"You're still leaving tomorrow, right? They can stay in the apartment. It's fine. There's enough room for them, and Taylor and I will just be right in the house. The fact the property is gated is a good thing for her."

"You really don't mind that Chelsea is staying in your place?"

Liv took longer to answer this time. "You were the one who still had a problem with her, Gem. We made our peace a long time ago. Things have changed in Haven Ridge."

"Yeah, I've noticed." The crunching of tires made her look toward the gate, and she saw the gray sheriff's SUV pulling up just outside the gate. "Hey, the deputy is here. I have to go."

"Okay. Just keep me posted. And Gem, be careful."

"I will. I'll be in touch. Love you, bye." She finished in a rush, stuffed her phone in her pocket, and strode down the gravel drive toward the gate, where the sheriff's deputy was already standing behind his open car door. He was younger than Gemma expected, perhaps mid-forties, with a craggy look that suggested a lot of time in the sun and a fit build beneath his Kevlar vest. A far cry from the bored, bloated deputies that had hassled them about parking off-road when they were in high school.

"I'm Deputy Dixon. You Gemma Van Buren?"

"I am." She punched the keypad on the inside of the gate to open the door and stepped back as it swung inward. "You can park up by the house."

He climbed back in his SUV and followed her slowly up to the house. Gemma shook off the feeling of being observed, analyzed, even though the deputy probably was sizing her up. She couldn't help but do the same thing anytime she met anyone in a professional capacity, and sometimes even outside that. She stood back while he parked behind the three cars taking up the cement pad and then stepped out of his vehicle.

"Her kids are up in the apartment. I thought it might be easier to talk inside the main house?"

He gave her a nod, and she slipped into the accessory unit where Chelsea was just helping the kids slide the baking sheets into the oven.

"He's here," she murmured, and Chelsea instantly paled. "It'll be okay. He's Thomas Rivas's uncle. He's one of us."

The flicker in Chelsea's eyes drew Gemma's attention to what she'd just said; the other woman's surprise couldn't match her own. *One of us.* How long had it actually been since she owned her place in Haven Ridge?

No, she knew exactly how long it had been. She'd cut her ties the moment she got back on that bus to Phoenix, feeling foolish and heartbroken, fifteen long years ago. The only big surprise now was that in her current heartbreak, she wasn't rushing to revoke that claim once more.

"Come on," Gemma said gently. "I'll be right there. I promise. It will be okay."

Chelsea gave a nod, and she looked so vulnerable and trusting that Gemma had difficulty drawing her next breath. She knew better than to assure anyone things that weren't hers to promise. She knew all too well how many ways talking to the authorities could go wrong for an abused spouse, and it was only some long-forgotten shred of hope that Haven Ridge might be different that led her to voice the words. But now that she had told her that—worse, that Chelsea believed her—it was Gemma's responsibility to make it true.

Deputy Dixon was waiting for them outside the apartment, speaking something in a low voice into the radio when they appeared. The minute he saw them, he replaced the mic onto his shoulder and turned down the speaker on the radio on his belt. "Shall we talk inside?"

Gemma led the few steps to the main house, unlocked the front door, and then brought them into the comfortably-appointed living room. The space had a slightly musty, disused smell from being shut up the past couple of days, despite the lingering vanilla aroma from the cupcakes. She lowered herself to the sofa and patted the cushion next to her reassuringly. Chelsea sank down on the edge, tension in every line of her body.

The deputy sat gingerly on the chair across from them, looking ill at ease in the soft surroundings. But his voice was gentle when he asked, "I see your face is bruised, Mrs. Meinke. Can you tell me what happened?"

The story that unfolded in halting, tear-choked words told a story that was worse than Gemma had hoped, but ultimately not a surprise. She'd heard the tales of far too many other women with abusive spouses to not know what some men could be capable of. Chelsea outlined a story of abuse starting just after their marriage eight years ago, beginning first with Doug establishing total control, first over her and then later, the twins; ending with increasing physical violence. This last episode was because she'd dared to criticize him for going through his niece's phone—which was the way he'd learned that Gemma had sent her contact information to Rebekah—and questioned him about his confrontation of Gemma.

The whole time, Chelsea focused on the deputy, carefully not looking at her former enemy, but when Gemma stretched out her hand, palm up, Chelsea grabbed it and squeezed so tightly Gemma felt her bones crunch.

The deputy made notes in his notebook. "I think the next step, Mrs. Meinke, would be to transport you to the hospital where you can be examined and your injuries photographed—"

"No," Chelsea said immediately. "I'm not leaving my children and I'm not dragging them along."

"Chelsea," Gemma said gently, "it would help your case . . ."

But Chelsea was resolute. Deputy Dixon gave both of them a sad smile. "I'll be right back." He excused himself, his service boots thudding hollowly on the wood floor as he let himself back out the front.

Gemma turned to Chelsea and squeezed her hand. "You did so well. That wasn't easy."

"Doug is going to kill me," she whispered.

"No. He is not going to kill you. That I can promise." Another promise she couldn't reasonably keep, but for reasons she couldn't even fully understand, she felt protective toward this woman. After all, had Chelsea ever had a healthy relationship modeled for her? Her mother's desperation to find someone to provide for her and her daughter had surely been what made her latch onto a married man. That had to have had some impact. Gemma and Chelsea were connected by their own parents' bad decisions, whether they liked it or not.

Deputy Dixon knocked on the door before letting himself in again. When he returned, he was holding a Polaroid camera. He held it up as a question, and Chelsea gave a little fearful nod.

Gemma stood back while the officer photographed

the bruises on her jaw. Then Chelsea slipped off her sweater and stood shivering in a tank top while he took photos of the finger-sized bruises up and down both arms. Gemma's stomach twisted while she choked back her rising anger. When the other woman looked to her for support, she struggled to give her a reassuring nod.

While Chelsea pulled her sweater back over her head, Gemma asked, "So what happens now?"

"I'll write up a report. And then we will go to her residence and arrest her husband."

Chelsea went still. "What? No. I just intended to get a restraining order—"

"And you still should," the deputy said gently. "But Colorado is a mandatory arrest state. If there's evidence of domestic violence or cause to believe there will be, we're required to arrest the aggressor. He'll be arraigned within twenty-four hours and most likely released on his own recognizance or a low bail, so you'll definitely need the TRO in order to prevent him from returning to the family home."

Chelsea sank onto the sofa, no doubt finally realizing the enormity of the step she had taken. Gemma went to her side and put an arm around her. No matter how badly she had been treated, it was no doubt still difficult to know she was the one responsible for her husband being arrested. Even harder when she knew how the Haven Ridge rumor mill worked; by the end of the day, it would be all over town.

Good, Gemma thought viciously. *He's the mayor of Haven Ridge. If he can't be held accountable for his actions, who can?*

And for a tiny second, she felt a wave of approval from . . . somewhere.

The officer collected his Polaroid equipment and the photos and walked with them to the front door of the house. But they'd barely breached the porch when the sound of male shouting drifted on the wind.

"That's Stephen," Gemma said in surprise, while at the same time Chelsea whispered, "Doug's here."

The officer said something into his radio that Gemma didn't catch, then broke into a jog toward the sound of the argument around the corner. She and Chelsea followed not far behind, then stopped short.

Stephen and Doug were facing off in front of the apartment door, Stephen looking furious but resolute while Doug screamed at him, spittle flying with every word like a rabid dog.

"You are not taking the children," Stephen said firmly. "Not when you're like this."

And then, before the deputy could intervene, Doug took a swing at Stephen.

Gemma gasped, but Stephen seemed ready for it, sidestepping the punch easily. He twisted Doug's outstretched arm upwards and dumped the angry man face first into the gravel.

Deputy Dixon was on the mayor in seconds, cuffing his other arm to the one Stephen still held immobile. He glanced at Stephen, who backed off immediately, looking more surprised than angry. Then the deputy hauled Doug to his feet and began to read him his rights. "Doug Meinke, you're under arrest—"

"For what?" Doug screamed, fighting the cuffs. "I didn't touch him."

"For assaulting your wife," Dixon said tightly, and from all the loathing in his voice, Gemma was suddenly reassured. Mayor or not, Doug wasn't getting out of this. There were witnesses to Chelsea's injuries, and even if there weren't, they'd just seen him assault Stephen.

Dixon continued with the Miranda warning and walked him toward the cruiser just as another patrol vehicle pulled up beyond the gate in a blaze of lights and sirens—the deputy had called for backup. Gemma slid an arm around Chelsea while she watched, wet-eyed and shocked as her husband was pushed into the back seat of the vehicle. He caught his wife's eye and spewed a barrage of obscenities at her.

Gemma expected Chelsea to shrink, but instead, some unexpected steel filled her. She drew herself up, marched over to the open door, and said with perfect equanimity, "If you plead guilty, I might consider letting you see your kids someday. Think about that tonight in your cell." And then she turned her back and walked past Gemma and Stephen through the apartment door, no doubt up to her children.

Gemma held onto the remnants of her attorney persona as Stephen approached her. "You okay?"

"I should be asking you that."

"I'm fine." He threw her a rueful smile. "The day Doug Meinke gets the drop on me is the day I check myself into the retirement home."

It was a comment begging for a laugh, but Gemma couldn't summon one even if she'd tried. Instead, she clutched her arms around herself, watching the sheriff slowly drive off of Liv's property. When at last the crunch of the tires on gravel had faded into the distance, he stepped in front of her so she had no choice but to look at him.

Instantly, she wished she hadn't. He looked just as heartsick as she felt, and the last thing she wanted to do was feel any kind of sympathy toward him.

But still, she let him take her hand. "Gemma, we need to talk. Let me explain."

"Was that or wasn't that your girlfriend?" She stared hard into his face, even as she willed him to prove her wrong, to say it had all been a big misunderstanding.

But he dropped his gaze. "Used to be. We broke up earlier this week. Or, I thought we had."

She wanted to believe him. She wanted to trust him to tell her the truth. But all she could think of was the familiar way that beautiful woman had walked up to him and kissed him, like she still had the right to do so. That wasn't the sign of a clean break. That wasn't the sign of someone who had grown up and learned from his past mistakes.

She pulled her hand from his. "The time to settle all this was *before* you told me you loved me." And she turned on her heel and followed Chelsea into the apartment.

CHAPTER TWENTY-EIGHT

GEMMA STOOD ON THE OTHER SIDE of the door, silent tears streaming down her face. Everything she'd just said to Stephen was true. She believed it down to her very soul. So why was there something crumpled in her chest where her heart should be?

But she didn't need anyone to answer that question for her. Against her better judgment, she'd fallen for him again. She'd let that kernel of love that had never died, nurtured by memory, grow into something that had no chance of survival. What did she always tell her clients? *When someone shows you who they are, believe them.* Just because he could be sweet and kind and his kisses set her ablaze like a shooting star didn't mean that he was the man for her or even a good person.

It just meant that she needed to finally put the past in the past.

Gemma steeled herself and dragged her sleeve across her face, smearing mascara on her jacket. If she looked even a fraction as bad as she felt, there was no way she could keep up the charade that everything was okay. But Chelsea was going through a real crisis, ending an abusive marriage, and she needed Gemma. Not Haven Ridge Gemma with her cutesy conversation hearts cookies and her unabated crush on the high school quarterback, but attorney Gemma, who could navigate the legal minefield of restraining orders and separations.

She could break down on her flight home tomorrow. Right now, she had work to do.

Gemma made a good enough show of it that it escaped the younger children, but the teens and Chelsea kept darting glances at her throughout the evening, as if they sensed not all was well. They'd decided that Chelsea and the twins would take the apartment, while Gemma and the teens went back to the main house. Gemma moved her things into Liv's room while Taylor took Rebekah's backpack and her own possessions back to her space. The twins, of course, thought it was a big adventure and spent a fair amount of time bouncing on the bed, helped along by the large quantity of snowball cookies they had consumed while the adults had been otherwise occupied. Taylor and Rebekah may or may not have eaten as many as the kids, judging from how few were left when Gemma went back upstairs.

Rebekah and Taylor went out for pizza *again*— killing Gemma's last possible chance to feed her niece something healthy—and Gemma sat down on the apartment sofa with Chelsea, who was still looking shell-shocked.

"I can't believe they arrested him," she whispered, caught between relief and horror. "What's going to happen now?"

"He'll be arraigned in the morning," Gemma said, though she was just guessing—her actual knowledge of the local sheriff's department was limited to what Deputy Dixon had told them. "We'll go to the courthouse first thing and fill out a request for a temporary restraining order, which will in all likelihood apply to the three of you, your kids' school, and your house. Benji Balden said he'd grant it. As soon as Doug is served, you can go home. And then you need to get a lawyer to help you through the process of figuring out a permanent restraining order, supervised visitation for the twins, and your divorce."

Chelsea seemed to cave in on herself. "Divorce."

"I assume that's where we're headed," Gemma said delicately. "You realize how unlikely it is that things will change for the better, right?"

"Considering he's been like this our whole marriage," Chelsea whispered, "then yes." She looked to Gemma suddenly. "Why can't you be my lawyer?"

"For one thing, I don't live here, and for another, I'm not licensed to practice in Colorado. But I can get you some recommendations for someone good. And Chelsea . . . you need to prepare yourself for a fight. I'm almost certain it will get nasty. You'll want the best attorney you can afford."

Chelsea just nodded, still clearly stunned. If Gemma had the time to walk her through the process, she wouldn't dump all this on her at the same time. But she'd be heading straight to the airport from the courthouse tomorrow. She didn't have time to do this easily and gently. Chelsea needed to know what she was up against, the importance of having someone who would fight as hard for her as her husband was going to fight against. Gemma knew all too well what happened when a woman was too passive in this process. Had her mother actually had a decent attorney, they might never have had to leave Haven Ridge.

Chelsea was lost in thought, so Gemma rose, placing a hand briefly on the other woman's shoulder as she passed, and headed back into the kitchen to clean up the leftover baking mess. As she scrubbed out the mixing bowls under a stream of hot water, she thought about how ghoulish her job must seem from the outside. Picking over the bones of a marriage, sorting through one person's pain for bits of information she could use as leverage against the other. Painting the other spouse in the worst possible light to get the best possible outcome for her clients.

It was exactly why she had always insisted that she only take cases she believed in, where she represented the wronged party. To do otherwise felt mercenary. Wrong. Immoral even. The end of a marriage wasn't something to be celebrated, no matter how it came about. Her job was to extract her client without any further personal damage.

She shut off the tap and set aside the bowl, the truth hitting her with the force of a sledgehammer. All this time she'd been dithering over what she should tell John Mercer, when there really had been no question. She had only a single option. A third option.

The girls weren't home with the pizzas yet, so Gemma grabbed her jacket and her phone and slipped downstairs onto the patio. She pulled her zipper to her chin and found John's cell number in her phone, dialed, pressed the phone to her ear while it rang.

"Gemma!" John answered on the third ring, genuine surprise in his voice. "I didn't expect to talk to you until tomorrow in the office."

"Yeah, about that. I had to change my flight. I won't be back in California until tomorrow night."

"That's fine," he said easily. "I'll put you on my calendar first thing Tuesday morning and we can—"

"John, I quit."

Gemma hadn't expected to put it so baldly, but the

minute the words slipped out, they felt absolutely right. She wasn't the one who was forcing her hand. She wasn't the one who was going back on a verbal agreement and pressuring her into a difficult decision. She didn't owe him her delicacy.

Apparently, John was just as surprised, because it took him several long moments to reply. "Gemma, do you realize what you're saying?"

"You've given me no choice, John. I can only do this job effectively as long as I stand by my personal principles. You're asking me—no, blackmailing me—into compromising those principles. I won't do it. So I quit."

"I see." John took another long pause. "I have to tell you, I thought—"

"You thought I'd cave. I know. I thought for a while that I would too. But coming back home has made me remember why I started doing this in the first place, and it's not to increase my billable hours or to raise the profile of your firm. It's to help spouses who have no other options. No one is going to make me victimize them."

She heard John's long exhale, could practically sense the moment when he realized he wasn't going to change her mind. "I'm sorry to hear that, Gemma. You know that I've always believed in you. I've always championed you here at the firm. But I'm afraid that this time it's out of my hands. We'll miss you."

"I appreciate that, John. I'll be in on Tuesday to get my things and fill out my severance paperwork." She only had a couple of open cases, which she regretted leaving behind, but she'd seen enough attorneys move through the firm in the past to know that staying on simply to close out those cases was impossible. The other associates at the firm were more than competent and far less picky than Gemma. They'd do fine for them, even though her colleagues would likely resent being assigned her remaining clients.

Another long pause and then John said with a touch of emotion, "I'll miss you here, Gemma. I regret that it came to this, but I wish you well with your future endeavors."

Somehow in those few words, he managed to convey just how sorry he was that he'd been forced to give her this ultimatum. If she'd ever had any question that this was coming from Eli Merivale, that was gone. And given that she was only at Merivale and Mercer because of John, she couldn't even be angry. Not now. Not anymore.

Not when confronted directly with the reason she'd gone into this profession.

She was still sitting outside in the cold, perched on a metal bistro chair with her arms wrapped around herself, when the girls pulled up in Chelsea's minivan. They walked toward her, each carrying a large pizza box. Taylor's expression turned concerned. "Aunt Gem? Are you okay?"

"I just quit my job." The words came out before she could consider that she was dumping information on a teenage girl.

But Taylor's eyes lit up. "Does that mean you're staying?"

Gemma shook her head, a sad smile coming to her lips. "Afraid not, Taylor. I'm still going home tomorrow. I'm just. . . going to be doing something different."

Taylor looked like she wanted to say something else, but Rebekah nudged her, and they went inside with the pizzas, leaving her alone in the cold night.

Gemma tipped her head back, taking in the spill of stars across the dark expanse above her. Until the storm had passed and she saw those bright dots in the sky, she hadn't even noticed they'd been obscured by clouds. If you lived perpetually in the storm, eventually you forgot what you were missing.

Stephen had awakened something in her that she hadn't known still existed. A desire for companionship. A need to be known, *truly known*, not just as a capable attorney or a crusader for her clients or the woman who baked to make herself and everyone around her feel better. She'd thought for a second that he was the one who could see her exactly as who she was and love her anyway. But if he couldn't understand that he should have just been honest with her from the start, then there was no hope for them.

Gemma knew she should go back up and check on everyone, but she didn't have the heart for it, nor did she have the ability to mask the pain that she knew must be plain on her face. Instead, she went into the house and went straight to Liv's beautiful simple bedroom. She wanted to call Liv and talk over what had just happened, but she knew she didn't have the words yet. Didn't have the heart. Instead, she showered in Liv's en suite and pulled on her pajamas. From down the hall, she could hear Taylor and Rebekah's voices coming from the other bedroom, so she made one last round through the house, checking the locks on doors and windows. And then she climbed into her friend's cushy bed, glad she and Liv were still close enough that she didn't feel the need to track down clean sheets or do laundry.

It was going to be a big day for Chelsea tomorrow. And she was going to need Gemma's support, never mind the fact that she was probably the last person on earth that the woman thought she'd be relying on. She couldn't afford to be wallowing in her own personal misery while a client—official or not—needed her.

This was what Gemma did. It was what she was good at.

Still, it felt like hours before she fell asleep, and as she drifted into blackness, she was vaguely aware of tears on her cheeks.

CHAPTER TWENTY-NINE

WHEN GEMMA'S ALARM WENT OFF far too early the next morning, she had no idea where she was. For a panicked moment, she sifted through all the possible locations— her house in California, the apartment—and finally landed on Liv's bed, the events of the day before rushing in with painful clarity. Chelsea and Doug. Stephen and Nikki. Her job. No wonder her body ached and her mind felt numb. Her life had literally imploded right before her eyes in a space of three hours.

She stumbled into the kitchen in her pajamas, surprised to find both Taylor and Rebekah dressed, if not completely awake, staring at the toaster as if they could make their bagels heat faster through sheer force of will. Gemma went straight to the coffee pot and scooped grounds into a new filter. "Consciousness coming right up. Give me five minutes."

Taylor leaned against the edge of the plywood countertop and studied her. "Are you okay, Aunt Gem?"

"No," she said honestly, not meeting her niece's eye. "Not really. But I will be."

"What happened?"

Gemma threw her a raw twist of a smile. "I'd rather not talk about it."

"Do I need to call Mr. Osborne out?" Taylor asked, dead serious. "You know he's already kind of on the principal's radar because of all the books he's teaching. All it would take is—"

"No," Gemma said firmly. "Stephen is a good teacher and you know it. Whatever happened between us has nothing to do with you, his job, or this town. Got me?"

Taylor nodded, sufficiently chastised. "Yeah. I just . . . we've got your back, Aunt Gem."

It was so sweet, even misguided as it was, that she slung an arm around each girl and pulled them in close. "Thanks, you two. That means a lot."

"Are you sure you won't stick around?" Taylor asked hopefully. "Make the Broken Hearts Bakery a real thing? We need one, and look how much good you could do here. If it weren't for you, Rebekah's aunt would still be stuck with that creep and her dad wouldn't be coming home."

"Your dad's coming home?" Gemma asked, surprised.

Rebekah gave her a cautious smile. "Yeah. I called him last night and told him what happened, what's been going on. He booked the next flight home. He said he shouldn't have left me alone for so long."

Gemma let out a long breath and squeezed the girl once more. "That's great. I'm so glad to hear that."

"Anyway," Taylor said, not to be distracted, "you should think about it. You know the apartment isn't going anywhere."

And once more, there was so much of Liv in her stepdaughter that it was hard to believe that they weren't blood. "I know. Now go and get your stuff. You're going to miss the bus."

The girls raced out the door a few minutes later, cream cheese-smeared bagels in hand, and Gemma picked up her phone to text Liv. Then she caught the time on the screen. 7:20. How on earth was it already so late? She had to make sure that Chelsea was already up so they could be at the county court buildings as soon as they opened. She raced back to her borrowed bedroom, slipped into her most professional clothing—which was still only a pair of dark jeans and a cashmere sweater—and twisted her hair up into a makeshift French twist. Then she went across to the apartment to check on Chelsea and the kids.

To her surprise, they were already awake, and Chelsea was busy fashioning Etta's hair into twin braids. "What are you doing?"

"Getting them ready for school," Chelsea said brightly, the fake cheer in her voice all too apparent to Gemma. "They love school, don't you, kiddos?"

"I don't," Etta said grumpily, crossing her arms.

"She forgot her favorite shoes," Chelsea stage-whispered to Gemma. "It's a tragedy." She planted a noisy kiss on her daughter's cheek and the little girl squirmed away, even though a tiny smile was starting to tip up her lips.

Seeing Chelsea with her kids melted the final bit of ice in her heart. Gemma tugged her out of earshot. "Are you sure that's a good idea? Until there's a restraining order, Doug will be able to pick them up from school. Not that I necessarily think he will, but I've seen spouses do a lot of insane things out of revenge."

"Oh, I wouldn't put it past him." Chelsea's eyes flashed. Clearly, she'd found her backbone overnight. "But the principal and their teacher are both friends of mine. They'll look out for them like they're their own kids."

Gemma nodded. At least Chelsea was thinking critically now, out of the initial panic mode. That would make all of this a lot easier. "Then let's take them to school. I'll follow you and we can go directly to the courthouse."

She saw Chelsea falter at the mention of the courthouse, but then she straightened her spine, eyes blazing in her bruised face. "Good. Let's do it."

Gemma followed Chelsea's car to school, waiting across the street while she walked them inside—and Gemma assumed, explained the situation to all the relevant school personnel—then led the way to the Chaffee County Combined Courts, which were in Salida. Like many of the regional courts, it looked more like a school with a low-slung light brick facade and a flagpole right in front of the entrance. Now Chelsea faltered a little, faced with the reality of what she was about to do.

Gemma shifted into advocate mode. She'd never been here, but all courts were more or less the same and a professional demeanor plus some polite inquiry could get you a long way. She got the right forms for the temporary civil restraining order, then drew Chelsea aside to help her fill out the information. Meanwhile, she was texting Benji, telling him that they were there and the request for the TRO was about to be filed. Benji texted back immediately that he would try to expedite the process for them. He wasn't the only judge who heard TRO requests, but he would make sure their hearing was on the docket and set as early in the day as possible.

And then there was nothing to do but wait. Gemma knew that even with Benji's efforts, it could be hours before they heard anything, so they walked the few blocks from the Salida courthouse to a small coffee shop on F street. As they walked, Gemma couldn't help but note how similar the town was to Haven Ridge, at least in age and architecture. But Salida had a feeling of life and freshness that Haven Ridge lacked. She paused at stand-alone building—barely more than a shack—on the corner that had nonetheless been turned into a vibrant, busy bakery with an ordering window and a cluster of bistro tables outside. Even with the cold temperatures, people sipped coffee and ate baked goods, their breath causing white clouds to hover over them like halos.

Chelsea threw Gemma a searching look. "That could be you. Tempted?"

Gemma smiled, a little wryly, as they started walking again. "Maybe a decade or two ago. You knew I wanted to run a bakery when I was a kid?"

"Everyone knew," Chelsea said with a little laugh. "Whenever it was your turn to bring birthday treats, you came in with these elaborate unicorn cupcakes and things. It surprised all of us when we heard you'd become an attorney."

Gemma turned to her in surprise.

"Oh, don't get me wrong, I'm sure you're good at it. And I for one am happy that you are. But . . ."

"But what?"

Chelsea laughed a little self-consciously. "I'm the last person who should be saying this."

"Come on. I think we're past that now."

"It's just that . . . you were always so happy. Almost annoyingly so." Chelsea threw her a wry look. "Why do you think I hated you so much?"

"Ouch."

"Like I said, I really don't have room to lecture you. But you just seem . . . sadder . . . now."

"I guess life will do that to you. Especially with what I do for work. It's hard to help people without becoming a little cynical."

"But do you have to be? Really? Why couldn't you open that bakery? Haven Ridge needs one."

Gemma laughed. "Now you sound like Taylor."

"She's a good girl," Chelsea said significantly. "Wise beyond her years."

Now she knew that Taylor and Rebekah had been up to something if they'd gotten Chelsea in on it. Gemma wanted to laugh at how quickly things had changed if they thought her oldest and bitterest rival would be the one to convince her that she should come back to Haven Ridge.

"I'm not coming back," she said. "There's nothing for me here."

"Because of Stephen?" When Gemma looked at her in surprise, Chelsea said, "If it makes you feel any better, I don't think he meant to hurt you. I see the way he looks at you. You've always been it for him. The old girlfriend never had a shot."

"Then he should have told her that," Gemma said stiffly. She didn't even ask how Chelsea knew. This town was too small for that, and they'd all known each other for much too long. "I can't be with someone who isn't honest with me."

"I get that. Believe me, I do. I just. . .there's a difference between someone's mistakes and who they actually are." She gave Gemma a significant look. "I know you don't think much of me or Doug. But I'm not stupid, Gemma. I knew what he was all along. I just overlooked it when I got pregnant because I wanted so badly for my kids to have a father. I knew what it was like growing up with a single mom and that was the last life I wanted for them." Her voice broke on the last words, but her eyes were still clear, her expression determined.

Gemma grabbed for Chelsea's hand. "You are nothing like your mom, I hope you know that."

"And Stephen is nothing like your dad." She let go of Gemma's hand. "You know, none of us expected you to come back here. None of us expected you to . . ."

"Shake everything up?" Gemma suggested wryly.

"Belong."

Gemma almost stumbled at that one word. Such a small thing, especially coming from the mouth of a former enemy, but how strange that it could mean so much. She darted a look at Chelsea, but the woman was staunchly not looking at her. She found her throat was so tight she couldn't force sound through it.

Was it true? Did she really belong in Haven Ridge? She'd convinced herself she was an outsider for so many years, thanks to the unkindness that she and her mother had faced, that she'd never even considered what they might think of her now. At least not beyond the superficial.

But there had been the way that she'd been voted captain of her Capture the Flag team and how they'd rallied around her. The way everyone had embraced the so-called Broken Hearts Bakery. The teen girls who just seemed so happy to have someone to whom they could talk openly and without judgment. Could there really be a place for her here?

She didn't find her voice until they walked back into the court building and Gemma checked with the clerk on the status of their filing while Chelsea sat nervously in the corner. She strode back to Chelsea. "Hearing is at one. I have just enough time to stand up with you and then I have to be off to the airport. Liv's plane comes in at two thirty."

"No, you don't have to wait. I'll be fine . . ."

Gemma shot her a look that caused Chelsea to trail off. "I'm here for you. You'll want to go back to Liv's house until you've been notified that the TRO has been served. Deputy Dixon said he'd do it for you."

Impulsively, Chelsea threw her arms around Gemma's neck. "Thank you, Gemma. I feel terrible about everything, then and now. I hope. . . I hope you do decide to come back." She pulled away and gave her a rueful smile. "If you'd consider it, I'd like to make it up to you. Maybe even be friends?"

And even with the ache that had settled into Gemma's heart because of Stephen, the words warmed her. "I think maybe we already are."

CHAPTER THIRTY

TRUE TO HER WORD, Gemma stayed long enough to stand beside Chelsea as she walked into the courtroom, shrinking a little bit as if the authority of the room was a physical weight. For Gemma, who had spent an inordinate amount of time in court for a family law attorney, it was just another room like any other she'd spent her adult life in. Though she did have to bite the inside of her cheek when she saw Benji in his black robes, sitting behind an engraved plaque that identified him as the *Hon. Benjamin Balden.* She knew they'd all grown up and changed, but he probably got the award for glow-up of the decade. Somehow being in charge of a courtroom had gone a long way to transforming him into someone with confidence and gravity.

By the time they walked out again, Chelsea had been awarded her TRO and Deputy Dixon was already parked in front of the courthouse, waiting to serve the paperwork. Gemma didn't think she was misreading the way the officer's gaze lingered on Chelsea with a bit more than just professional concern. At least it seemed like she might have someone looking out for her while things settled. Even if Gemma wouldn't be here to see how everything shook out in the short term.

And then the two women were standing by Liv's SUV. "Thank you, Gemma," Chelsea said quietly, one hand picking nervously at the cuticles of the other. "You didn't have to help me. After how awful I was to you when we were kids, I might not have were I in your situation."

"I think you might have," Gemma said, but she really had no idea if that was true or not. After all they'd been through, she doubted she would ever count Chelsea among her very best friends, but she didn't think she was the evil shrew that she'd once believed. "High school wasn't exactly a picnic for either of us. For that matter, adulthood isn't turning out to be perfect either."

"Yeah." Chelsea swallowed hard, her eyes going shiny. She blinked the tears away quickly. "I have no idea how I'm going to talk to the twins about this. But you made me realize that I didn't need to just shut up and take it anymore. Like I always have."

And that gave Gemma just one more insight into Chelsea's life and why she might have been so mean to Gemma back then, especially if she'd always perceived her as happy. Gemma sighed and then folded her into a long, tight hug.

"Take care of yourself and your children," she said. "And if you need me, you know how to reach me."

Chelsea nodded. Gemma unlocked the car door and climbed into the front seat, but before she could close the door, Chelsea asked, "What are you going to do about Stephen? Are you going to talk to him?"

The pang in her heart at those words nearly took her breath away. "I don't know yet."

It was a question that Gemma turned over and over in her head through the whole drive to the airport. The roads had been cleared down to bare pavement, so even that didn't require her entire concentration, leaving part of her mind to mull over what Chelsea had said. Did it actually make any difference in the end? Maybe Stephen had thought his relationship with Nikki was over, but Nikki certainly hadn't. So how could she be sure that he wouldn't do the same thing to her? Did she really want to be with a man who had twice now gotten involved with someone else the minute his last girlfriend was out of the picture? That wasn't a coincidence. That was a character flaw.

And that was the thing that she'd always told her clients when they started to explain away their spouse's bad behavior. Anyone who would do it once would do it again. Everyone made mistakes, but repeated mistakes were deep-seated cracks in the foundation that wouldn't be fixed by love or anything else.

By the time she turned into the tiny parking lot of the Gunnison-Crested Butte Regional Airport, she was no closer to knowing what to do, and she felt almost physically ill, achy and clammy, at what even a conversation would reveal. As angry as she had been at Amber, now she was in the position of being the other woman. The very thought chafed her raw.

Gemma did her best to put on a happy expression, but when Liv came barreling toward her with as much exuberance as she had a week ago, she knew it was an abject failure. Liv took one look at her and said, "Oh, honey."

"I'm fine," Gemma lied. Liv looked good. Relaxed, refreshed. The week away had been just what she needed, apparently, to reset her life. Gemma's had been reset too, but she imagined she looked as wrung out as she felt when Liv gave her that reproving *who-do-you-think-you're-fooling* look.

"Okay, I'm not fine. I'm actually a wreck. Let's get your stuff to the car and we can catch up. My suitcase is still in the back."

Gemma walked with Liv out of the baggage claim area and back to her SUV. Hopefully Liv had gotten some clarity on her own situation. "Have you decided what you want to do about work yet? About moving?"

"I haven't," Liv said with a heavy sigh. "I did explain the situation with Taylor and told them that I had to explore the legal ramifications before I made a decision. They seemed to understand that, said I could stay on from Colorado until I decided. I'm not sure they're going to give me all the way to July, though." She shrugged, the ultimatum visibly weighing her down. "It's not exactly ideal, having it hanging over my head like this, but it gives me time to get Taylor finished with the school year and decide what we're going to do."

"Do you *want* to move to New York?"

Liv glanced at her. "I'm not sure. Why do you say it like that?"

Gemma swallowed down her automatic response. Maybe it was no coincidence that she'd found out about Stephen's lie of omission at the same time she learned her best friend and niece might not even be staying in Colorado. It potentially saved her from making a huge, bad decision. She fudged her answer. "I just know it's not what you hoped. You love Haven Ridge."

"I do. But I guess you can just as easily hop a plane to New York as you can here, right?" Liv threw her a look and Gemma could see that she was trying hard to look at the positives. Gemma stopped right there in the middle of the parking lot and put her arms around her friend.

Liv hugged her back tightly, her voice muffled in Gemma's hair. "I'll be okay. Everything works out as it's meant to in the end, even if we can't see it right now."

"Yeah," Gemma whispered. "I have to believe that."

Liv pulled back and stared hard at her, searching. "How long are you going to make me pretend I don't know what's going on?"

Gemma crumpled in her friend's arms. "Taylor told you."

"Yeah, she told me. She was furious, by the way. Had all sorts of revenge fantasies planned."

Gemma let out a watery laugh. "Yeah. I had to stop her and Rebekah from trying to ruin his teaching career. Not that I wasn't tempted, mind you."

"I'm so sorry, Gemma. I would have said something if I'd thought . . ."

Gemma froze. "Wait. You knew? About Nikki?"

Liv grimaced. "Kind of? We don't talk about those sorts of things much, but he told me . . . oh, it must have been three months ago . . . that it wasn't working out with her. I'm surprised it took so long for him to break it off. Wait, he did break it off with her, didn't he?"

"So he says. She didn't seem to get the message." Gemma exhaled in a long, heavy whoosh. "You know he actually asked me to stay? Come back to Haven Ridge? He told me the town needed me. The worst thing is, I was actually considering it."

Liv squealed and clapped her hand over her mouth. "I don't know how to feel right now. I want you to come back. Of course I do . . . but . . ."

"Yeah. I know. I've got a lot of things to think about, and so do you." She hugged Liv tightly once more. "And right now, I should go get checked in. The last thing I want to do is get stuck here another night."

Liv sighed, but she held onto her as long as she could. "I'm sorry, Gem. I should have said something earlier. I just never dreamed . . ."

"You and me both." Gemma forced a smile. "Give Taylor another hug for me. And go easy on Chelsea, she's been through a lot today."

"You got it."

Gemma blew her an air kiss, grabbed her suitcase, and started for the tiny airport terminal. Before she'd gotten more than a dozen feet, Liv called out to her.

"Gem? For the record, I think Stephen is right. Haven Ridge does need you."

Gemma gave her a little wave of acknowledgment and continued into the terminal. Maybe it did. But in the last week, she'd experienced enough highs and lows to wish for her steady, normal, pressure-cooker life in LA. The bigger question wasn't whether Haven Ridge needed her, but whether she really needed *it*.

The big advantage to the Gunnison airport was that it took nearly no time to get through security, and despite cutting it so close to her boarding time, the desk near the gate was completely empty when she arrived. She flopped down on one of the vinyl seats—which were really individual chairs hooked together, like they had in the high school multi-purpose room, not even real airport seats—and pulled out her phone.

3:05. Stephen would be getting out of his last class now, but she vaguely recalled he had speech practice right now. Also, she wasn't all that keen on getting into a potentially emotionally-charged discussion in an airport, but the alternative was to make the whole trip back with this sick, roiling pit in her stomach. She needed to settle this.

She opened up her messaging app and began to tap out a simple message to Stephen: **Call me.**

At that exact moment, an airline staff member stepped up to the gate and spoke into a microphone. "Mountain State 396 to Denver boarding now at Gate 2."

Gemma looked at the message, ready to send, and quickly hit the delete key before she shoved her phone into her pocket. Later. She'd send it when she got to Denver and had some time to talk.

Except their plane sat at the gate for an extra forty minutes in Gunnison and then circled the airport in Denver for an extra hour due to high winds. By the time the tiny jet touched down at DIA and rolled up to the jetway, her flight to Los Angeles was already boarding and she and another passenger had to sprint the length of the terminal to their departure gate. They were just announcing the final call for the flight when she stumbled up to the gate, fumbling for the boarding pass in her phone's airline app.

"Just in time," the airline employee said brightly, and Gemma managed a weak smile.

For all her rush, though, the two hours to Los Angeles gave her far too much time to think and far too few answers. Every contact with Stephen replayed on a loop through her mind, hitching on that moment where Nikki had kissed him and Gemma had realized their time together had again just been a fantasy. A fraud. It instantly transported her back to high school, left her standing alone in a peach satin prom dress while the boy she loved smiled at another girl like he'd once smiled at her. And despite how well she'd thought she'd put her past behind her, those same feelings came rushing back as if no time had passed at all.

She was worthless. Forgettable. Just a way to pass the time until someone better came along. And someone better *always* came along.

Gemma didn't even realize she was crying until the older woman beside her handed her a travel package of tissues. She gave her a sympathetic look and patted her hand reassuringly before she went back to her cozy mystery novel, as if it was perfectly normal for a grown woman to cry on an airplane.

Well, why isn't it? Why should everyone else get to fall apart and not you?

Because she'd prided herself on her self-control, her common sense, her refusal to be taken in by matters of the heart. She'd told Liv that it was hard to date because men ran at the first mention of her line of work, but the reality was, she ended every one of those relationships before she could fall in love. It didn't take a therapist to recognize now that the two most important male relationships in her life had ended with feelings of abandonment, and now she didn't put herself in a position to get hurt.

Until she went back to Haven Ridge and realized that her feelings for Stephen had never completely gone away, just gotten buried, petrified, preserved in amber like a relic from another era. And somewhere deep inside her, she'd thought that if she could only revive that relationship, she could rewrite the past and make it like none of the pain had ever happened.

But real life didn't work that way. Just because you ignored the hurt didn't mean it had healed.

Gemma pulled a tissue from the pack and dabbed at her face, then wiped her nose. She probably could have used therapy ten or fifteen years ago. Maybe then she wouldn't be sitting here, sobbing on a plane over a guy who had never really been hers in the first place.

She closed her eyes and leaned her head back against the headrest, the dry, recycled cabin air making her tear-stained face feel tight and sticky. What on earth did she do now? It wasn't an exaggeration to say that the things that had been important to her were now all gone. She didn't have a job, which meant if she didn't do some-thing fast, she wouldn't have enough money to pay her mortgage. She didn't have anyone who actually cared about her in LA, and except for that brief shining moment when she thought there might be a future between her and Stephen, no real reason to go back to Haven Ridge.

But even through the ache in her heart, she realized that was a lie. What if she didn't look at this as everything she had counted on falling apart, slipping out of her hands? What if she looked at this as a clean slate? An opportunity to reevaluate everything she thought was so important to her? A chance to ask hard questions of herself?

Had she chosen law because she loved it and wanted to help people or because she thought it was insurance against becoming her mother?

Did she stay in Los Angeles because she hated Haven Ridge or because her relative anonymity in LA meant she couldn't get hurt?

Now that she had no obligations, what did she want to do with her life?

In that moment, thirty-five thousand feet in the air somewhere over Arizona, Gemma began to mentally unravel every *should* and *must* and *won't* she'd told herself since she was sixteen years old and realized her dad wasn't the person she thought he was. By the time they touched down in Los Angeles, even if she didn't quite know *what* she wanted to do next, at least she finally understood why.

CHAPTER THIRTY-ONE

GEMMA WAITED until she had disembarked the plane and made her way through the aging 1970s carapace of Los Angeles International Airport to the taxi stand before she switched on her phone. It struggled to find a signal for several long minutes, but just as she reached the front of the line, it erupted in a cascade of pings and notifications.

Plenty of messages from her office, several of them from HR, and a couple from surprised colleagues. News had traveled fast. Four texts and two missed calls from Stephen, which she ignored for the time being. And a single concerned text from Liv: **Are you okay?**

Gemma slid into the back seat of the cab and gave the driver her address, then tapped out a reply: **I think so. Ask me after I'm done with HR at work tomorrow and I'm officially unemployed.**

Wait, what?

Oh, that was right. She'd been so distracted by Chelsea and the news that Stephen had a girlfriend, she hadn't even told Liv that she'd quit her job. Quickly, she tapped out an abbreviated explanation of what had happened and waited.

Good for you, Gem. I'm proud of you. What are you going to do now?

Not sure. I don't have to decide immediately, but I have to decide immediately, if you know what I mean.

Liv just sent back the laughing-with-sweat-droplet emoji, which pretty much summed up all Gemma's feelings about her life today. She still wasn't sure if she was making the biggest mistake ever or if she was narrowly avoiding disaster. There remained a knot in her stomach and a heavy weight on her chest, but oddly, her mind felt clear. And if she were being honest, a little excited. Maybe it was the kind of excited you got before you flung yourself out of an open airplane door, hoping your chute opened as intended, but at least it didn't feel like sorrow.

It felt like getting a second chance.

Gemma watched the scenery from LAX back into Santa Monica as if she was seeing it for the first time, the shifting neighborhoods, the congested rush-hour traffic, the occasional glimpse of the ocean before they turned back inland. When the taxi finally pulled up in front of her tiny ranch as the sun was giving up its final rays, she couldn't help but feel like she was standing outside of herself, or maybe split in two. One part of her felt relief at being back in her quaint neighborhood and the home that had been her retreat these past years. The other part felt as if it was foreign, part of a life that had turned out to be a dream. How was it possible that after only a week back in Haven Ridge, it had begun to feel more real and vibrant and part of her world than the city in which she'd spent the last decade?

Gemma smiled at the driver and thanked him as she climbed out of the car and pulled her small roller case out after her, then walked up the cracked cement driveway, waiting for the feeling of oddness to go away.

It didn't.

She pushed open the door, breathed in the floral-scented, slightly stale air, and flipped on the lights. Rolled her case into the entrance. Let her eyes roam over the carefully chosen decor painted in shades of white and gray and blue and pale wood—all coastal colors meant to remind her that she was biking distance from the beach. Her Ocean Breeze candle stood on the back of the sofa table, waiting to reinforce that impression—it was one of the first things she did when she returned from a trip or even a long work day to chase away the scent of disuse.

And yet the thing she yearned for was that particular combination of dirt and pine and sagebrush that characterized Colorado, the dry crispness of the air that conveyed the altitude, even when the clouds didn't look close enough to touch. The way the smell of the air changed when a storm was coming in. How the sunsets splashed the sky like a cloud-dotted watercolor, all pinks and oranges and yellow streaked across the pale expanse of blue.

Only then did she realize that she might have lived in California for a decade, but Colorado was and always would be home.

Gemma sank down on the edge of her linen-covered, down-cushioned sofa, sinking into its squashy comfort, a little bit stunned by the thought. She ran her fingers over the slubby texture of the upholstery, trying to anchor herself here, as if somehow that would bring back the feeling of belonging and comfort that she'd always felt when she stepped through the door. But it was ruined now.

Her heart yearned for old brick buildings and wide-open vistas and mountains and mud-splattered trucks and everything that made Haven Ridge what it was. Her niece and her best friend and the townspeople who had either decided to embrace her or maybe had never stopped. Chelsea with a fierce love for her children that led her to escape her husband, even though she was scared. Mallory who had come to Haven Ridge and inserted herself into the town's fabric, no doubt as charmed by the very things that Gemma now missed.

Even without Stephen, there were people and places and things that were calling her back home. She had just needed to put to rest that old calloused pain before she could open herself to them again. She'd needed to understand that sometimes people *could* change—really understand it in her heart, not just her head.

Stephen's betrayal didn't undo that.

The idea was simultaneously terrifying and thrilling. She couldn't be sure she wouldn't wake up tomorrow and change her mind. But she did know that this was a decision she had to make for herself, apart from whatever she might feel for Stephen and whatever explanation he might have for his behavior. Her newly scrubbed heart was tender and oh so vulnerable, and she couldn't be sure that a good explanation and a heartfelt apology wouldn't make the decision for her.

She unlocked her phone and deleted his messages and texts, unread.

* * *

It should have taken longer to quit her job. But when Gemma showed up at the office of Merivale and Mercer the next day, dressed in her usual suit and heels—she did have an image to uphold, even if her work uniform felt foreign after the last ten days in Haven Ridge—it took her less than an hour to dismantle her employment at the firm. John was sorry, of course, and still a little surprised that she had opted for the "nuclear option" (his words, not hers), but he didn't try to convince her to stay. Maybe it was something in her voice or her expression, but he evidently could see that her mind was made up. And it was.

HR was as professional as always. Gemma signed all the required forms terminating her employment and ensuring her confidentiality, handed over her laptop and files, and emptied her desk into a big banker box from the supply closet. There was precious little there—the expensive pen she'd bought to celebrate passing the bar, a bag of Kona coffee, a handful of energy bars she ate on days she didn't have time to leave the office. She removed her framed degrees from the wall very last, staring for a second at the nails left behind, expecting to feel a twinge of regret.

But there was nothing of the sort. Nervousness, yes. Maybe even a little excitement. But in that moment, she knew for certain that she'd done the only thing she could possibly do in the situation. Maybe the thing she should have done earlier, if only she could have come to grips with her past a little sooner.

Gemma walked out of the office slowly and quietly, raising a hand with a smile to associates who looked up from phone calls or offered quick, subtle nods from the conference room. No going-away parties here, no exuberant goodbyes. Just as well. She'd respected her colleagues and she'd enjoyed working with them, but she wouldn't call them friends. In few weeks, when there was a new attorney sitting in her office, it would be like she'd never been there at all.

"Gemma!"

A frantic voice caught her just as she was pushing through the double glass doors toward the elevators directly opposite. She caught the door with her elbow before it swung shut and turned to find Alicia, the receptionist, racing towards her, a blue greeting card envelope in her hand. "You're leaving already?"

Gemma glanced down at her box of stuff. "Looks like it. There wasn't all that much to clear out in the end."

Alicia stared at her like she couldn't believe it. "What are you going to do? You got a better offer elsewhere, didn't you?"

She smiled. It was kind of sweet that the receptionist automatically assumed that she'd been poached for more money by another firm. She wouldn't ruin her assumptions by telling her that she'd quit so she didn't get fired.

But no, that wasn't entirely true either. Her forced time off had conveniently coincided with Liv's trip, but even if it hadn't, Gemma would never have left her best friend in the lurch, and she would have come to the same conclusions. It was just that John and Eli's ultimatum had made her decision that much easier.

"Not exactly," she said slowly. "I'm moving back to Colorado."

"I guess I don't blame you, though that was fast." Alicia narrowed her eyes. "Is there a man involved?"

Gemma let out a little laugh. Apparently the breakup hadn't shattered the woman's hopelessly romantic tendencies. "No, no man involved. I just realized I missed my hometown. And they need someone like me there."

"Well, they're lucky to have you. Even if we'll miss you." Impulsively, the receptionist threw her arms around Gemma—at least the best she could around the banker's box—and squeezed her. "Thanks for all the advice. And all the pastries." She realized she was still holding the envelope and dropped it on top of Gemma's pile of things. "You can open that later."

"Thanks, Alicia. Take care of yourself, okay?"

"I could say the same to you, Gemma." Alicia smiled and held the door for her so she could break free toward the elevator. She stood there until the car came and Gemma gave her a little wave goodbye as the doors slid closed.

As the elevator descended silently to the main floor, Gemma let out a breath. She hadn't meant to say it so baldly. Had convinced herself that she was still considering whether she should find another job here in Los Angeles or move back to Colorado. But when faced with the question, the truth had spilled out almost without her knowledge.

She was going home.

She called Liv with the news, and predictably, her best friend was over the moon. Gemma had to hold the phone away from her ear so her friend's squeal didn't pierce an eardrum. "Oh my word, I'm so excited. Do you know what you're going to do yet? Do you have any plans?"

"I have a lot of things to unravel here. I have to put my house on the market, for one thing. Find someplace to live in Haven Ridge—"

"Pfft," Liv said immediately. "You'll live here. The apartment will be open soon. Doug got served with the restraining order, and I suspect Andrew had a very stern talk with him when he did, because Doug vacated their house immediately. Chelsea's going home tonight."

"That's great!" Gemma said, and she meant it. "But who's Andrew?"

"Deputy Dixon," Liv said, and there was a teasing thread in her tone. "It seems that he asked Chelsea to call him by his first name."

"Oh, he did, did he?" It would be some time before Chelsea was ready to move on—Gemma had observed all too well the impact of a rough marriage and divorce—but the fact that she had someone looking out for her would no doubt remind her to stay open to the possibilities. Proof that just because the man you loved turned out not to be the man he portrayed himself to be didn't mean that you wouldn't find happiness. Someday. With someone else.

Almost as if she could sense Gemma's change of mood over the open line, she asked quietly, "Have you talked to Stephen?"

"No. He called and left messages, but I'm not ready to talk to him. I need to do this on my own. I need to make sure that I'm moving back for the right reasons." She should have left it at that, because she hated the needy, hopeful sound of her own voice when she asked, "Have you talked to him?"

"No, but Taylor is pissed at him. She asked her guidance counselor if she could transfer out of his class."

"What'd they say?"

"No, of course, because he's the only one who teaches sophomore lit. I told her to treat him with respect, but I think she's still giving him the cold shoulder. She wants to quit speech."

"No!" Gemma's heart plummeted. "That's the last thing I want her to do! I feel so guilty now."

"Don't worry," Liv said wryly. "She might be willing to sacrifice her academic achievement, but she's not willing to let him ruin the speech meet for her after you two raised enough money for them to rent a bus *and* stay overnight in a nice hotel."

Gemma laughed, relieved and a little amused. That sounded like Taylor. At least she didn't need to have the guilt over her niece's change of plans hanging over her.

"But honestly, Gem, how are you? Really?"

That took a bit of thought to unravel. Finally she said, "It hurts. For that brief time, I was really happy. I had hope that maybe things would work out between me and Stephen. And now that's been yanked away. But I think it needed to happen. All this time, I've been so determined not to hinge my happiness on a man that I think I was hinging my happiness on *not* having a man, and I've been missing out." Gemma took a deep breath and let it out slowly, glad that it was just a sigh and not a sob. "The fact that I could even think about having a relationship with him and this . . . betrayal . . . didn't completely break me makes me think I could have a relationship with someone else."

"Wow, Gem, that's . . . huge." Liv sounded impressed. "I'm not there yet, it's too soon, but it kind of gives me hope for myself. I miss Jason every day, but I know he wouldn't want me to be alone forever. I just . . . still don't want to be with anyone but him." There was a hitch in Liv's voice, and it tugged on Gemma's heart. Just another reason she needed to go back, even if Liv was only there for another four months. The fact she'd stayed away so long for a job that she'd given up on a week's consideration made her feel like she'd been a bad friend, selfish.

"Liv—"

"Don't you start guilt-tripping yourself, Gemma Van Buren. I know you. This is not your responsibility. And no matter how glad I am going to be to have you back, that doesn't mean I wouldn't want you to stay there if that would make you happy."

"I know. And what makes me happy is coming home."

Liv fell silent and when she spoke again, she was quiet. "I'm just really glad that you're my person. Even if you weren't here, just knowing you were out there if I needed you . . . I couldn't have survived without you."

Tears pricked Gemma's eyes. "I love you, Liv. I feel the same way."

And of all the reasons she could have uprooted her life and made a big change for, maybe that one was the best.

CHAPTER THIRTY-TWO

STEPHEN COULDN'T REMEMBER the last time he'd been so miserable.

No, he could. It had been the last time he'd done something so colossally stupid that Gemma had walked away from him forever and refused to acknowledge his existence for almost a decade and a half. Except this time it was worse. Because last time, it had been done out of childish ignorance and insecurity, and he hadn't had the slightest idea what he was giving up by cheating on Gemma with Amber. They'd been little more than kids, after all, still raw material, not yet formed into the people they'd be someday.

But this time he had no excuse, because he knew exactly what he had lost. What an amazing, unique, one-of-a-kind person he'd had in Gemma Van Buren for a few shining moments, a woman he was lucky had even deigned to look his way. And he'd still managed to crater his only chance of happiness with her.

After repeated calls and messages, Gemma had finally responded with a short, terse text: **Please stop. I'm not ready to talk to you.** At first, his hopes had risen—the implied *yet* in the statement hinted that perhaps there would come a time when they could work it out. But when days and then weeks passed with no contact, he finally gave up. He'd tried talking to Liv, but while she looked at him with sympathy, she'd simply said, "Gemma is my best friend. If I have to take sides on this one, it's going to be hers." He didn't press. Gemma deserved the loyalty. It had just been his last-ditch effort to get a message to her, to convey how little he'd meant to hurt her, how much he already missed her.

Nikki, on the other hand, had taken the break-up shockingly well: a Priority Mail box had arrived with a few things—his favorite sweatshirt, a nice metal-handled razor, a few old books—and a sticky note that said *Wishing you the best. No hard feelings. N.* He almost felt like he should be insulted that he'd meant so little to her that she'd shrugged it off. Then again, it just proved that he probably should have been more honest about his feelings instead of letting the geographical distance do all the heavy lifting.

He was starting to realize that he'd done a lot of stupid things out of fear in his life.

He threw himself back into the myriad things that he'd ignored during the week Gemma had been there, finishing up his schoolwork, working on the lesson plans for his new books. It was only when he was planning out the unit on *Little Women* for AmLit as a replacement for Sylvia Plath's *The Bell Jar* that he stopped to question why.

What exactly was Edgar Daughtler going to do if he refused? Fire him? Leave the school without a literature teacher for all four grades? And given who had most likely been the driving force behind the objections, how much weight would they really hold anyway? Word of Chelsea's restraining order against Doug had spread like wildfire throughout the town, and from what Stephen had heard, the man had hunkered down in a motel in Buena Vista, afraid to show his face, while Chelsea walked freely through the town with her children.

They had certainly come a long way since high school.

The Friday afternoon after Gemma had left, Stephen knocked on Daughtler's door and poked his head in. "Can I speak with you?"

"Sure, Stephen, come in." The principal lowered the lid of his laptop and folded his hands atop it. "What's on your mind?"

Stephen remained standing. "I rescind my alternate lesson plans for my classes. I'm teaching the books I prepared."

Daughtler stared at him for a long moment. "I don't understand."

"There's nothing wrong with the books, Edgar. They're accepted classic works of literature. The people who have objections to the material are delusional about what's actually going on in their own town if they think this is going to corrupt our youth. Or they're just choosing not to see it because it's easier to be ignorant. How are we ever going to teach this generation to do better than their parents if all we ever do is reinforce the status quo?"

"I see." The principal steepled his fingers, a sure sign that he was hedging. "You realize that the school board, and by extension, I, have the final say on the curriculum. If you refuse to change it, I'm within my rights to fire you."

"I understand that. I also know that you'll have angry parents who don't understand why their kids' literature class is being taken over by the football coach instead of someone qualified to teach the material."

Daughtler stared at him for a long moment, and the

corner of his mouth lifted in the barest hint of a smile. "You might be right about that. And as much as I'm tempted to let you believe that taking a stand was what won me over, the truth is, the main objectors don't have the same standing that they once had here."

"Doug Meinke."

"Among others of his cronies—" Daughtler coughed— "excuse me, supporters. In fact, I don't know if you've heard yet, but Meinke just resigned his office."

Stephen took a step back, stunned. "You're kidding. Why?"

"Something to do with fifteen hundred signatures on a recall petition this week alone. Which is in itself impressive since there's less than a thousand people who actually live within town limits. Turns out that the surrounding unincorporated areas don't take kindly to spousal abusers either."

"That's . . . good news then. So you won't oppose my book choices?"

Daughtler shook his head. "Not unless I hear from the majority of the parents that they object. Which I would find surprising."

Now it all made sense. The mayor had been loath to allow the students to delve into Stephen's decidedly feminist curriculum, lest it cast light on what was going on in his own house. So instead, he'd harnessed latent racism among some of his cronies to press his agenda and hide his motivations. It still reflected an ugly side of Haven Ridge, but it was a relief to find perhaps the attitudes weren't as widespread as he'd thought.

But he voiced none of that out loud; he simply nodded. "Thank you, sir. I appreciate your support."

Daughtler waved a hand in dismissal. But just as Stephen got to the door, he called out, "You know there's going to be a recall election next month."

"Oh? For mayor?" He hadn't really thought about what happened when one resigned, but it made sense that they'd need to quickly elect a replacement.

"You ever consider throwing your hat in the ring?"

If he thought he'd been stunned before, it was nothing compared to how he felt now. "Me? Why?"

"I saw how you stepped up for the community when I was out of town last weekend. It was a good idea opening the shelter, and from what I saw, the festival was a huge success. Of course, that's school business, and I'm just not ready to give up my position here. But I think you would be surprised by how many people would back you should you volunteer."

"Are you that eager to get rid of me?" he asked, defaulting to humor while his mind buzzed with shock.

"Oh no, I would expect you to continue teaching literature. After all, we need you here. But given that mayor is a part-time job anyway and you're already doing some of the community building duties without being paid. . . I don't see why you couldn't do double duty. I'd be willing to endorse you."

For the first time in his life, Stephen was well and truly stunned speechless. "I don't know what to say."

"You don't have to say anything. Just think about it."

Stephen nodded and slipped out, closing the door behind him. What had just happened? He had stood up to his boss regarding his curriculum and come out with a de facto endorsement for a part-time job as mayor. Did he even want such a thing?

More importantly, if he had the opportunity to do more good here, could he actually pass it up?

Unbidden, his mind turned back to Gemma. Besides his personal grief at her absence, the town was also missing out on her presence. She'd brought a life and a passion to Haven Ridge, even just briefly. He'd seen how the town reacted to her, how they embraced her the second time around. Heck, she'd made enough of an impression on his sophomore girls that practically the whole class was giving him the cold shoulder now. It was Taylor, of course, leading the charge, but he'd overheard enough conversations to realize that she was known as "Aunt Gemma" among all Taylor's friends.

He knew nothing about how to run a town, but he knew plenty about how not to run it. Honestly, what did he have to lose, besides face? That wasn't worth much at this point anyway, though had anyone cared about his love life outside a handful of teenage girls, it might.

Your dad would certainly be proud, came the wry, somewhat bitter inner voice. In his mind, the only thing better than being the high school quarterback would be holding town office.

You're going to have to stand up to him sometime, that voice came again, but this time he dismissed it. It was one thing to stand up for his principles as a teacher, when it came to his job and what he believed about the education of young minds. It was another to try to sway a man who had been set in his ways for longer than Stephen had been alive. Standing up to his father about anything now would be more unkind than it would be useful. The time to rebel would have been when they'd pressured him to forget about Gemma and move on to someone more suitable, like Amber. When it might have actually made a difference in the trajectory of his life. Before the fear of not letting others down had been hard-coded into his personal operating instructions.

Because that's what this was all about, wasn't it? His fear of letting people down. The need to keep his dad happy so he didn't scream or throw things at him—an avoidance technique he had learned from his mom— had transferred into a desire to keep everyone around him happy, even when it wasn't the right thing to do. Dating Amber. Not being honest with Nikki. Caving to Daughtler. Heck, even letting the school administration push their unwanted responsibilities on him. He'd never thought he was a coward, but now it was hard to see himself as anything but. It made him ashamed. And embarrassed.

And determined to stop that cycle before it could continue to dominate the rest of his life.

Because Gemma had been right when she'd looked at him and dismissed him as being weak and untrustworthy, even if it wasn't for the same reasons. He didn't want to be that person anymore.

Not just for her. But for himself and everyone around him who counted on him.

CHAPTER THIRTY-THREE

IF QUITTING HER JOB WAS EASIER than Gemma expected, selling her house and leaving the state turned out to be more involved than she'd ever dreamed. She'd somehow thought her move out of the tiny Victorian in Haven Ridge as a teen had prepared her, but she hadn't appreciated how little she'd had to do and how much her mom had handled. Now that she had her own house, one in which she'd lived—and collected *stuff*—for five years, she realized what a daunting undertaking it was.

Fortunately, the house had been remodeled right before she moved in, so there were only a few minor repairs to be done, which she handled herself or called a handyman to complete. Still, the Realtor wanted her to stage the spare bedroom, which Gemma was currently using as an office, as an actual sleeping space, which meant that she needed to put her desk, bookshelves, and extensive book collection—both law school books and her personal reading material—into storage. And if she was going to pack all that stuff up, she might as well pack everything she didn't need at the same time. Which was how she ended up with a living room full of boxes, a steel container in her driveway, and a pounding headache two days before she was supposed to put her house on the market.

To be fair, it wasn't only the state of her living room that was causing the headache. In between cleaning, packing, and arranging, Gemma was trying to sort the process of getting licensure to practice law in Colorado. Turned out that Colorado admitted out-of-state attorneys to the bar through a process called Admission on Motion, but only if they were licensed in one of forty-one states with which it had bar reciprocity. Naturally, California wasn't one of those states.

Even after more research, she *thought* she could apply and simply take the Multi-State Professional Responsibility Exam again, since it had been more than five years since she sat the exam in California. She just hadn't had time to actually call and clarify matters.

And maybe she didn't want to be discouraged in her decision if for some reason she needed to retake the bar exam in Colorado. God help her. It was bad enough the first time around after plenty of study.

But that was something to stress about another time, when she didn't have to move stacks of boxes higher than her head out into the storage container in her driveway. She had just dollied another stack of book boxes out her front door, down a borrowed ramp, and into the container when a Ford Focus rolled up in front of her house. She squinted at it in curiosity—her neighborhood was soundly anchored with young professionals, so there wasn't much traffic during the day while everyone was at work—but dismissed it as she went inside for another load. This time when she wheeled another stack out, she jolted to a stop so hard that the top box slid forward on a sure trajectory to the concrete.

Stephen darted forward and caught the box before it could drop, then pushed it back into place on the top of the stack. "What do you have in this thing? Bricks?"

"Close enough, law books." Gemma answered automatically, her mouth working faster than her brain right now. Surely she was imagining things. It could not be Stephen, standing on her sidewalk in a pair of jeans and a flannel button-down that looked laughably out of place, more ill at ease than she'd ever seen him. But then it would have to be, because she'd never seen him with such uncertainty etching his face, wouldn't have even been able to imagine it. "What are you doing here?"

"You wouldn't answer my phone calls or return my texts."

"And that required coming here?" Gemma's gaze skittered away as she levered the hand truck backwards with a grunt. While she was muscling boxes into storage, she could pretend that exertion and not nervousness—or maybe elation—was behind the sudden speed of her heartbeat.

"Let me." He slid in beside her and took the dolly from her hands, their shoulders brushing and sending a shiver of awareness down the entire left side of her body. He rolled the boxes into the container with ease and called, his voice both echoing and muffled, "Just put these anywhere on the stack?"

"Yeah," she called back. She grasped her hands in front of her, broke them apart, stuck them in the back pockets of her jeans in a way she hoped seemed casual just as he came back out with the empty dolly. "What are you doing here?" she asked again, hoping this time he'd give her an answer that actually made sense.

"Can we go inside and talk?"

Gemma swallowed and nodded, jerking her head as a sign that he should follow her into the house. She wove through the stacks of boxes in the entrance and went directly to the kitchen. "Do you want something to drink?"

"No, thank you."

Gemma got herself one of the glasses still in her cupboards—she'd be driving the essentials to Colorado rather than shipping them—and filled a glass from the dispenser on the fridge. She knew she was stalling, and the whole time she could feel Stephen's eyes fixed on her. Of course he'd show up when she was sweaty and streaked with dust, wearing a pair of ripped jeans— nothing so stylish as artistically ripped, just old—and a T-shirt that was just a little too tight. She couldn't begin to fathom why he would be here, what was so important he had to say it in person.

Or maybe didn't want to.

After she'd drained half the glass and set it on the counter with a sharp crack, he finally spoke. "Gemma, I'm sorry."

She didn't say anything. Couldn't even if she wanted to.

"I should have told you about Nikki."

"Yeah," she said, her voice coming out croaky, constricted from her tight throat. She cleared her throat and tried again. "You should have."

"It looked bad. And it hurt you. And I'm sorry. But you need to know the truth. It was kind of a weird situation."

Wait, that wasn't exactly what she'd expected to come out of his mouth. *Sorry I cheated on my girlfriend with you. Sorry I gave you the wrong idea about us.* "I don't understand."

"When I left Utah, Nikki and I decided that we were going to take some time to figure out what we wanted. But we were both so busy, we never really defined our relationship. So we just got stuck in limbo. I don't know why we didn't break up sooner. I think neither of us liked the idea of being completely alone, and neither of us wanted to be the one to actually end it. Which is stupid. It's obvious we didn't love each other."

He looked around for a place to sit, but her barstools were already stacked and wrapped in stretch film, so he had to settle for cocking a hip against the counter. "The fact is, when we talked the week before you arrived, I told her this wasn't working anymore and if neither of us were willing to compromise, we should call it quits. I took that to mean we were broken up. I never dreamed she was going to come to Colorado as some big romantic gesture. If I'd had any idea she didn't think it was over, I would have said something."

Gemma stared at him, taking in his body language, his unflinching gaze. He was telling the truth. Something unwound inside her, the knots that had formed in her gut the minute she saw Nikki loosening. "Thank you," she said finally. "I understand where you're coming from. I just wish I'd have known. Heck, the entire town thought you were still taken, and here I am running around with you, oblivious to the fact they all think you're cheating with me!"

He looked heartsick. "I should have said something. But I was just so wrapped up in everything that was happening. And for the record, everyone knows the truth now. No one thinks you're the other woman."

Her heart lifted in sudden wild hope, but it fell just as quickly. For all his earnestness, he hadn't said anything about wanting to be with her. He hadn't said he missed her or loved her or even liked her. He simply wanted to straighten out the aspersions cast on his character. Maybe he just didn't want her to hate him— or maybe Taylor's cold war was becoming bothersome.

She rubbed the back of her neck uncomfortably.

"Stephen, why are you here? If you just wanted to clear the air, it could have waited until I got back."

"What do you mean?"

"I'm moving back to Haven Ridge." She waved a hand at the disaster that was her home. "What do you think all this is about?"

His mouth dropped open. "I just assumed because you quit your job, you couldn't afford your house anymore. You said that if you had to quit. . ."

Gemma started laughing. This whole thing was starting to feel ridiculous, a series of misunderstandings that could have been resolved with a phone conversation. But that was exactly why she hadn't taken his calls. Because deep down she didn't believe that he was the person that the situation made him seem, and she knew if her doubts were put to rest, she'd jump at the chance to be with him. That she'd drop everything here and move back there so she could live out the life that she'd always envisioned for herself, before her dad and the move and Stephen's betrayal. She could never know if she was moving forward or simply living in the past.

"No," she said finally. "I'm moving back to Haven Ridge. I'm coming home. It's time. So, you see, you could have saved yourself a long trip if you had just waited a month or two."

"No," he said quietly. "I couldn't have waited."

And the hope that had slowly been dying in her heart was fanned back to life, even as she warned herself that she was setting herself up for a fall.

Stephen circled the island that divided them so that he was standing so close she had to look up at him. "I couldn't stand the idea that you thought I was just passing time with you. That you didn't understand what you mean to me. What you've always meant to me."

Gemma swallowed hard, licked her lips, held by the

intensity in those glorious hazel eyes. "And what is that?" She wasn't trying to make him prove himself; she truly couldn't trust her own read of the situation.

He reached out and took her hand, placed her palm against his heart so she could feel the steady beat beneath the thin layer of flannel. "Even when we were sixteen and I was stupid enough to let you get away, I knew that we were meant to be together. I let everyone tell me that it was impossible, that we were too young to know who we wanted to spend our lives with, and so I made bad decisions. I hurt you. But I never forgot you, no matter how hard I tried. I told myself the reason I never felt the same way about anyone was because that was first love, first infatuation, and those things just go away as we grow up. As we learn to know better."

He squeezed her hand and lifted it to his lips. "But then I saw you again and I knew the truth. You've always been the one I wanted. I never stopped. And I am so sorry that I hurt you, then and now. If you'll give me another chance, I will never stop making it up to you."

Gemma stared up at him, her breath caught in her throat, tears glimmering in her eyes while her heart cracked wide open. Secretly, she'd always dreamed of this moment. Secretly, she'd always thought that he was the one. And yet . . .

"We can't go back," she whispered, hating how the energy drained from his face. "I don't deny that what we had was real, no matter how young we were. I loved you, truly. But just because we belonged together back then doesn't mean we make sense now."

He looked sick now, stricken. He slowly let go of her hand. "Gemma—"

"If we're going to make a go of this, we have to start over."

He blinked at her. "What?"

She smiled now, knowing it was cruel of her to make him go through that moment of horror, but she had gone through the same. "I've thought a lot about us, Stephen. About what would happen if we got back together. We can't go back to the past. I wouldn't want to. If we're going to have any chance of happiness, we need to move forward. Clean slate. Right here, right now."

The color had returned to his expression, along with the hope. "What does that mean exactly?"

"We have almost a decade to catch up on, Stephen. We're different people than we were when we were together. And just because we're still attracted to each other—" the understatement of the century— "doesn't mean that we still fit."

"But. . ."

Gemma smiled now. "But I would really like the chance to find out."

Stephen broke into a grin and it felt like the sun coming out behind clouds. He reached for her and then thought better and asked, "Can I hug you?"

She laughed. "Yes, you can hug me."

He pulled her close, so her cheek was pressed against his shoulder, her senses enveloped in his particular scent of cotton and cologne and fresh air that seemed to persist even here. "So does this mean you'll let me take you out to dinner?" he asked, his voice muffled in her hair.

She laughed, suddenly the lightest she'd felt since the first time she'd left Haven Ridge. She didn't know what was going to happen in the future. She didn't even know who she would be. Would she still be an attorney? A baker? Would she and Stephen be together forever? Or would they conclude that their only future was as friends? She couldn't say, couldn't see that far, but she knew that whatever happened, she'd been brought back to Haven Ridge to put the past to rest and face the future with hope and excitement.

She pulled back from Stephen, who was still waiting for the answer to his question with anticipation in his eyes, and gave the only answer that felt right, to his question, to all of it together.

"I think it's a wonderful place to start."

EPILOGUE

Three months later

GEMMA STOOD before the 1890s brick building on the corner of Dogwood Street and Delaware Avenue, a single thought running through her head over and over.

She was out of her mind.

At the time, it had seemed like a good idea to put the entirety of the proceeds from the sale of her Santa Monica house into a building in Haven Ridge that could house two businesses and a residence—it would save her the pressure of having to maintain rent on three different locations, especially while she was getting settled. But now, looking at the blank and rather dirty slate she had to work with—not to mention the container sitting at the curb waiting to be unpacked—she was beginning to think that perhaps her dreams had outpaced her ability to accomplish them.

"Is there a reason you're still standing on the sidewalk or are we just admiring the view?" Stephen stepped up behind her and slid his arms around her waist, pressing a kiss to the top of her head.

Gemma leaned back against him for a moment, allowing herself to savor his warmth, the feel of his strong arms around her. She would have thought that after a month back in Haven Ridge in which they'd spent nearly every waking, non-work hour getting to know each other again, butterflies would have ceased to materialize in her stomach every time he came near. But it seemed that she would never get over the wonder of being with him again in Haven Ridge after so many years apart.

Or maybe those flutters were the twinges of nervousness that had been dogging her since she signed the loan paperwork yesterday morning. She twisted in his embrace to face him and looped her arms around his neck. "Right now, I'm rethinking my life choices."

Laughter rumbled in his chest as he bent to kiss her. "Then clearly I have not been doing my job."

Gemma allowed herself to sink into his kiss for a few seconds before she pulled away, smiling. "Not about you. Never about you. About the building."

"Ah. Well, it stands to reason. It's not every day that you buy an entire historic city block."

Gemma laughed, though the exaggeration felt painfully close to the truth. "You're supposed to be making me feel better, not worse."

"How's this, then?" He stepped back, his hands going to her shoulders while he looked her in the eyes. "You are as brilliant as you are beautiful, and if anyone could make this work, it would be you. Haven Ridge is lucky to have you back."

"Oh, are we giving more pep talks?" Liv materialized on the sidewalk beside Gemma with a grin for Stephen. "Which is it this time? The building, the bakery, or her exam?"

"The building." Stephen glanced at his watch. "She

doesn't usually start freaking out about the exam until after dinner."

Gemma rolled her eyes, but she couldn't help but laugh at the accuracy. Returning to Haven Ridge hadn't just meant reuniting with Stephen and Liv separately, but the reforming of the tight little trio they'd once been in high school. Even when they ganged up to tease her about her Type-A anxieties—or maybe because of it—it felt like no time had passed at all.

Liv clapped her hands. "So, are we getting this tour you promised us or what?"

Gemma stepped away from Stephen and dug in her bag for her keys. She hadn't been in the building since she put in the offer a month ago; she'd wanted to take her first look as an owner with the two people in the world who meant the most to her, the ones who had been responsible for bringing her back home. She found the key on the ring, unlocked the front door of the retail space, and stepped inside.

"Here it is," she said. "The future home of the Broken Hearts Bakery."

Thanks to the previous occupant—Sugar Dreams, the now-defunct bakery that Mallory had mentioned during Gemma's first trip to the Brick House Cafe—the interior was already outfitted with everything she needed to get up and running in a short period of time. Which was a good thing, because she had her first customer already lined up; Mallory had made it clear that the cafe would be her best and most reliable account. That, of course, came with its own set of worries—the need to quickly scale up her recipes to suit bakery production, for example—but it also made the idea of owning her own retail space seem far less risky.

She even had a potential manager lined up. Now that Chelsea's divorce was in-process, the woman was looking for a full-time job that wouldn't take her too far from the twins . . . and she just so happened to have experience managing a business. Of course, it had been a dental office, but people were people. Gemma had no doubt that the woman—who had, not surprisingly, been one of her biggest cheerleaders since she got back— could manage cookies and cupcakes just as well.

Stephen and Liv crawled over the place, exclaiming over the features and equipment that a home baker could only dream about—a Hobart floor mixer! an automatic dough sheeter!—Liv already detailing her ideas for redesigning the retail space. When they'd pored over every last inch of the bakery, Gemma led them back out to the sidewalk, through a separate door into the narrow stairwell, and up to the second floor.

"The future Law Offices of Gemma Van Buren," she announced, unlocking this door with a second key and standing aside.

Liv went through first. "It's . . . historic."

"If historic means old," Stephen said *sotto voce.*

Gemma gave him a shove, earning a laugh. "It needs work. But it's a studio, which I thought made it a pretty good space for an office. Especially considering the kitchen is barely more than a break room anyway." She kept her voice confident, even though her heart had fallen a little on her second look. She'd remembered the industrial-looking melamine cabinets and sad 1970s fridge in the kitchen, but now the sight of grimy moldings, battered hardwoods, and peeling paint made her question the potential she'd seen in it upon her first viewing.

But Liv, it seemed, was warming up to the space. "Heart pine floors . . . real plaster moldings . . . this could be gorgeous. And you've got an original fireplace! Tell me that won't be comforting to your clients in the winter. You can put a couple of chairs here and serve coffee or tea and baked goods from downstairs."

"Get a free dozen cookies with every divorce," Gemma whispered to Stephen, and he grinned at the echo of her earlier sarcastic words.

"Okay, now show us your place," Liv said.

"You asked for it," Gemma muttered. She led them up to the top floor, unlocked the door, and let them enter before her.

Even Liv couldn't put on a brave face when she stepped into the third space. "Oh Gemma."

"I know." Her apartment—what was supposed to be her apartment—was something out of an episode of *Hoarders*. Stacks of boxes mixed with old furniture, jumbled together with antique doors and windows, cleaning supplies, and what looked like a lifetime's collection of *National Geographic* magazines. "Jayden and his wife bought the building intending to turn the upper two floors into vacation rentals, but they only managed to finish the bakery before they had to move. But Liv. . .look." Gemma led her best friend into the bathroom—almost wholly vintage and surprisingly intact—and pointed to the apartment's main selling point.

"A claw foot tub!" Liv clapped her hands in delight. "Now it all makes sense. A woman would put up with a lot of hassle for one of those."

They didn't linger—there wasn't enough room to walk around, for one thing—and Gemma led them back out onto the landing, then down the stairs. "You'll be stuck with me at your place a little longer, Liv. It's going to take some time."

"Some time?" she shot back. "It's going to take an army."

"Which fortunately," Stephen said, holding open the door on the bottom floor for Gemma, "we have."

Gemma came to a halt on the sidewalk, too shocked

to continue. Spread out before her was a crowd of people—what seemed to be half of the town. A group of teenagers stood off to the side, clustered around Taylor. Several dozen men and women stood by, headed by Chelsea and Mallory. Granny Pearl was there with a cluster of senior citizens, waving merrily. And every single person was wearing work clothes and gloves, carrying mops and buckets and hammers. Beaming at her as if it were a surprise party.

Gemma struggled to find her voice for several seconds. "I don't understand. How—?"

Chelsea stepped forward, smiling. Her outward appearance was unchanged, but there was something in her bearing—chin lifted, back straight—that made her seem like an entirely different person than the one Gemma remembered, whether fifteen years ago or four months ago. "We're so glad to have you back here in Haven Ridge. We want to help, if you'll let us."

Gemma pressed a hand to her chest, overwhelmed. She looked between Stephen and Liv. "Did you two do this?"

"No, actually," Stephen said with a smile. "You can thank our new mayor for that." He nodded toward Thomas, who was making his way through the crowd.

Gemma laughed and accepted Thomas's brief hug. "I still can't get used to that, Mr. Mayor. How's life as Haven Ridge's fearless leader?"

Thomas grinned at her. "Busier than you'd expect. I still think Stephen would have made the better candidate, but I'll admit there is something to be said for carrying on the family tradition." He sobered. "Granny Pearl has always said that when the town turned its back on you and your mom, it was the beginning of the end for it. So it's up to us to make things right. On behalf of Haven Ridge, allow me to welcome you home."

Gemma looked around at the gathered townspeople, their images blurring suddenly in her vision. Stephen slipped an arm around her, pulling her close enough to plant a kiss on the top of her head, as if he sensed how suddenly overwhelmed she was by the unexpected show of support. Liv reached for her hand while the rest of the crowd waited expectantly for her reply.

She found she couldn't speak. All she could do was smile and give a single nod of agreement.

In an instant, the crowd dispersed into all three floors of the building, directed by the very effective team of Chelsea and Mallory. Gemma stayed where she was, enveloped in Stephen's warmth, bolstered by the squeeze of Liv's hand.

After fourteen years of longing and hoping and striving, she was finally home.

ABOUT THE AUTHOR

Carla Laureano could never decide what she wanted to be when she grew up, so she decided to become a novelist–and she must be kinda okay at it because she's won two RWA RITA® Awards. When she's not writing, she can be found cooking and trying to read through her TBR shelf, which she estimates will be finished in 2054. She currently lives in Denver, Colorado with her husband, two teen sons, and an opinionated cat named Willow.

Made in the USA
Coppell, TX
07 May 2023